A SEASON
IN THE
SOUTH

by Marci Alborghetti

To Sara —
Maybe the next one
will be about Ogunquit!
Love,
Marci

✝ **Resurrection Press**
An Imprint of
CATHOLIC BOOK PUBLISHING CO.
Totowa • New Jersey

DEDICATION

For God, Who has given me abundant blessings.
To Charlie, the best of them.

—·—·—·—·—·—·—

First published in March, 2003 by Resurrection Press, Catholic Book Publishing Company.

Copyright © 2003 by Marci Alborghetti

ISBN 1-878718-78-9

Library of Congress Catalog Number: 2002115855

Cover design by Cindy Dunne

Printed in Canada

1 2 3 4 5 6 7 8 9

CONTENTS

ACKNOWLEDGEMENTS

FIRST and always, I thank God for being the kind of Companion to me that He is to Maggie/Margaret. I am so grateful.

I owe a debt of gratitude to my insightful and incisive readers: Evelyn Casey, Gwen Costello, Maxine Dean, Anne-Megan Kelly-Edmunds, Tom Rezendes and my husband, Charlie Duffy. They all contributed immeasurably to the book's content and my confidence. I want to thank Sue, who's name I respectfully borrowed and who's generous, gentle spirit was never far from me as I wrote. I thrived on Emilie Cerar's encouragement and excitement as the story unfolded.

The St. Francis Cancer Center is a vital and wondrous place, and I was honored to include it in the text. So is the University of Hartford, though its Performing Arts Center in the Northend of Hartford is still a dream-in-the-making. I know it will be every bit as wonderful as I've made it.

Within the context of the story, this book is something of a love letter to Key West. The place and its people, particularly those who were so very kind to me in my days there, remain always in my heart and mind.

Finally, I thank the men and women who have shared with me over the years their "cancer" stories. Some of them are my closest friends; some I encountered only once or twice. They have all touched my heart and broadened my spirit. They made this book possible.

CHAPTER 1

FEAR OF FLYING

WHAT bothered her most was that the pilot hadn't said a word. Their awfully small plane had just bounced down and then, abruptly, shot back up off the short runway. Margaret knew that wasn't supposed to happen, and, from the gasps and moans of the other 18 passengers, so did they. And the pilot hadn't said a word.

Even now, as they slowly circled back over tiny Key West, the southernmost island of the United States (or, as her husband had pointed out blandly, "as far away as you can get without actually leaving the country") the pilot remained silent. Margaret really thought he should say something. A lie would do fine. After all, no one actually wanted to know if he'd overshot the runway, or if another plane had been about to smash into theirs. But he could say something comforting, jovial even, to reassure them that he knew what he was doing. That he was actually *there*.

She was more disturbed by his silence than by the fact that they might have come close to crashing. And this was odd, since until now, she'd been terrified of flying. She'd never flown before. Harry had laughed thirty years ago when she rejected his parents' gift of a Hawaiian honeymoon because she was too afraid. He'd stopped laughing when he realized she really wouldn't go. She had not been to visit her own parents since they retired to Sun City seven years ago. "Sometime soon," she'd tell her mother over the phone, both knowing it was a polite dodge. So much, she knew now, had been a polite dodge.

Maybe that's why everyone had had such a hard time believing her when she told them about this trip. She'd waited until Christmas when both girls were home. *Christmas in Connecticut.* Well, it would never be the same anyway. The doctor had taken care of that. Or rather, the radiologist, because as she'd learned over the past eight months (*was it only eight months?*), it is the radiologist who actually "makes the call," as they say. It is the radiologist who "reads the pictures."

It was the radiologist, whose name Harry had never learned to pronounce, who told her in May that the mammogram showed a small lump in the top left quadrant of her left breast. She remembered thinking, it sounds like a map . . . take a left at the belly button, a right at the clavicle and stop just past the nipple. Caroline, her eldest, had not been amused. Of course, Caroline was trying to get pregnant and her typical intensity had clarified around the issue of Women and Their Health. That's how Margaret thought of her daughter's obsession, as if it were a title or an announcement for some seminar.

Caroline, considered the whiz kid of the St. Francis hospital public relations department in Hartford, was brisk and efficient when told about the lump. Her brilliant daughter's mind worked so fast. She didn't even have to stop and think before she started talking. "Now Mom, the first thing is a needle biopsy. They have these machines now that make it much more accurate. It'll be benign. You have no history. Gran never had breast cancer, did she? No. OK, then it's sure to be benign. But just in case, I'll start researching oncologists. I know how much you like Dr. Elgin, but we are NOT leaving this to a family doctor, no matter HOW much you and Dad like him. The guy's not getting any younger, is he? I'll check around at the hospital. But I know it'll be benign."

Everyone said the same. Harry. His sister, Kath and her husband, George. Their best friends, Mike and Macy. Abby, her assistant at the paper. Even her younger daughter, Christine, a dance major at the University of Hartford's Hartt School and a much more emotional version of Caroline, immediately followed her initial wail of "Oh Mom!" with a typically unfocused litany, "But, it's nothing. It's got to be nothing. We've got no history, right? No one in our family, right? What about on Dad's side—oh, but that wouldn't matter for you, would it!? Mom, just get the biopsy over with. It'll be nothing, right? What do they call it? Benign, right? It will be benign."

It wasn't. Margaret knew from the moment she heard Dr. Riatshahna's lilting musical voice on the phone (*they actually give you news like this over the phone!*) that it would not be benign. That's still how she thought of it, not benign. She still couldn't bring herself to say the other word. Malignant. Even knowing it would not be benign, when she heard the word, malignant, she felt the nausea rising and had to drop the phone and lunge for the sink. Afterwards, as she wiped her mouth, she wondered why she'd expected them to say "not benign," instead of the other. It was stupid, really. Or as Caroline had said, almost angrily, "Mom, you've got to get over being so naive. This is the real world now."

Harry had said very little. He'd looked mildly surprised when she told him about the mammogram. He hadn't offered to drive with her to the biopsy even though it was nearly an hour from their home near the beach in Old Saybrook to the doctor in Hartford. Caroline had gone with her; actually, Margaret had driven herself but Caroline had been waiting at the office of the doctor she'd recommended. He was affiliated with St. Francis. Margaret soon learned that there were doctors affiliated with St. Francis in just about every other building on the streets and blocks surrounding the monolith hospital. All the times she'd visited Caroline in Hartford, she'd never imagined all those buildings were doctors' offices. She found it amazing, all the things she hadn't known before. Maybe Caroline was right: she was in the real world now. Or, at least, a different one.

Harry had not asked about the biopsy results, but when she told him it was not benign, he'd at least tried to respond. He'd stopped in the middle of pulling off his tie, his back to her. She could almost see him swallowing hard and trying to figure out what was expected of him. He turned and took her hand awkwardly. He did not pull her on the bed to sit with him. He did not pull her onto the bed to hold her. He cleared his throat and said, "Well, what do you do next?" Not "we." "You."

She didn't ask him to accompany her to the oncologist. She did not wake him when she left shortly after dawn that day, first riding along the shore road to watch the early morning sun spread glowing fingers across Long Island Sound. She drove by Fenwood and Fenwick, past the silent, dew-blanketed golf course, and over the causeway, where a few people were already striding rapidly along on their morning walk, suspended over the moving water. She loved this drive. She would have moved to Old Saybrook just for this drive.

She stopped at a Berlin Turnpike diner for a greasy grilled cheese sandwich with french fries she'd never have eaten a week ago and was surprised to realize she'd never eaten out alone before. She arrived in Hartford an hour before she was to meet Caroline and Christine at the oncologist's office. Christine had offered to come home from Hartt and drive with her, but she'd refused, wanting this hour. She parked downtown, in the lot across from Saint Patrick-Saint Anthony, the church Caroline and her rather humorless young husband, Tom, attended. Margaret had not thought to stop at her own church in Old Saybrook; she'd come directly here. She'd been here many times since Caroline had moved to Hartford six years ago and "discovered" the church run by liberal-minded Franciscan friars. From the time she was a child, Caroline had believed nothing was real until she discovered it. But Margaret had immediately understood why Caroline was so taken with this church. Though Harry grumbled about the downtown location and the friars' almost obsessive focus on serving the "urban poor," it seemed like a place Jesus would approve of. It was where Margaret yearned to spend a quiet hour before her two o'clock appointment.

Arriving just as the noon Mass was ending, she sat in the back pew and watched, surprised at the number of people. It seemed the offices around the church had emptied out just for a weekday Mass. She doubted this many people attended her church at home on Sunday. She spent her hour in the shadows, listening to the blood rush in her ears. As hard as she tried, it was as close as she could get to a prayer.

When she met Christine and Caroline in the waiting room of Dr. Toser's office at the St. Francis Cancer Center, she marveled yet again at how different her daughters were. Caroline, her perfect size eight form dressed for success in a navy Chanel suit, was intensely focused. Her eyes never left the receptionist as if she could will the poor woman to call

Margaret's name. She had made this referral, and she was determined it would go well. Caroline had needed to control things from the time she was a toddler; Margaret often mused that they should have never waited five years to give her a little sister. Caroline had been running things much too long by then.

By contrast, Christine seemed incapable of running a bath. Maybe her sister's propensity for taking charge had robbed her of incentive. She had, as Harry was fond of pointing out, no discipline. She'd changed her major four times before deciding on Fine Arts with a major in Dance ("of all things," scoffed Tom, an unrelenting social worker who believed that a life not spent in service was a life wasted). With her pale, freckled skin and tiny frame, Christine had a waif-like air about her. That day in the waiting room, she looked like a fidgeting four-year-old waiting for her first dentist appointment.

Dressed in Levi's and a University of Hartford sweatshirt, Christine seemed to be struggling mightily to keep herself from fleeing the room. Her eyes darted from the gentle Monet prints on the rose-colored walls to the young twins clinging to a harried looking Puerto Rican woman across the room. Her glance occasionally fell on Margaret, but she would nervously look away with a vague smile every time her mother met her look. She'd done the same thing as a little girl when she got caught at something, Margaret had thought, always offering that goofy unfocused smile even as her gaze slipped away.

Margaret had decided right at that moment not to tell her parents. They were far enough away so that they'd never find out. Unless. The girls were bad enough; she would not put her parents through this. Especially her mother. The truth was she couldn't imagine trying to cope with her mother's reaction *and* the disease.

Both girls had entered the consulting room with her. Margaret had been drawn to Dr. Toser from the start. A tall, slender woman with cropped dark hair and creamy coffee colored skin, she had frank dark eyes that managed to communicate both compassion and strength. Caroline had done well choosing this doctor. She will not let me off the hook, Margaret thought calmly. And as Dr. Toser began speaking the unspeakable, she knew it was true.

It was still light when she got home that night. She remembered thinking it was so nice to have it light at 7:30. It was too early in the season for cicadas, but she could hear the tiny cries of the peeper toads from the pond across the street. Harry was waiting for her, a look of vague annoyance on his face. Most people would not have noticed. It had taken her years to learn to read his signs. The tiny frown creasing his high forehead. The slightly raised eyebrows arching toward the graying receded hairline. The occasional small tic that meant a clenched jaw.

Poor Harry. Caroline had phoned him at work and given him, as she later assured her mother, "an earful." If he'd thought to avoid hearing about Margaret's day, his elder daughter had dashed that hope with a stern lecture on the meaning of love, support and involvement. Margaret knew her husband did not intend to be cold and disengaged. It was just his way. An only child who'd been sheltered by her parents, Margaret had been a young, naive bride. At 21, fresh out of secretarial school, she'd been swept off her feet by Harry's quiet stoicism, and told herself he would eventually reveal to her, and only her, the passionate emotions that must be roiling just below the surface.

He didn't and there weren't. Harry, she'd slowly learned, detested emotional displays. By then, she'd come to fully understand her mother's favorite saying, "You made your bed; you lie in it." Her parents were perfectly happy with Harry, and anxiously turned her over to him, believing their overly romantic daughter needed a good Catholic man with a stern guiding hand. And, truly, Harry was a good Catholic man, though the stern guiding hand was more like hands off. He'd even given in to her abject fear of flying to Hawaii for their honeymoon, accepting the equivalent in a cash gift from his parents just to avoid an argument. She'd often wondered if things might have been different if she'd forced herself to take that trip. Or if he'd insisted she go. After his initial surprise, and her first glimpse of the telltale signs of irritation, he'd not discussed it further with her. Harry had seldom criticized her in their three decades together; admonishment might have led to confrontation, and confrontation was something he detested.

His penchant for avoiding it had served him well in his work. When they'd married, he was already managing Old Saybrook's only office supply store, having won over the owner with his two years of college and quiet confidence. Eventually the store had been acquired by a large chain, and Harry easily slipped into the role of company man. When computers hit the office and home markets with a vengeance, his rational nature lent itself well to the field. Now, at 54, he could teach just about anyone to use a computer, and then sell them the one perfectly matched to their needs. He spent hours every night on their computer at home. Margaret was mildly amused by the fact that her husband communicated better online than across the kitchen table.

He was waiting for her on the deck that May evening when she rounded the corner to their backyard. For some reason they always used the kitchen door, parking the cars in the front and walking round to the back. Now she wondered about it. "Why do we always use the back door?" she asked him. He held her look for a beat, and then sighing, shook his head and went inside.

She followed, wondering why *he* was exasperated. *She* was the one who had cancer. Was he worried she'd start asking other questions? Like, will you come with me to the surgery? Like, will you take me for the chemo treatments? Like, why are we still married? And why don't we get counseling? Or why can't we try Retrouvaille? Mike and Macy had raved about what Retrouvaille had done for their marriage, and their faith for that matter. But every time they mentioned it, almost gushing, Harry would look away, as if embarrassed. So Margaret had never asked.

And she didn't now. Instead she began to recite what Dr. Toser had told her about the treatment. Harry cut her off with a short, "I already spoke to Caroline." He knew that she was scheduled for surgery next Monday. They called it a lumpectomy, but Dr. Toser also said they would remove nodes and enough tissue to, hopefully, achieve "clean" margins. As if she'd ever feel clean again. He knew that surgery would be followed by six months of chemo, administered in four cycles, once a week for six weeks with breaks between cycles. He knew that chemo would be followed by six weeks of radiation.

He knew that she'd be cut, poisoned, and burned. And that all that still might not work. She might still be, well, not benign.

And all poor Harry could manage was "I already spoke to Caroline."

In the end, he'd offered to take her to the surgery. Caroline must have done quite a job on him. Margaret was in the hospital two days, and he visited both evenings, taking the third day off to bring her home again. On the silent ride home she wondered if he was worried about how many computers would go unsold.

She was on her own when it came to the chemo. She knew better than to expect him to drive her to Hartford every Monday and wait for hours while she sat in the glaring white antiseptic room, watching poison drip into her veins. Those were the good days. The bad days were when the fingerprick blood test at the beginning showed a too-low white cell count. That meant she couldn't have the chemo. Instead, she had to have a series of shots to boost her immune system so that she could resume the chemo next week. The first time it happened, she thought how strange it was to be both relieved and frightened at the same time. She couldn't help being relieved to avoid the nausea and horrible listlessness that followed chemo treatments. She couldn't help being relieved at the thought of enjoying food again for more than two days in a row. Or just keeping it down.

But her relief was vastly tempered by Dr. Toser's explanation, "You need every treatment. The program is designed to give you the maximum benefit in terms of completely eradicating the cancer. We removed the lump and the surrounding nodes, but the chemo-radiation combination is our insurance." Margaret began praying for a good white cell count. Funny, that she could pray for something like white cells, but she couldn't manage to pray for healing. She'd sort of lost the hang of prayer.

Which is why she decided to ruin the remnants of Christmas with the announcement about Key West. She'd gotten through the chemo and five weeks of radiation in something of a daze, never once allowing herself to stop and think. It felt to her like everyone around her was in charge, and she was simply following orders. She was, as Macy said, "wrapped in cotton batting." Macy, with her extensive experience in counseling lingo, told Margaret that the numbness was a natural reaction, necessary to get her through the horror of learning about cancer and the nightmare of surgery and treatment.

All that was fine with Margaret. She wasn't anxious to feel anything more than she was feeling. Even at her job, she went on automatic pilot, leaving much of the work of running the paper to Abby. Abby was as good an assistant as any editor could hope for; indeed, Margaret often thought the earnest girl took their work a little too seriously. After all, the *Saybrook Crier* was not exactly *The New York Times*. It was mostly a matter of collecting enough advertisement revenue to have a decent number of copy pages each week. The news was mostly press releases, budget issues and small town gossip. Margaret had been editor for over ten years, often acting as photographer, chief writer, copy editor, and layout artist.

That had changed when Abby came along two years ago and took on many of those tasks herself. Though she initially seemed no more than a child, she considered herself a journalist and was determined to act the part. For all the attention she paid it, the paper might as well have been *The Times*. She even managed to attend town meetings and budget hearings, enabling the *Crier* to offer readers a little more information than meeting minutes. She also brought the paper into the age of technology, computerizing the layout and helping Sharon, their business manager, update accounts. If Abby had wondered why the wife of the town's technology wizard was such a computer idiot, she never said. Harry had never offered to overhaul the *Crier's* systems, and Margaret had never asked. The paper, at least, was hers.

So Abby was perfectly capable of taking over while Margaret underwent treatments. The efficient 24-year-old made a point of showing Margaret every issue's layout, bringing it to the house when Margaret was too sick to go to the office. Finding herself suddenly uninterested in the paper she'd shepherded and nurtured for a decade, Margaret was still grateful for Abby's weekly visits. Abby, it seemed, was the only person left in her life who could talk about something besides cancer. She was the only one who didn't have a story about a mother, sister, aunt, friend, who'd "lost a breast," or "beat the odds," or "lost the battle," or "went for the whole mastectomy." She was the only one who never pressed Margaret with advice on antioxidants, estrogen replacement therapy, breast reconstruction, group therapy, macrobiotic diets, recurrence rates, yoga, and centering prayer. Centering prayer, one of Caroline's urgent suggestions, was Margaret's favorite: she couldn't even pray off-center anymore, how was she supposed to learn centering prayer now?

It was during one of Abby's visits that Margaret had a melt-down. It was just before Christmas, in the sixth week of radiation, which Dr. Toser described as the "booster dose" week. Margaret was, as Caroline triumphantly put it, "almost home free." It sometimes seemed to Margaret that Caroline thought *she* was battling cancer.

But then, when Margaret was almost home free, an amazing thing happened. The cotton batting unraveled. And suddenly, she was vulnerable to every emotion and fear she'd buried for over six months. On the Monday of the booster week, in the middle of Abby's solemn description of a town council meeting, Margaret interrupted her.

"I don't know how to pray anymore."

Closing her mouth, Abby regarded Margaret through over-sized, perfectly round spectacles. Her elfin face, surrounded by coppery cork-screw curls, was utterly still. Abby had a way of listening with her whole face. It was all Margaret needed. She poured out words she hadn't known were in her, words she could never say to Caroline or Christine or Harry, *especially* not Harry. Words of pain, confusion, fear. Words of how she dreaded leaving her daughters before seeing how their lives would work out. Words of how losing her hair had sickened her almost as much as the chemo. Words of a resentment so violent it made Margaret ashamed. Words of her inability to pray or to hear God anymore. Words of terror that there would be no answer if she asked.

When she finished, she was soaked in sweat, her cheeks wet with tears unshed for nearly eight months. Abby sat silently for a moment, her eyes searching Margaret's face. Then, with the lit Christmas tree glowing behind her, Abby asked, "So what are you going to do?"

Do? Margaret had no idea. It had never occurred to her that she could *do* anything. It seemed that everything had been done *to* her. The cancer, the surgery, the scar, the gut-churning chemo, the ravaging radiation, even the loss of her thick, dark hair, the one vanity she'd cherished. Had she done any of this to herself? No. It had all been done to her. By who—God? Had God done all this to her? Was it a punishment for two healthy daughters and a relatively unscathed life?

Abby waited. "What am I supposed to do?" Margaret asked plaintively, wincing a little at the whine in her own voice.

Abby responded simply, "What do you want to do?"

"Leave."

It was out before Margaret even realized she'd said it. It was out before she even realized that it was exactly what she wanted to do. She wanted to leave Caroline's strident battle against her cancer. She wanted to leave Christine's fragile uncertainty. She wanted to leave Harry's detachment. She wanted to leave Kath and George's over-solicitousness. She wanted to leave Macy's smug platitudes. She wanted to leave Dr. Toser's comforting confidence. She wanted to leave the home where she'd spent entirely too much of the past months vomiting and refusing to look at herself in the mirror. She wanted to leave the *Crier,* with all its nonsense and minutiae, completely in the capable hands of the surprising young woman sitting here with her.

And there was something deeper to her need than the desire for escape. She had the sickening, sinking feeling that she would never find God again if she stayed. Week after week, she'd stopped at St. Patrick-St. Anthony's on her way to treatments. And week after week, she sat there, deaf and mute. Every weekend, if she wasn't too sick, she'd dutifully accompany Harry to church, but Mass had become little more than an obligation.

This emptiness, this silence, had shaken Margaret to her very core. She'd never been someone who recited prayers by rote and attended services with the same level of involvement as she shopped or slept. For as long as she could remember, she'd felt God's presence. From early childhood, she'd understood that she had a companion in Him. Her mother still told anyone polite enough to listen how she could leave Margaret alone for hours and, perfect only child that she was, she never needed to be amused. Was it because she was an only child that she'd come so close to God? Was that why she'd never in her life felt without Him?

Until now.

Yet Margaret had a feeling that it wasn't God Who had gone away. It was she who had lost touch with Him.

Abby, still watching her, finally asked, "Where?" When Margaret looked at her blankly, she repeated, "Where? When you leave, where will you go?"

Bless the girl, thought Margaret, she'd said "When," not "If." And in that statement, Abby had transformed Margaret's blurted unthinkable wish into reality. The *Crier* layout was forgotten as they devoted the rest of that afternoon to planning Margaret's escape. Abby was the one who'd suggested Key West. Self-proclaimed writer that she was, she was fascinated by the place, though she'd never herself been there.

"It's where writers *go*," she insisted, as if Margaret was anything more than a glorified copy editor. As if Margaret was in search of a place to write instead of a place to pray. To survive.

So Key West it was. Abby brought over a file of travel and tourism articles and brochures the very next day. Margaret felt a pang at the sight of the carefully collected information. Was she stealing Abby's dream? But Abby, in her uncanny way, dismissed the unspoken worry. "As soon as I save enough, I'll spend a winter there myself, working on a novel," she'd said confidently, and Margaret knew she was leaving the paper in hands more capable than her own. By day's end they'd purchased a one-way ticket and rented a cottage. They'd planned everything. Except how Margaret would tell her family.

She decided to tell Dr. Toser first, refusing to consider the possibility that she'd nix the idea. After her last radiation treatment, Margaret found herself again in Dr. Toser's office, but this time her palms were damp from a different kind of worry. How could she feel more nervous at the prospect of losing her escape than she had seven months earlier at the prospect of losing her life?

Contrary to her fears, the doctor was enthusiastic. Taking Margaret's hands in hers, she said, "Some say the relationship between a woman and her oncologist is one of the most intimate bonds either will experience. I don't know if it's true. I do know there's something missing in you, something you hold close and don't share. I've seen it, or maybe, the lack of it. We can only cure your body, you have to do the rest."

"*Am* I cured?" It was the question Margaret had dreaded asking.

"I don't know," Dr. Toser returned her gaze without blinking, "but today, the cancer's gone."

Christmas was three days away. Fortunately, her parents had opted for a Caribbean cruise instead of a traditional holiday in Old Saybrook. There would still be a full house on Christmas day: Christine and a Nigerian student named Abu who had nowhere to go for Christmas, Caroline and Tom, Kath and George, Mike and Macy, and, of course, Harry. She'd decided to tell them all together; there seemed no point in telling Harry first. His would be the life least disrupted by her absence.

She'd waited until they'd all returned to the living room to have mince and pumpkin pie by the Christmas tree. It was the loveliest tree they'd had in years. Christine, Caroline and Abu had put it up the first of December while Margaret was at radiation. She was so relieved to have it up and decorated that days passed before she noticed what a beautiful job they'd done. Now it shimmered in the twilight as her family and friends finished dessert, chatting idly. She remembered the touching grace Christine had said before dinner, thanking God for giving their mother, wife and friend back to them.

"I'm going away," she said abruptly.

Abu began clapping enthusiastically, thinking this was good news. But he subsided after a quick glance at the others. Before questions could ravish the silence that descended, she rushed on, "January 7. The day after Epiphany. That way I'll be able to take the tree down on the 6th, like always." She ran out of words. Macy on the other hand, was just winding up. "*Where* are you going? Why? Are you getting alternative treatments? Is it that Spiritual Health monastery I told you about? How long will you be gone for? Is Harry going?"

The words ran together, swirling around Margaret, but all she saw was Christine's expression of confused anguish. She didn't need to look at Caroline to know her features would be arranged in outraged righteousness—the same look she'd had as a baby just before she started to wail. But it was Christine's wordless hurt that transfixed Margaret until she looked away and said, "Harry isn't going. No one's going. Just me."

And it had been just her who'd boarded the American Airlines jet this morning at 6:45. She'd asked Harry to drive her to the airport, thinking it would be their last chance to break the silence that had fallen Christmas day and hung like a pall over their home. Harry had risen from his easy chair that day and left the room just after she'd admitted she had no idea when she'd return. As Caroline shrieked, "Who leaves on a trip and *doesn't know when they're coming back? What do you mean you don't know? What about Easter? What about the baby? What about the christening? You hate to fly!"* her father disappeared into the den. In a moment they all heard the whir of the computer starting up.

He hadn't spoken to Margaret since, except for the half-sarcastic, half-bemused remark about Key West and to refuse her request to take her to the airport. When Macy came at 4 a.m. to pick her up, Harry had rolled over and sat up in their bed, his back straight against the mahogany headboard. She remembered how she'd fallen in love with that pose of his in bed; he'd looked so strong, so stolid.

All night long, this past night, he'd held her, still silent. As she bent to brush her lips over his forehead while Macy waited, her car headlights beaming misty light into the dark pre-dawn, he asked, "Would counseling or Retrouvaille make a difference? If I agreed?"

"I don't know," she said, echoing Dr. Toser. At the bedroom door she turned back to him, "Maybe. Maybe when I come back."

Caroline and Christine were waiting at the airport, Caroline's face set in stubborn disapproval. Margaret noticed how her belly had grown around the new baby. Christine looked both bruised and brave, smiling tentative encouragement through unchecked tears. Macy hugged her good-bye after she checked her bags, whispering some nonsense of how proud she was of Margaret's "new-found independence." The girls lingered, waiting with her for the security check line to grow shorter.

There was really nothing left to say. Caroline had harangued her for an entire week after Christmas, using every tactic she knew to discourage her, and when that failed, to make her feel guilty. By the end of it, they were both worn out, and Margaret was still going. Now Christine merely held her mother's hand, while Caroline blew out a long-suffering sigh. Still unable to give up, she muttered, "*Tom* didn't even want me to come here. *He* said it was like giving you approval."

Sounds just like him, thought Margaret, refusing to be baited. Instead she put her free hand on Caroline's round little belly and laid her head on her eldest daughter's shoulder. Caroline burst into tears, crying, "Mommy, how can I have this baby *without you?*"

"The same way I had you, my darling," she said softly, as Christine sobbed softly with her sister. "And you'll have Tom with you. I didn't have Dad to help me; men didn't come to births back then."

"Is this about Dad?" Caroline sniffed.

"No, Caro. It's about me."

* * *

The plane touched down safely in Key West on the pilot's second try. Everyone burst into relieved applause, but Margaret felt sure they weren't clapping for the still silent pilot. They were clapping in spite of him. She'd never seen such a small airport. It matched the tiny airstrip and the tiny plane they'd boarded in Miami. Of course, she'd never seen an airport at all from this perspective. She'd always just been the one to see people off or greet them.

She disembarked to a smothering blast of heat. She breathed it in, forgetting everything she'd ever known about January. Stopping short on the simmering tarmac, she let the heat bathe her, washing away memories of the cold room where she'd endured so many chemo treatments. No matter how heavy the sweater she'd worn, she could never warm up during those hours. Or afterwards. Until this moment, when the heat obliterated the very definition of cold. She felt something shift within her as if thawing in places she hadn't known were frozen.

She walked toward the airport, no more than a sprawling shack, really. She found herself moving more slowly, the very atmosphere here was languid. Palm trees around the perimeter of the airstrip drifted in the hot breeze. Carrying one small bag, she entered the shack, passed rows of chairs that constituted the gate area, and went to fetch her other bags. Already, she knew she'd packed too much. The baggage area was a sort of opening in one wall through which sturdy youngsters in shorts and T-shirts slung the luggage. Hiking her carry-on up onto her shoulder, she firmly grasped one suitcase in each hand. Perspiring, she was seized with the fear she hadn't felt on the plane. What was she doing? She barely had enough strength to drag the bags out of the general fray; what had ever made her think she could pull this off? Caroline was right. *She'd had cancer!* A panic that had never overtaken her through months of surgery, chemo and radiation now threatened to overwhelm her.

A pulse pounding in her ears, her eyes raked frantically over the airport. No one in the crowd took notice until a soft, lilting voice asked, "Are you all right, ma'am?" Whirling around to face him, she saw a massively built, middle-aged black man. His flowered shirt exposed bulging muscles, and he wore many ropes and chains around his neck, some strung with shells and beads. He took off a mirrored pair of sunglasses to peer more closely at her. He stood behind a table piled high with T-shirts he was selling. Margaret's eyes fell on a brilliant magenta shirt covered with writing. She took a step closer to read it.

"When God finished creating the world, He turned it upside down and shook it, and everyone who couldn't hang on ended up in Key West."

Loosening her grip on her bags, Margaret looked up and returned his gaze with a small smile, "Yes, I am. I am all right. How much for that one?"

CHAPTER 2

MAGGIE

ARTHUR, the T-shirt salesman, tried to talk her out of it, pointing out that the shirt was an extra-large, and "you're nothing but bird-size." But Margaret insisted, asking him if she could pay with her credit card. He grinned hugely and held out his broad palm for the card. He glanced at it, whipped it through the little machine he kept with a cash box on a small table beside him, and handed the shirt to her with a flourish. "Here you are, Miss Maggie," he declared, and for the second time since arriving she came to an abrupt stop.

Maggie. No one had ever called her that before. She let it dance through her mind and decided she liked it. His voice made it sound musical, and she was absurdly pleased with herself for recognizing his accent as Jamaican. One of her radiation technicians had been Jamaican, and her singing voice had often lulled Margaret away from images of burning flesh. Arthur, gesturing at her two bulging suitcases, asked, "You renting or cabbing?"

Another thing she hadn't considered. Arthur studied her confused expression for a few seconds and then decided, "Renting. By the looks of that luggage, you'll be here for a time and may want the car. If you don't you can always bring it back here. Nothing on this island's more than ten minutes away." Then, sweeping his cash box and card machine into a tan leather duffel bag, he slung it onto his shoulder and took up one of her bags in each hand. Leaving his T-shirts untended, he ignored the caravan of flamingo-pink Key West taxi cabs and headed toward the small rental car counter.

Inexpressible gratitude flooded her as she followed, clutching her T-shirt and not bothering to worry that a large Jamaican stranger was striding away with everything she owned. Not a stranger, she corrected herself. A friend. Named Arthur. My first Key West friend.

By the time she reached the counter, he was already flirting with the thin blond girl behind the Hertz sign. Arthur talked the blushing girl into a discount, and though Maggie had been perfectly ready to pay the standard fee, she got the sage-colored Tercel for 10 days while only paying for a week. She followed Arthur to the car, marveling at how easily he bantered the waiting cabbies out of their grumbling about him stealing a potential fare. Was there anything this man couldn't handle? Did everyone on this island move through life with such happy ease?

After tossing her over-stuffed bags into the trunk as if they were a couple of backpacks, he slammed the trunk closed and handed her the keys. Looking at her closely, he asked with some trepidation, "You do know where you're going, don't you, Maggie?

And wasn't that the real question.

Summoning up a semblance of the courage she knew she'd need as soon as he left, she smiled and pulled out the scrap on which Abby had written the address of her rented cottage. "Southard Street," she answered proudly, showing him the directions from the airport as if it were a map to buried treasure.

He offered that lovely, broad grin and leaned in as if to embrace her, but then he hesitated and patted her arm awkwardly instead. "Stop back and let me know how you're doing," he said. As she watched him take long, languid steps back to the airport, she felt strangely bereft, yearning for that hug. Why hadn't *she* hugged *him?*

The inside of the car was broiling. Though the windows had been wisely left open and the upholstery was light beige, the Key West sun had done its work. She didn't think she'd ever felt such intense heat. She lost her chance to experience anything close to a tropical climate thirty years ago when she rejected the Hawaiian honeymoon. She'd passed her whole adult life never knowing what she'd missed. Was missing. And she couldn't help but wonder, as she sat breathing in the melting leather scent of her first rented car, what else she'd missed.

Arthur was right: nothing in Key West was very far from the airport. But the maze-like drive to Southard Street took her through entirely new worlds—more than one. The sweep of the ocean stunned her as soon as she turned left out of the airport onto North Roosevelt, the wide boulevard that circled half the island. There was an expanse of shimmering blue to her right, the horizon nearly indistinguishable as the azure sky met an endless ocean. This couldn't be the same angry, gray Atlantic that sulked along the shores of Connecticut. Trees and bushes grew right out of the water here as if all living things rooted on the ocean floor felt compelled to stretch for the sky. She'd never seen anything like these lone trees reaching from the sea to the sun, and without thinking, she whispered in awe, "Look what You did!"

The sound of her voice immediately set her heart pounding. Her palms were suddenly slick with sweat, and she trembled as she pulled the car over. She'd uttered a prayer! She'd spoken to God! After all these months. And she'd done it in the old familiar way, without really thinking about it. She'd done it without forming the words, without making a formal petition. As if she was talking to her Friend. Again.

She lay her head on the steering column and wept.

Resting her face there, she tried not to think. She would not ruin this moment by trying to analyze what it meant or plan how to finish mending the Friendship. She would do no more than savor this blessing and taste the salt tears seeping from her closed eyes. The muted rhythm of passing cars lulled her into a deeper sense of peace.

Until a sharp rap on her window made her bolt upright, banging the ridge of her nose on the wheel for good measure. A ragged-looking man was peering in at her from the passenger window. He rapped again, mouthing words she could barely hear over the air conditioner and through the closed window, "Lady, you OK in there?"

His face and beard were streaked with dirt, and long, gray hair was matted under a yellow knit cap. He seemed to be dressed more for New England than Key West in torn trousers, a long-sleeved orange jersey under a purple T-shirt, thick white wool socks that were astonishingly clean, and scuffed loafers that looked as if the soles were just about gone. Several beat-up keys hung from a thin, frayed rope around his neck. A piece of purple yarn, tied like a choker, held a cross formed by two nails soldered together.

Dismissing a vague concern about what Harry would say, she pressed the window button, and he stopped knocking as glass was replaced by air.

"Lady, you OK?" he repeated, his surprisingly clear dark eyes filled with worry.

"I think so," she answered slowly, "At least, I think I will be."

"OK," he smiled, revealing teeth ruined by years of inattention. He started to turn away, and she called impulsively, "Can I give you a ride somewhere?"

"No, Lady," he chuckled, "See, I live here." He gestured to a tangled clump of brush below the boulevard, just at the water line. Craning, Maggie looked over the street barrier and noticed a Wal-Mart shopping crate filled with lumpy black plastic bags. A Bible was cradled in the small carriage head. She could barely make out an old couch, its torn upholstery revealing mustard-colored foam stuffing, nestled in the thick undergrowth.

"I live here," he repeated, pointing and nodding reassuringly at her. Strangely comforted, she shifted out of park and drove off waving.

In direct contrast to the living oceanscape on her right, pure tourism reigned on her left. Restaurants, hotels, fast food chains, play grounds and malls abounded, increasing in density as she crossed the intersection where Route One, which started in Maine, ended in Key West. It was not the car's hyper-efficient air conditioning that made her shiver as she remembered how just that morning, Macy had driven along Route One in Old Saybrook on their way to the airport. She had an odd feeling that perhaps she really had left Margaret behind on that old highway, and that Maggie had emerged here to discover the other end of Route One.

Soon, both sides of the boulevard grew more crowded. The ocean side was dotted with water sports concessions offering everything from wind-surfing, kayaking and snorkeling to what she'd always thought of as water motorcycles—those noisy wave-riding machines that churned up the water.

She hadn't been driving for more than ten minutes and already she sensed what it was like to live somewhere where life revolved around the water as much as the land. New England, for all its celebrated coasts and rocky shores, did not belong to the Atlantic the way this place did. Here, the sea and land seemed to merge into one entity, a collaboration. At home, they remained starkly separate, often on the verge of war.

Now there were larger malls with super-sized grocery chains and familiar stores like Tru-Value, Home Depot, and Barnes & Noble. She felt a surprising twinge of disappointment at this evidence of normal life. Then she laughed at her outsized fantasies: apparently she wasn't Alice gone down the rabbit hole to an extraordinary place wholly populated by new and exotic creatures. New and exotic creatures wouldn't have much need for Tru-Value.

She soon passed through what appeared to be a commercial fishing compound with corridors of boats and trawlers for hire. Abby had told her that some of the upper Keys were havens for serious fishermen, though this looked pretty serious to her. Signs offered all-day and weekend fishing trips, some boasting impressive catches and listing the different types and sizes of fish they specialized in. Several boats, with names like Marlin Hunter, Catch-Up, and Harpoon, displayed their morning's catch—massive, glistening carcasses—over the side. She'd always thought of fishing either as a whimsical hobby or an actual job, but never as a vocation.

Within moments she crossed White Street, the unofficial boundary between New Town, through which she'd just driven, and Old Town Key West. If New Town had seemed a hodge-podge of tropical isle and commercialism, Old Town was a combination of quaint Caribbean village and Las Vegas-by-the-sea, all crammed into a few square miles. That small space included everything from houses so humble they might be called shanties to stucco mansions. With no warning, these sweet, lazy neighborhoods would abruptly flow into Duval Street, the teeming coast-to-coast road that gives Key West its worldwide reputation for nonconformity.

But Maggie had not yet reached Duval. Abby's directions took her to a corner on Southard, a few blocks back from Duval, into a quiet, pleasant-looking neighborhood. Other than a woman with a large straw hat working in her garden, Maggie saw no one on the street. She felt deflated. Abby had described Key West as a place packed with people, vibrant with life, offering a surprising sight on every corner. Except for the heat, this lovely little block might have been in a charming Vermont village.

All that changed when she pulled up to the curb. The huge, seemingly deserted Victorian house across the street erupted. A thin, pale woman burst from a side door, waving her arms and shrieking unintelligibly. Flying to the picket fence on the very border of her property, she continued shouting. Her slim form and swift movements had given the initial impression of a middle-aged woman, but from this closer distance, Maggie could see she was well into her seventies, perhaps even eighty. The paleness of her skin had been achieved by a layer of white powder so thick it might have been applied with a putty knife. Her uncombed black hair was coarse and white at the roots, springing from a careless middle part, and she was wiry rather than slender, the tendons in her neck taut with tension as she continued her diatribe.

It took Maggie a moment to realize it was directed at her.

"At least she doesn't have her broom today," observed a dry voice. Maggie swiveled her head around to see the man who'd emerged from a large house on the property where she was to stay. Of medium height, his slender figure also suggested muscular strength, but it was a much healthier version, born of good humor and hard work rather than crazed rage. His black and silver hair was long, but neatly trimmed like the beard that had grown in mostly gray. He wore white shorts, white athletic socks, and a white cotton T-shirt with a single word emblazoned in black capital letters: LANDLORD.

Grateful for the hint, Maggie watched while he shook his head, a look of bemused resignation on his face as he eyed his neighbor who now accompanied her garbled shouts with a series of wide, brusque, sweeping motions. *Perhaps she thinks she does have her broom?*

Maggie hadn't realized she'd speculated aloud until LANDLORD answered, "Nah. She just wants you to move your car."

"But," Maggie ventured tentatively, "I'm not parked on her side of the road."

"Doesn't matter. She gets like this anytime someone parks on either side of the street, on either side of her house. Anyone. She gets the cops here regularly."

"The cops?" squeaked Maggie.

"Oh yeah," said LANDLORD, sighing elaborately. "She comes from one of the old island families—a real life Conch." Seeing Maggie's perplexed look, he explained, "In Key West, Conchs are people who were actually born on the island. They're fiercely protective of the name—or designation, you could call it. It's like a heritage for them, the thing that separates them from all us newcomers. They can get pretty snotty about it, too. If you move here and stay for decades—*and* they like you—you might get to be a Fresh-water Conch, but never the real thing.

"Anyway, folks say this one across the street has a fortune stored up somewhere. Probably stuffed in an iron lung and buried under the porch for all I know. So the cops pay attention to her. They never really hassle anyone, but they do pay attention to her. Try to mollify her. And she does have the law on her side."

"It's against the law to *park?*" Maggie asked.

"You'd be surprised at what's against the law here . . . and what isn't."

With that, LANDLORD offered a crooked grin, and his somber face was transformed into a creased map of wry humor. When he stuck out his hand, Maggie realized she was still in the car and stepped out awkwardly to take the proffered hand. His grip was warm and surprisingly dry, given the thick heat. "I'm Mark," he said, "and you must be our new tenant. Margaret, right?"

"Yes," she answered, and then added self-consciously. "Actually, it's Maggie."

"OK," he said easily, taking the keys and opening the trunk for her luggage. Raising his voice for the benefit of the figure across the street who was still pacing wildly, he explained, "We'll move the car later." The black-clad crone retreated to her house, muttering, her hands in the air in a gesture of frustrated defeat.

As Mark hefted her bags, Maggie asked uncertainly, "Does she really have a broom?"

"You'll see," he answered enigmatically, treating her to that same quizzical grin.

They passed through a waist-high, white picket fence gate with a bell on the latch. Her careful, New England mind registered with relief the fact that no one could enter without being heard. Almost immediately she chided herself for the observation, determined to leave her cautious nature where she'd left her name.

The fence encircled a property that had looked deceptively small from the street. It was perhaps a half acre, no larger than her yard in Old Saybrook, but this space was much more densely planned, as if the owners had worked to make the most of their land. She would soon learn that land was a precious—and fiercely coveted—commodity in Key West. One of the island's largest industries, besides tourism, was construction.

There was one large house, two stories and rambling with a well-worn porch fronting Southard Street. Two small cottages were situated close behind the house, with the larger bungalow sharing a wall with the main home. The smaller cottage, though only an arm's span away, was altogether separate and appeared newer then the other two structures. One wall looked to be on the property's border line, but on closer inspection the sliding glass doors that comprised most of that wall opened onto a tiny flagstone patio, separated from the neighbor's house by a live fence of tangled vegetation. Its coat of white paint with green trim looked fresh and clean, and the miniature porch had been carefully swept. Two glistening windows on either side of the door seemed to look out at her curiously, beckoning. A single wooden chair, also bright green, waited comfortably on the porch.

But it was the door yard that won Maggie's heart. The small front porches on both cottages opened onto a charming tableau that recalled the secret gardens of childhood fairy tales. She'd always wanted such a yard: it had no grass. Instead, flowers and moss and ivy all but overflowed onto the flat stones that served as the only walking path through the vibrant mass of growth. The stones branched off from the gate into three paths, each leading to one home. A huge banyan tree towered above everything, offering copious shade to the house and cottages. Such a lavish display would have been ridiculous in her staid, conservative neighborhood. But it was the kind of artfully arranged disarray that she'd always yearned for as, year after year, she tended her small, square, perfectly planned garden with its meticulously trimmed borders.

A stone fountain in front of the smallest cottage gurgled under the tree, water bubbling out of a pitcher held by a marble angel. The angel wore a look of such peace that it brought unwitting tears to Maggie's eyes.

This cottage was hers. She just knew it. It had to be.

In the large house every window was open to catch whatever small breeze might stir, though Maggie could feel none. Her eyes widened as she realized they didn't have air conditioning. Noting her surprise, Mark gave a short bark of laughter and said by way of explanation, "Used to live in Australia. Among other places. The heat doesn't faze us much." Well it does me, she thought silently, alarmed at the thought of trying to sleep in a sweltering cottage, no matter how cozy it may be.

"That's where we live, Lily and me," said Mark, pointing to the main house. *Lily,* she thought, the wife. Somehow it was hard to imagine such a delicately-named creature married to this basic, no-nonsense man. Would she be the fine-boned, fragile, pale creature her name implied? Maggie suddenly felt ungainly and discomfited. She self-consciously adjusted the scarf-wrapped straw hat that covered her new bristly hair. She'd thought the scarf an elegant touch, but now it just seemed ridiculous. No scarf, no matter how pretty, could change the fact that she was practically bald underneath it. To add insult to injury, what little hair that had grown back had come in white. Not thick and dark, the way it had been. Not even a soft, sophisticated silver. Pure white. And coarse, so that it stuck up like a long crew cut.

She was acutely aware of the scar and still-healing radiation burns so carefully concealed by her dark cotton jersey. Were perspiration stains now spreading on the dark blue material? Lily probably didn't sweat. She had, after all, lived in

Australia where Mark had no doubt carefully guarded her frail nature from all excesses of climate and population. It was easy to imagine him shielding her from any discomfort or discourtesy. Maggie imagined her as lovely and gentle, the kind of woman who could draw protectiveness from any man.

This image, at least on first glance, was not far wrong. When Lily suddenly materialized, it took Maggie a moment to realize she'd been seated the whole time on a wrought iron bench partly hidden behind the massive banyan tree. Had she been watching and listening? Had Mark known she was there? Maggie studied the graceful woman who moved unhurriedly from behind the tree into the light.

She was lithe and pretty, just as Maggie had imagined. Macy might have called her petite, but she was not diminutive like Abby or even Christine. She was possessed of a stylishness that could not be dismissed. Though nearly as tall as Mark, she somehow appeared much smaller. Perhaps it was her way of looking up at him through half-closed eyes. Alabaster skin and fine bones in the slender oval of her face made otherwise even and unremarkable features seem almost exotic. A slight slant to her gold-flecked hazel eyes added to that effect, and straight ash blond hair created a perfect frame.

Maggie sensed Lily had been studying her with the same level of intensity. She slowly extended a slender hand with long fingers, and Maggie took it, feeling the delicate bones in a limp, tentative clasp. She met Maggie's eyes in one swift glance and then quickly lowered her lashes. In that flashing moment, Maggie understood that this woman was neither sneak nor siren. She was merely shy, and evidently painfully so. Maggie could read it in her eyes, a look of uncertainty and panic not unlike the one she glimpsed all too often in Christine's eyes. Lately, she'd seen it a few times in the mirror as well.

Already Lily was slipping away, retreating toward the main house as she murmured, "Mark will show you the cottage. Do let us know if you need anything." As she disappeared around the corner, Mark followed her with his eyes. A wistful expression had replaced the sardonic amusement on his face.

He caught Maggie observing him and, gesturing to the cottage she'd already chosen, said gruffly, "It's this one. We deposited your check for January and February. If you want to stay longer, we'll need to know by February 15. Your key's inside. It may stick in the humidity. Everything here sticks."

He was already on the porch and through the door, but she followed more slowly, watching the main house for any sign of Lily. There was none.

The cottage was as enchanting inside as out. Though tiny, the layout made good use of the available space. She entered into what appeared to be one long room, which encompassed a compact but efficient kitchen and a living/dining area with a small glass-topped table and pretty wicker chairs. A lazily revolving ceiling fan softly stirred the air. There was also a couch upholstered in bright green and yellow flowers on a white background and a Mac Personal Computer. "As you can see, you're not the first writer to stay here. Feel free to use the computer," Mark offered, "And what you do is your business, but the couch'll come in handy if you have any guests."

Wrong on both counts, thought Maggie. I'm *not* a writer. I'll *not* be using the computer. And I'm *not* having any overnight guests. In fact, she thought, I'm not even going to *tell* anyone at home about the couch. It would sound too much like an invitation. Except to Harry. She doubted he'd care. She said none of this to Mark, merely commenting, "It's lovely. I will let you know if I decide to stay longer."

He was all business now, showing her the tiny bedroom and bath at the back of the cottage. She was relieved to see a small air conditioner in the bedroom, but not so pleased to see that one entire wall of the bedroom was a window. Without a curtain or blinds. Impatiently banishing visions of strangers in the dark watching her thrash around on the narrow single bed in what passed for sleep these days, she focused on Mark's recital. "Trash day is Tuesday. There're some black, plastic bags under the sink. Tie 'em up good and put 'em just outside the fence. You can do it very late on Monday, but Tuesday's better if you don't want to get Elvira all rattled."

Maggie blinked. "Is that really her name?"

He rolled his eyes and started out. On impulse she asked, "Where's Duval Street?"

Without turning he called over his shoulder, "Head down the street a couple blocks, and you can't miss it. No one can. All roads lead to Duval."

Two hours later she'd unpacked, taken a long shower, towel-dried her head—couldn't really call it hair, changed into a short-sleeved yellow jersey dress, turned the air conditioner on full blast, and tried to relax with a book. That proved harder than she thought. *Tuesdays with Morrie* might not have been the perfect choice for this particular trip and time. She soon put it aside and wandered out onto the porch. It was too early for dinner; she'd promised Abby to fully exploit the Key West lifestyle and never eat before nine. It was barely six now and the mystery of Duval Street still beckoned. Exchanging her neon blue flip-flops—another ludicrous purchase—for brown espadrilles, she slipped her key and some money into the generously cut dress pockets and headed in the direction Mark had indicated.

She'd not walked a block before Duval Street began to prove its extraordinary reputation. As soon as she turned the corner onto Southard, she saw the wide intersection a few blocks ahead. It overflowed with light and noise and energy, robbing the early January dusk of all its bleak, looming power.

She glimpsed shops and slow-moving cars and more people than she'd seen since leaving the airport in Miami. Walking up the narrow twilit street, she had the odd impression of being in a dark, lonely tunnel that would, momentarily, empty into a lively, raucous city. A year ago she would have turned around and fled back to the secret garden and hidden cottage.

Now she hastened her pace. She'd been in the tunnel too long.

Technically, Duval was only a street, but it may as well have been a city. She reached the corner of Southard and Duval and stopped, breathless. Wherever she looked there was light and motion, and the street did, indeed, stretch from one coast to the other. Mark had said it connected the Atlantic Ocean to the Gulf of Mexico, but she thought that must be an exaggeration. She should get a map. Or maybe not. Harry swore by maps; she could never understand them. She always wanted specific directions with landmarks and street signs when she was going to a strange place.

Looking around, she knew she'd arrived in the strangest place she'd ever been, but instead of the jolt of fear she might have expected, she felt a surge of excitement. "Thank You," she whispered and then laughed at herself for the secrecy: here, she could shout aloud to God and no one would look askance at her.

Joining the lazy flow of humanity, she began to wander down Duval. Few people here moved with any conviction, or as if they definitely had someplace to go. People stood about in small groups on the sidewalk, chatting or calling to those passing in cars. Virtually every store and shop opened onto the street, giving the impression that none had doors. She might have been wandering with thousands of others in the world's largest open air mall. It seemed no one was in a hurry, and she had to deliberately slow her typical Connecticut winter pace. There was no cold to escape here, and the encroaching night had been permanently displaced by the pulsing glow of Duval.

She lost count of the restaurants that offered daily specials and, by the looks of some patrons at this relatively early hour, seductive happy hour libations. Many restaurants had blackboards on the sidewalks listing their menus, and just about every eating and drinking establishment offered outdoor dining. From the tiniest beer and burger joint to large theme chains like Planet Hollywood and elegant, pricey cafes featuring dishes she'd never even heard of, all had set up tables and chairs on patios or roofs or just off the street. Tiny white lights were draped over fences and bushes and slender trees; they were hung from balconies and wound around table umbrellas; they flowed from eaves and canopies. It was as if Christmas never ended here.

People clustered around the menu boards, and she glanced at several in passing. Shark Mediterranean? Shark? Who ate shark? One menu listed Grilled Dolphin with a Rum and Pineapple Salsa, and then added: *"THIS IS NOT FLIPPER: Dolphin is a type of white-fleshed fish, comparable to Mahi-mahi."* Mahi-mahi? Where were the swordfish and salmon and flounder? Where were the fish and chips and fried clams and fried scallops? Her most extensive experience with fish was trying to disguise it enough so Harry would eat it on Fridays during Lent.

The thought of eating Grilled Dolphin with a Rum and Pineapple Salsa outside in this balmy night under thousands of twinkling lights as the mass of humanity surged around her was slightly dizzying. Just twelve hours ago, she'd been seated in a plane anxiously watching them de-ice the wings in the steel gray January dawn. Suddenly, it was all too much. She should have just brought a sandwich back to the cottage and gone to bed. The first day—the traveling day, Macy called it—of any trip was always the worst. She would go back now. Back. Could she even find her way back? She knew Southard was off Duval, but exactly where? She'd gotten so caught up in meandering, that she wasn't sure which direction. Where was the intersection? There was a labyrinth of streets off Duval, and many of them led into their own dark, confusing little warrens.

She leaned on a stone wall and breathed deeply. Wait, she told herself. Clear your mind. Slowly she made her way to some sweeping stone steps that led up to a massive, steepled Episcopal church. A few other weary travelers rested on the steps, including a filthy woman in a dirty, faded denim dress with a bottle of something in a crumpled bag. Motionless, she might have been sleeping, but for the occasional repetitive movement of bringing the bottle to her lips. The others sharing the church entrance, a well-dressed older couple drinking bottled water, a shaggy looking young man reading a thick book, and an exhausted young mother with two toddlers— one asleep and one energetically sucking his thumb—took no notice of the bag lady.

It was such a contrast, this large quiet haven. An Anglican oasis, it seemed as if it should be set on a corner in London, not a few yards away from the Hard Rock Cafe and the Hog's Breath Saloon. Maggie collapsed gratefully on the steps, leaning her back against the solid stone. It even seemed cooler here off the street and away from the over-heated cars and glaring lights. She found herself facing a large sign that introduced the church to passersby. Reading it, she closed her eyes to hold the image of the words in her mind for as long as possible.

BE STILL AND KNOW THAT I AM GOD.

She would not be overwhelmed. She would not retreat. This—this life, this *difference*—was what she'd come for, what Abby had described so avidly. Flipper on the grill would not send her scurrying back into her tunnel. And she *wasn't* lost, but even if she was, all she had to do was flag down one of the ubiquitous pink cabs and give the driver her address.

But not yet. It was not even eight, and she'd barely covered a quarter of Duval, never mind all the mysterious, winding streets that branched off the main way. She would continue on and explore. She'd find a place for dinner, definitely a place where she could sit out in the night. Maybe she'd even stop somewhere first for a glass of cool white wine. At home they always drank red wine. Harry had read some medical report that suggested red wine was good for the heart. She missed white wine, cold and dry. She'd never gotten accustomed to the unchilled red; at room temperature, it had always tasted like prune juice.

Lest her resolve fail, she rose abruptly, and then fell back as the world began to spin. She landed hard on her butt and one hand, but even the pain couldn't cut through the spinning. Dazed and dizzy, she couldn't remember whether to breathe slowly or fast, whether to fix her eyes on one spot or keep them closed. Nausea, aggravated by extreme hunger, threatened. Why hadn't she thought to eat something? Had she had anything since the bran muffin she split with Macy at the airport this morning? She couldn't remember. The whirling continued; she became flushed and sweaty as panic set in with a vengeance.

She felt the cool hand on her wrist before she saw the woman.

She found her dizziness dissipating as she focused on the hand gently gripping her arm. It was pale and strong, the skin stretched thin to the point of translucence, with corded blue veins showing through. Maggie could feel every bone, and yet, there was a comforting strength in this grasp. Her eyes traveled slowly up a slender arm, freckled with age, to a very long, very thin neck. A head seemed to hover over this extraordinary neck, almost as if it was not attached, beaming down at Maggie like a disembodied moon against the dark, night sky. The face, a glorious maze of wrinkles bronzed by the southern sun and fringed with wispy white-blond hair, bobbed slightly as the woman fixed dark eyes, brimming with concern, on Maggie.

Her voice, low and resonant, made it clear that she tempered sympathy with practicality. "You're dehydrated," she said, nodding sagely, and now the long neck and amazing face dipped and rose in long, slow strokes. "Drink this," she directed, pulling a long bottle of water from a copious straw shoulder bag.

"You carry water in your purse." Maggie observed rather stupidly before obediently taking a long swallow.

"Of course I carry water," the woman observed archly, "Everyone in Key West carries water; anyone with any sense, that is. Something you obviously lack, my dear." Maggie almost giggled out loud, though she knew the laughter would be tinged with hysteria. At home everyone considered her the queen of common sense. And here, a mere day's span from home, this odd old woman was accusing her of senselessness. Perhaps she truly had gone through the looking glass.

"I'm Marie," the woman said briskly, watching vigilantly as Maggie slowly finished the tepid water, "and you are?"

"Oh, I'm sorry!" exclaimed Maggie, almost choking on the last swallow, embarrassed by her rudeness, "I'm . . . I'm Maggie."

"You sure?" Marie asked, her eyebrows quirking quizzically. Before Maggie, now blushing, could answer, she continued, "No matter. And you may as well stop apologizing right now. Key West is not a place for regrets. Very few people who come here end up being the same person who arrived.

Everyone on this island is a work-in-progress. Down here, we're living proof that God gives us infinite chances."

This struck Maggie with a force that was almost sacred. Who was this woman who'd filled her with such relief and comfort in only a few moments?

It seemed she was about to find out. "Come along," Marie commanded, taking the empty water bottle and putting it back in her bag.

"But . . . where?" asked Maggie tentatively, still light-headed, "I guess I got myself lost."

"I'm stunned to hear it," Marie declared with a grim smile, "First, some food, and then I'll find your way home for you. You *do* at least know the address, don't you?"

"Yes, of course," Maggie answered with a trace of irritability. She wasn't a complete fool, after all.

"Of course you're not," Marie answered, and before Maggie realized she'd not spoken the protest aloud, Marie added, "But perhaps you shouldn't have gone wandering off on your first night."

Torn between defending herself and asking how Marie knew all this, Maggie had no chance to do either. Marie was already moving away.

Maggie's impression of a lovely ancient crane crystallized as she watched Marie descend the remaining steps, moving with a slow, dignified gait that perfectly matched her long, slender limbs. Anyone else might have appeared awkward, but Marie merely gave the impression of an exotic creature who had adapted her movements to this earthly plane. Maggie could easily imagine her rising from the steps and soaring aloft, her true nature revealed in heavenly flight. Turning back to her, Marie shattered that breathtaking vision, saying impatiently, "Well? Are you coming?"

For all her elongated frame, Marie moved with a slow, almost heavy, grace, and Maggie easily kept up. "We'll go to

Mangoes; it's right by the corner of Duval and Southard, and I can get you home from there easily." Marie said decisively, "I'm half-starved myself. Thought that blasted meeting would never end."

"Meeting?" Maggie asked, realizing she had no idea where Marie had come from.

"In the church," Marie said patiently, "Where you were on the steps? Didn't you know that was the Episcopal church?"

"Well, yes, but was there a service? Umm, do they have Communion?"

Maggie could sense Marie rolling her eyes mentally as she answered, "You must be Catholic. Yes, they have Holy Eucharist. But no, it was not a Mass. It was an ecumenical meeting of church representatives from all over the island. We're trying to plan some kind of joint Lent and Easter program. We do it every year. But, as usual, no one could agree on anything. I thought it would drag on until dawn. Honestly. Sometimes I think ecumenism is nothing more than a nice idea."

Not wanting to be intrusive, Maggie asked tentatively, "Are you Episcopal?"

"Catholic. Eucharistic Minister, to be specific. Couldn't you tell?" Marie emitted a short, dry chuckle, and Maggie was too embarrassed to admit she'd always thought the Eucharistic Ministers at home were a bit show-offish. She, herself, had never felt worthy to distribute the Body and Blood of Christ.

As they walked Marie pointed out selected sights: Fast Buck Freddie's, which perversely sounded like a flea market and was actually an exclusive department store, Jimmy Buffett's famed Margaritaville, from which sounds of tonight's rock and roll band warming up blared, and Ripley's Believe It Or Not Odditorium. Maggie couldn't imagine how she'd missed so much in her wanderings. When they passed

Chico's, an upscale clothing store, Marie waved briskly to a reed thin, beautiful Black woman with flawless mahogany skin. Dressed completely from gorgeous, glittering earrings to simple elegant sandals in Chico garb, she might have been a model. At the very least, she was one of the shop's best advertisements.

"That's Glendalynn," said Marie matter-of-factly, "She's the Baptist representative to the ecumenical planning committee. She had to work tonight. I'll fill her in later."

Maggie, still gaping at the woman's stunning beauty, repeated incredulously, "She's a Baptist? I thought they were ... more ..."

"Dowdy?" Marie filled in, and Maggie looked away, feeling foolish. Marie patted her arm gently, "Don't worry. Things here are not what you've known, or what you might expect. You'll get accustomed to it. Would you believe it if I told you that Glendalynn left a successful law practice in D.C. to come live here and manage the store? She came down one winter on vacation and never went back. Not even to get her belongings. She just had everything she wanted shipped down here. Part of it was that she'd had it with the practice of law, but part of it is what some call the Key West syndrome. There are people who come here, vacation, and go home satisfied that they've 'done' Key West. And then there are those of us who come here— sometimes at 20, sometimes at 70—and know, for the first time, that we're home."

Emboldened by curiosity, Maggie asked, "Was it that way for you?"

Taking her arm, Marie led her up to Mangoe's outside entrance. "Why don't I tell you while we eat?"

CHAPTER 3

MARIE, LILY AND THE STRANGER

THE next morning, wakened by the sun burning through the window-wall of her tiny bedroom, Maggie had the same gut-dropping moment between sleep and waking that she'd been having for almost nine months. The moment when her slumbering mind woke to the slashing reality of one word: Cancer.

But this morning for some reason—was it that she'd actually slept through the night for the first time in memory?—her racing mind slowed sooner, and the wrenching vision of her body being invaded faded more quickly. Without deliberate thought, images from the previous evening replaced the pulsing terror, and she smiled a little thinking of Marie.

She'd been greeted at Mangoes like visiting royalty. The young maitre'd, a stunning Val Kilmer look-alike, shed his haughty demeanor as soon as Marie loped into sight. He all but leapt from his elevated platform where he'd been coolly greeting new arrivals from behind a sleek blond wood podium. Abandoning his leather-bound reservation journal, he enthusiastically embraced Marie as if she were his long-lost mother, or grandmother. "Where've you all been?" he queried earnestly in a soft, southern drawl. "It's been ages since we've seen you for dinner."

"Oh," said Marie, flapping one of her long hands dismissively, "It's The Season, isn't it?" As if that explained everything. Later, after Robert had seated them with much pomp at a prime street-viewing table in the lively canopied restaurant, Maggie asked what she'd meant. Marie answered, "Most of us year-round Key Westers go into hibernation from New Year's to Easter. The Season. The time of year when we're overrun with tourists, and you can't even make it down Duval to run an errand. You haven't seen the worst of it yet. Wait until Spring break when all the kids come here to drink themselves silly at the sunset celebrations. It's a wonder they don't end up brain damaged. Wait until March when the bikers start arriving by the hundreds. Some of the hotels refuse to rent to young people, because they'll end up with a half-dozen kids in one room. And then, there's Mardigras. You can't imagine what it's like."

Maggie couldn't, but she was stirred at the thought of such sights, *such life!* It didn't even occur to her to tell Marie that she might not be here in two months.

Marie continued, "So for those three months, we natives stick to ourselves. Hardly ever go up to Duval Street or Sunset on Mallory Square. If we go out at all, it's to local places like Mo's that most of the tourists don't know about. The real Conchs—the folks born here—some of them really detest the tourists. I've seen bumper stickers that say, 'IF IT'S THE SEASON, WHY CAN'T WE SHOOT 'EM?' Of course, no one likes to admit that tourism is the main economy here. The

only economy, if truth be told. So, it's really a love-hate relationship. I don't mind The Season so much. We spend a lot of
time planning the Lent and Easter festivals. That's where I was
tonight, lucky for you, my dear!"

Marie, it turned out, was not only a Eucharistic Minister
at St. Peter's, the island's large Catholic church, she was also
the parish representative on the Lent/Easter ecumenical
planning committee. They used the acronym LEAST, "as in the
least of your brothers," Marie supplied helpfully. Despite her
frustration with that night's meeting, she spoke of the LEAST
festival with deep pleasure and of her parish with pride.
Maggie was reminded of Caroline's commitment to St.
Patrick-St. Anthony as Marie described St. Peter's.

The parish grounds sprawled over several acres and
included a large church, rectory, parish center and school.
The congregation was mixed, or as Marie said, "diverse," heavily influenced by Cuban and Caribbean immigrants. Three
priests, one of whom had been smuggled out of Cuba as a
child, all spoke fluent Spanish and offered *Misa en Español*
every Sunday at noon. They also kept chickens and roosters
in their dooryard, not an unusual practice in Key West.

Marie had taken time from this description to order for
them, and they sipped Mangoritas, a cafe concoction that
came in huge goblets with spears of pineapple, orange
wedges and limes. Maggie had never tasted anything so deli-
cious in her life. She was savoring the luscious drink, when
Marie had changed the subject with no warning at all. "What
were you doing just about passed out on the steps of that
church?" she asked abruptly.

Maggie swallowed the wrong way and had a short
choking fit before she could answer. Whether it was fatigue
or simply a need to confide in someone in this unfamiliar
place, she'd told Marie everything. The words had poured
out so easily, she'd not considered that it was the first time

she'd actually spoken of the whole experience. The cancer. The treatment. Dr. Toser. Abby's unselfish offering of Key West. That frightening, exhilarating Christmas Day. Caroline's outraged protest. Christine's heart-breaking uncertainty. She said little about Harry, and Marie, exhibiting unusual restraint, did not ask. Instead she posed a typically blunt question.

"Were you scared?"

"Not at first," Maggie answered slowly, thinking about it, "I really didn't get scared until it was over."

"Me either."

Maggie had stared, probably open-mouthed now that she thought of it, as Marie matter-of-factly recounted her own battle with cancer. It had been over a decade ago, which meant that she'd probably won, but she'd lost her right breast to a radical mastectomy in the process. "A casualty of war," she told Maggie with her lopsided grin, adding that she'd not thought twice about choosing the most extreme "battle plan."

"Women today, they look for all kinds of alternatives. Choices. Second and third opinions. Herbs. Naturopathy. All that. Anything to avoid losing a breast. And I don't blame them. God bless them! They *should* question everything. Women are more sophisticated now, less trusting," declared Marie. "But that wasn't for me. I wanted them to get it all, and I didn't mind that my breast had to go if that was the surest way. Not a bit. Never understood the big attraction there anyway. It's not like I had much to show off in the first place. And I didn't breast-feed my sons, so there wasn't any sentimental value to me."

As Maggie struggled mightily to keep her eyes from straying to Marie's chest, the older woman continued in her direct way. "I never regretted it either. Nor did Calvin, my husband. He died two years ago, and never once in the nine years between the surgery and when he died did he complain or even give me an odd look. I remember feeling anxious the first time I undressed in front of him afterwards. I even mumbled something about how ugly it was going to be, to prepare him, you know. But he never flinched, never frowned or gasped, nothing like that at all. Instead, without saying a word, he held me and gently ran his finger along that long angry scar. And just before he kissed me, he murmured, "Not ugly at all. That scar? It's a blessing. It's the reason you're here with me."

When the tears filled Maggie's eyes, she'd looked away, not sure what she felt more deeply: the inexpressible poignancy of the exchange between Marie and Calvin, or a bruising envy. She couldn't even imagine herself and Harry sharing such a moment.

Their meals had arrived then, and they filled the charged silence by attending to their brimming plates. Marie had ordered them each one of Mangoes' elaborate signature salads, telling Maggie, "You shouldn't have anything heavy now anyway. And this'll help replace some of the fluid you've lost."

Whatever Maggie's motive for vigorously attacking her overfilled plate, she soon discovered that the food merited her full attention. At home, salad was iceberg lettuce, and except in July and August, a few tired tomatoes that often tasted more like paperboard than sun-ripened fruit. She'd always doused winter salads in heavy Italian dressing just to give them some flavor.

But Mangoes' salads barely needed dressing at all, and the light raspberry balsamic vinaigrette merely enhanced the whole composition. A copious mound of spring greens formed the base, covered with julienne yellow, red and purple (*purple!*) peppers; freshly shredded carrots, currants, sliced fresh figs and chunks of flavorful, blue-veined gorgonzola. A generous sprinkling of spiced walnut halves covered the mountain of vegetables, fruits and cheese. Maggie thought it almost too lovely to eat. Almost.

She and Marie had devoured at least half their salads and split the warm, aromatic contents of a bread basket that included everything from whole grain rolls to pumpkin muffins studded with almonds and dried cranberries, before either spoke. Maggie asked wonderingly, "Are the portions always this generous?"

Surveying the remains of her plate, Marie replied thoughtfully, "It's probably fair to say that they're happy to see me."

They'd finished in companionable silence, and though Maggie couldn't imagine eating any more, Marie insisted they split a slice of Mangoes' famous Key Lime pie, explaining, "Everyone else in the world thinks we invented Key Lime pie down here—or Key Lime anything, for that matter! Truth is, we import 'em." That sobering little fact did nothing to detract from the puckering delight Maggie took in her first taste.

When they left a half hour later, Maggie was amazed to discover it was past midnight. It was the first time she'd looked at her watch in hours. She'd smiled to herself, thinking that Abby would be pleased at how she'd spent her first Key West evening. Somehow, Maggie knew that this ageless, forthright woman had provided more revelation and excitement than any of the reputedly wild temptations of Key West night life.

Mangoes was almost directly across from the corner of Duval and Southard, and Marie had lead Maggie to her own little gate within five minutes. Maggie was pleased to learn that Marie lived only two blocks away. "It's a cute little place," Marie had said of her home, "Bought it when Calvin and I thought we had all the time in the world . . . and didn't nec-

essarily want to spend all of it in Missouri." She'd pronounced
it Missour-a, and there was no self-pity in her voice as she concluded, "Well, we didn't have all the time in the world—who
does!—but we made the best of what we had. That is surely
true."

With that she patted Maggie awkwardly on the shoulder
and turned away. Maggie had stood watching her until she'd
faded into the night. A few minutes later, Maggie was asleep,
comforted by the image of Marie just a stone's throw away.
She did not dream.

Loud knocking shattered her reverie, and she jumped
from her bed, calling, "Just a minute," as she pulled on shorts
and a T-shirt. Mark was waiting on the porch. In one hand he
held a mug of coffee, in the other a super-sized can of Raid.

"Breakfast?" asked Maggie, raising her eyebrows at the
can of Raid.

"Ah, she has a sense of humor," said Mark, "And she'll
need one. Did I mention the termites? They're eating the
place away at an astounding rate even as we speak."

Maggie, her good humor dissipated, stared at him. "I
thought you said this place was brand new," she said, glancing worriedly around the cottage. "I mean, it does *look* brand
new."

"It is," he answered shortly, "Doesn't matter. They're voracious. They'll take down every structure on the island eventually. And then we'll build 'em up again. Conchs say, 'What
the hurricanes don't get, the termites will.' Sort of a local
joke."

Ha, ha, thought Maggie, thinking he might have dis-
closed this tidbit of local trivia before taking her money.
Noting her expression Mark said, "It's not as bad as it sounds.
They won't bother you. They don't eat people or anything."
Half his mouth lifted in that enigmatic smirk. "I'm going to
spray around the foundation now, and then I'll leave the can.

When you see any of the little monsters, just spray 'em and slay 'em."

Now truly alarmed, Maggie asked, "Right now? You're going to spray that poison right now? It's not even eight o'clock."

Treating her to another eye roll, Mark said, "Um, hello? Some of us have to work, you know. Or did you think I made our living off a couple of low-end rents?"

Embarrassed, Maggie swallowed further protest. She had been about to mention that she wasn't thrilled with the idea of having a house filled with poison. She still wasn't convinced her own body had rid itself of the toxins masquerading as medicine. Just the smell of the bug spray would fill her with nausea. She could almost feel it coming, rising in her throat. But she wouldn't let Mark see that; wouldn't tell him anything about the poisons in her life. Averting her gaze she pressed her lips together and went about gathering up her wallet and purse, hoping she wouldn't humiliate herself by breaking down in front of this changeable, sardonic man.

He must have been observing carefully because his voice was softer when he spoke. "Look, you haven't had a chance to get any groceries. Why don't you just step around the yard. Lily's having breakfast on the porch. The company would be good for her. I know she'd enjoy it," he said in the hearty manner of someone trying to convince himself.

Maggie was far from sure that the beautiful, reticent woman she'd met yesterday would welcome any company, much less hers. Indeed, she'd much rather ask him for directions to a good breakfast place within walking distance, but Mark's expression had changed from slightly annoyed to slightly hopeful. She nodded her assent and started out. Still sensing her distress he made a dubious effort to reassure her about the termites. "One good spraying should take care of things for awhile. And after I'm done I'll open all the windows, even the sliders," he said nodding at the glass door that opened onto the tiny, vine-besieged patio.

She gave him a swift searching look. Did he know? Was he patronizing her? Had he glimpsed her scar? Could he tell from her ridiculous hair? But his face was blank, and he turned abruptly to the task at hand. Breathing raggedly, she stepped out onto the porch. He called after her, "'Course when you come back, the place'll be crawling with geckos. You know, those little lizards? But don't worry, they won't bother you. And they don't eat the walls either."

Maggie shot him what she hoped was a dirty look, but he'd already turned away. She swore his shoulders were shaking with laughter as she banged the screen door behind her and entered the door yard. She briefly toyed with the idea of walking out into the street, making sure she jingled the gate bell loud enough for him to know she was *not* going to share breakfast with his mute wife. In fact she yearned to do just that, keep walking until she came to a funky little diner or even a Dunkin Donuts. The prospect of spending an awkward, wordless breakfast with a fragile woman who agonized in the presence of anyone but her husband was not inviting.

"Bet I know what You want me to do," Maggie whispered in a small show of exasperation, her eyes flickering heavenward. And receiving no answer to the contrary, she turned on the garden path and walked slowly around the big house.

Lily's haunted eyes were riveted to the space Maggie filled simply by turning the corner. Whether the woman had heard her coming or had known that her husband would force this company on her, she was clearly expecting Maggie. But as soon as Maggie met her eyes, she looked rapidly away. Sighing inwardly at this unhopeful display, Maggie girded herself with a small hitch of her shoulders and stolidly stepped onto the porch steps.

"Mark told me to come and have breakfast with you, but if you'd rather be alone ... "

When there was no reply, Maggie, both irked and relieved, ventured, "I don't want to impose," and started to descend the whitewashed stairs.

"Please" Lily said in a low, breathless voice, though whether she wanted company or simply didn't want to counter her husband's wishes, Maggie couldn't tell. She hesitated, refusing to move again unless Lily invited her up. Without speaking Lily gestured to an empty chair, and Maggie took it. A wrought iron table was set for breakfast with coffee, raisin scones, and fresh melon. Maggie, unaccustomed to massive midnight suppers like the one she'd shared with Marie, was surprised when the sight of the food brought on a deep hunger pang. For so many months food had become something to avoid, if not dread; here, she seemed to be rediscovering her appetite with a vengeance.

Pouring herself a cup of coffee and reaching for a still warm scone from the napkin lined basket, Maggie noticed a book open by Lily's plate. "Don't let me keep you from your book," she said, "My husband always reads through breakfast, so I'm used to it." She'd meant it to sound bantering, and was taken aback at how aggrieved her own voice sounded.

Lily must have noticed because her eyes narrowed, and she said softly, "I never read until after Mark's gone."

Of course you don't, thought Maggie sourly, and then immediately upbraided herself for what was nothing more than pure envy. For all this woman's frailty, she clearly had achieved a degree of intimacy with her husband that Maggie had long since despaired of. Seeing it hurt. "I haven't even called my husband yet." The words were out before she'd even considered saying them. She and Lily exchanged a long look, both slightly shocked at this admission. Then Lily smiled slightly, kindly, and rose saying, "I'll get some more coffee. And butter for these scones. Mark loves them plain, but I always think they're dry as dust without butter."

They spent an hour together, talking unhurriedly, while they devoured the remaining scones slathered in butter and a rich strawberry jam Lily had also brought from the kitchen. Maggie was glad to see that the lithe, delicate woman had an appetite as voracious as her own. Licking the last of the jam off her finger, she wondered idly if her appetite would ever return to normal. Talk about the pendulum swinging back! For months, she could barely eat; now she could barely stop.

Lily, less self-conscious now that she felt more comfortable, filled in some blanks for Maggie. She and Mark had met twelve years ago in Australia, where she was the development director at a small private college. Mark was hired as a Professor of Economics when the dean of the business school lured him away from the University of Hawaii. He'd already made a name for himself as a brilliant maverick in the field. When he abandoned his position in Hawaii, he'd also left behind a wife and two children. They'd tried unsuccessfully for an annulment, but when they were refused, his wife had fought the divorce. By the time Mark had arrived in Sydney, he was battered and torn by a bitter divorce proceeding.

"He was," Lily recalled with a small, wry smile, "not interested in women. To put it mildly."

Nor was she interested in him. Indeed, an introverted beauty who'd been painfully fighting off unwanted advances since her teenage years, Lily was both disconcertingly shy and fiercely protective of her own privacy. She noticed Mark—"it's hard to ignore that kind of confidence . . . and arrogance!"—but would barely return his occasional gruff greeting. In the end it was her very reticence that attracted him.

"I think he realized that someone as shy as me would never give him the same hard time his ex had," she said with just a touch of sadness. Maggie was about to protest that there must have been more to the attraction than that, but then stopped herself. She, of all people, should know better than to judge the depth, or lack thereof, of any relationship. Still, she told Lily, "However it started, you certainly seem extraordinarily close now."

"We are" Lily agreed softly, the translucent skin of her face and neck growing pink. After a moment she continued, "Anyway, we got married and lived over there for five years. Mark was considered a wonderful asset to the college, but he began to chafe under the pressure and the attention that comes at small private school. To make matters worse, the school was launching a development campaign; they were trying to grow both their endowment and their reputation for academics. Mark started ignoring departmental meetings and parties; he graded on a basis that was all his own; he spent more time publishing articles than reading papers. And he didn't want me working the 70-hour weeks they demanded from me during the campaign. I didn't mind the hours, but all of a sudden, sitting in my office and writing grants and fund-raising letters wasn't enough anymore. I had to go out and meet prospective donors, host fund-raisers, that sort of thing. I hated it, and it drove Mark crazy to see me so upset."

The solution, they'd decided, was to work another year, save as much money as they could, and return to the states. Disillusioned with teaching, Mark wanted work that would allow him to use both his business sense and his body. A colleague from Hawaii who had settled in Key West told of a thriving island that depended on both tourism and construction. Mark had no desire to go back to Hawaii, and Lily, who'd been raised in Australia, liked the idea of a near-tropical climate.

"So, six years ago we bought this place, intending to fix up and rent the two cottages," Lily concluded, "Mark's great with building-type stuff, so he did most of the work himself. He does the books for us and also works on various other construction jobs around the island. Eventually, we'll rent out the first floor of this house, too. We've all the room we need upstairs, and we could use the income. I've never really found a job like the one in Australia, although I work part-time writing brochures and ad copy for the Hilton. I tried bartending—there's always a huge demand for that here—but it made me too nervous."

She looked away for a moment, just as Mark rounded the corner. His eyes widened when he saw them together, and Maggie thought she detected a spark of pleasure in his astonishment. "You're still here," he said, trying not to make it sound like a question.

"Did I need permission?" she asked a little archly, softening it with a small grin.

He responded with his own. "No, no, I think it's great," he answered, and it was obvious that he was speaking his approval more to Lily than Maggie. He bounded up the steps and brushed his lips over his wife's forehead. "I think it's just great," he repeated, looking directly at her. She swiftly raised her eyes to his, blushing with pleasure at his approbation.

He turned to Maggie. "I finished spraying. Give it a few hours before you go back in, especially if you're sensitive to that stuff. I left the windows and sliders open and turned on the air conditioner fan, but it'll still take a while to dissipate. Not much of a breeze today."

"Is there ever?" Maggie asked curiously.

"Sorry, you missed the hurricane season," he said, chuckling as Lily rolled her eyes in mock reproval. He touched her face briefly and started away toward that small truck parked on Southard Street in front of their house, adding, "I'm already late for that new job on Truman Street. Should be back around five, hon. Save my spot."

Lily shook her head affectionately, but her eyes followed him hungrily as he quickly checked the tool box in the bed of the truck and slid behind the driver's seat. Even after he'd waved jauntily, she watched the truck until it disappeared. She looked slightly startled when her eyes wandered back to Maggie, who realized with surprise that Lily had forgotten she was there. To ease the moment Maggie asked, "What did he mean about saving his spot?"

Lily smiled faintly. "You really can't imagine how desperate the parking situation is here. We used to put a cone right there in front of the house where he likes to park, but the police told us we couldn't. We tried No Parking signs, but people just ignored them. We even tried the one that a lot of people around here use: Don't Even THINK Of Parking Here, but it didn't do any good. You wouldn't believe how rude people can be. So it's sort of a joke between us: as if I'd ever go out there and try to keep some obnoxious, irate driver from parking. Of course, Mark would never want me to. But sometimes I wish I could."

Maggie, privately thinking it might be good for her to do just that, said, "Maybe one day you'll surprise him."

Lily shot her an unexpected and frankly appraising gaze. Lifting her chin a little, she asked, "Would you like to use our phone to call your husband? Maybe you'll surprise him."

Touché, thought Maggie, returning Lily's steady gaze with a slow, rueful smile. The silence that fell between them was oddly comforting, perhaps for its honesty. Gradually, Lily also smiled, inclining her head slightly in acknowledgment of the shared moment. Maggie said, "Thanks, but I think I'll wait on that."

Lily nodded, "Maybe you shouldn't wait too long."

"Maybe not," Maggie answered.

Rising, she asked, "Do I need to move my car? I forgot all about it."

Lily breathed out a small, quiet laugh. "I think Mark's getting a kick out of driving our friend across the way nuts. Or more nuts than usual. He'll probably have you move it tonight, but there's no rush."

"What will I do long-term?"

"You'll probably just have to park where you find a space as close to the house as possible. It's not illegal to park on the street, it's just that you can't leave a car in any one spot for more than a day or so. Sometimes, Mark ends up two or three blocks away. We've been thinking of paving over some of the door yard to make a driveway, but I'm resisting the idea. I just got it looking the way I want."

"And it's beautiful. You shouldn't pave it," declared Maggie indignantly, visions of her cool marble angel being replaced by a sizzling rectangular tarmac. "I don't mind moving the car every day."

"You may find you don't need it," suggested Lily, "I hardly ever drive. Besides the parking issue, most of the roads are harrowingly narrow, and Old Town drivers are maniacs. Except for Mark's work or when we have to go into New Town to shop, we tend to bike or walk everywhere. You can always borrow one of the bikes."

The idea of being careless, though initially a bit of a shock, was appealing to Maggie. She remembered a woman who often received chemo in the cubicle next to hers at St. Francis. Joan, her name was, Joan, Maggie now remembered, and she would always say, "Cancer's a blessing. You know why? Because it's taught me what's important. It's taught me to simplify. Simplify, simplify, simplify." She used to drive Maggie crazy, but lately she'd come to appreciate this mantra. After all, wasn't that exactly what Maggie had decided to do? Simplify, simplify, simplify? Try to figure out what really mattered?

She avoided the fact that right now what seemed to really matter was figuring out a way to get rid of her rental car instead of calling her husband. Silently she prayed, I hope You're going to sort this all out for me, because I obviously can't do it on my own.

Aloud, she asked Lily, "What will I do about food? I've only seen one grocery store, and that was in New Town on the way in."

Lily explained that there was a decent little store only three and a half blocks away. "Quite a few Old Town residents use it. Mark and I usually only go to the superstore once every two weeks and use this smaller place for in-between. It's an easy walk, and they have a pretty good deli and bakery."

Maggie, increasingly enamored of envisioning herself dependent only on her feet and, occasionally, a borrowed bike, said, "I've got the car for a few more days. Maybe I'll just return it afterwards instead of renewing the lease." It would give her a chance to say hello to Arthur at the airport, show him how well she was doing.

Lily told her how to get to the neighborhood grocery store, but suggested she first take a drive over to the "only beach worth seeing here."

Maggie, who'd seen nothing but coastline from the plane, was perplexed by the remark until Lily explained, "The real attraction of Key West is the coral reef, not our beaches. They're pretty crummy compared to most islands especially in the Caribbean. In fact, some of the big waterfront hotels actually had sand brought in—imported, Mark says—just to make a tiny beach for their guests. The only real, unspoiled beach is one most people don't even know about—and we try to keep it that way! It's quite a pretty stretch of sand and usually just about deserted. It used to be part of a naval base; the Navy used to be a big deal here. The beach at Fort Zachary Taylor. You should check it out while you still have a car; it's too far to walk."

Maggie decided to go to the beach first and pick up groceries on the way back. She didn't particularly want to return to her little haven until the scent of poison had passed. Lily gave her directions, but when Maggie invited her to come along, her bright gaze dimmed and slid away as she murmured something about having to finish a new ad for the hotel.

Maggie headed directly to her car, not stopping for a bathing suit. She'd brought one, knowing full well she'd never wear it. She'd never felt all that comfortable in a bathing suit before her surgery; she surely wouldn't wear it now, displaying her cut and burned skin for all to see. Bringing it had been more an act of false courage than anything else.

Ten minutes later she'd parked in a near-empty lot, and was climbing a shaded knoll dotted with scrub and pine trees. She could see why the place was such a secret. After she'd crossed Duval, the road had become almost lonely, even more so after she passed Truman Annex, a large gated residential community. There was no beach in sight, even as she hiked up the small incline.

And then there was.

It took her breath away. The calm, serene expanse of water she'd passed yesterday on the way in from the airport was nowhere to be seen. In its place was a wild, surging ocean, its waves crashing on a long, slender pull of sun-whitened beach. No more than a hundred people were scattered over the sand, reclining in sling-back chairs or on colorful towels. No one took notice of her as she stood, catching her breath on the crest of the wooded copse that sloped down to the beach and into the frothy ocean. The sand was coarse and pebbly, and the drop into the sea precipitous, but that only spiked the thrill of unfettered joy fluttering through her. No lifeguard here. She wondered if this was how it felt to discover a new land, a wild and untouched place where danger and hope strove side-by-side.

She'd never much believed in mysticism or, if she were to be honest, even miracles; but she knew in one breathless moment that she would not be surprised to see Jesus strolling along this coast, perhaps stooping to make signs in the sand. She need only close her eyes to bring the vision alive.

She found herself abruptly disappointed that she'd left the cottage without so much as a towel. She had nowhere to sit, nowhere to leave her bag and sunglasses. But why not sit in the sand? Why not kick off her espadrilles, leave them by her bag, and stroll down the beach? Her mother, who would disapprove of such a wanton display, was in Sun City. Her husband, who would roll his eyes at her carelessness, was at his computer store. Her daughters, who would be alarmed at any departure from the norm they clung to, were in Connecticut.

And not one of the people on this beach cared one whit for what she did.

She'd walked for about fifteen minutes, feeling less self-conscious with every rough-hewn step, before she fully realized just how warm the water was. She still couldn't believe this was the same Atlantic whose frigid waters could evoke shrieks even in the middle of August. Without giving herself a chance to stop and think, she plunged into the waves, shorts, shirt and all. The swift, deep drop immediately dunked her, and she rose to the surface soaked and sputtering with unexpected laughter. She remembered how her daughters used to tease her for refusing to get her hair wet whenever they went swimming. Now, rather than being grateful for their absence, she wished for just this moment, that they were here.

She swam a little, now feeling a bit foolish at the thought of emerging with her sodden clothes clinging to her. But the few people this far down along the beach were paying no attention to her whatsoever, and the sun would rapidly dry her clothes. By the time she'd walked back to her bag and glasses, undisturbed as she'd known they would be, she was almost completely dry. Who needed a towel.

Without bothering to check her watch to see if it was lunch time, she stopped at the little snack stand on the cusp of the knoll and studied the menu. Ignoring the few healthy offerings—salads and a plain grilled chicken sandwich—she ordered a cheese dog, and then marveled at herself when she ate it. Good thing she'd lost so much weight on chemo.

"From the looks of your plunge into the waves down there, this must be your first visit to our best kept secret."

Whirling to face the voice, her guard shot up. *He'd been watching her!*

He looked innocent enough in a white, button down shirt with the sleeves rolled up, khaki shorts, and brown loafers. He might have been 45 or 65 with his short, carefully barbered silver hair and closely shaven face. Clearly fit, he was of medium build and fairly tall, maybe six foot. His eyes were pale blue, almost the color of water, clear and bright with curiosity. He held an open bottle of Aquafina water in his hand. He didn't look like a psychopath, but she stared at him all the same. Surely psychopaths didn't carry around Aquafina.

"I'm sorry, I didn't mean to startle you," he said with what appeared to be genuine regret, "It's just that I know almost everyone who comes down here, and I'd not seen you before."

"My landlady told me about it," she answered automatically and immediately chided herself for being so forthcoming. *What are you thinking?* her mind shouted even as her voice, seemingly acting of its own volition, added, "It's my second day here."

He nodded encouragingly, expecting her to go on. Now she truly felt like an idiot. She turned away abruptly and started to walk rapidly away, wondering why she hadn't done so from the first. He called after her, "I really am sorry. My name is Patrick," but she merely increased her pace and swept one hand behind her as if to shoo him away or perhaps communicate her own inadequacy.

He raised his voice once more, "You've got mustard on your shirt—in case you want to go home and soak it."

Wishing with all her might that a crack might open in the parking lot and swallow her whole, she quickly looked down to see the stain, not just one discreet spot but a splatter of yellow that might have been the first stroke of an abstract painting. She all but moaned aloud, covering the last few yards to her car in almost a run. She slammed the door and drove off with undue speed, not daring to look back and see if he was laughing at her.

At least it was on your stomach and not your chest, the voice in her mind chuckled. Very funny, she fumed back, but then she was laughing too. Really laughing, the kind of laugh that peals out and continues in blessed release.

She was still giggling and wiping away tears when she pulled up to the grocery store and went in. Wondering why she'd spent so many years relying on copious lists, she bought what she wanted. Lily had cautioned her to get plenty of bottled water, but beyond that, she picked up whatever struck her fancy: everything from avocados, bran muffins and kiwi to chocolate chunk cookies the size of her fist (FOUR FULL OUNCES EACH, the hand-lettered bakery sign boasted) and several pints of Ben & Jerry's Phish Food frozen yogurt (Chocolate Frozen Yogurt with Swirls of Marshmallow and Caramel with Fudge Fish, as the label explained). Harry had always dismissed it as disgusting, so she'd never tried it. They always had vanilla. She didn't think she'd be buying any vanilla for awhile.

Weighted down with bags, she tentatively entered her cottage not knowing what she feared most: the carcasses of murdered termites or the lingering aroma of Raid. She found neither and gratefully concentrated on storing her food. She discovered, to her delight, that the large refrigerator was brand new. She found new appliances thrilling, especially refrigerators with their pristine interiors, unstained by exploding diet coke bottles or smashed cherries, and their sturdy, gleaming, rust-free exteriors. She'd had three brand new refrigerators in the thirty years she and Harry had been married, and the day each arrived felt like a birthday to her.

Turning with great pleasure to survey her domain, she saw something else new in the apartment. A new phone rested on the desk by the front window, already attached to a jack that was probably also used for the computer. A note, in elegant sloping script, rested on the phone.

Meant to have this in when you arrived. Feel free to make toll calls. L.

Right, thought Maggie, not knowing whether to smile at Lily's cleverness or frown at the implication. She sat gingerly at the desk. Glared at the phone. She *had* called Caroline from the airport in Miami yesterday to reassure her that all was well. And Caroline had not managed to bully her into saying when she would next call. She had not called Harry, but surely Caro had burned up the lines to both her father and sister as soon as they'd rung off.

Harry probably wouldn't care whether she called or not. He was probably having the time of his life, working at the store until the wee hours of the January night, and then eating take-out at his computer when he got home. CNN would be blaring. She used to really hate that. As if the newspapers and evening news were not filled with enough bad news, they had to saturate themselves with it all night? Harry probably kept it on around the clock now and wouldn't even hear the phone.

What did Lily know, anyway?

After four rings the machine picked up. She was right, he was still at work. After all, it was barely mid-afternoon. What had she expected? She listened to her disembodied voice: *"Hello. You've reached Harry and Margaret, but we can't come to the phone just now. Please leave a message, and we'll call you back as soon as possible."* The tone blared and she swallowed. "Hi, it's me. I'm here. Everything's fine. Will you let the girls know I called? Um. There's a new refrigerator in my cottage. Well. Love you."

She sat staring at the phone, waiting for her heart to slow down. What was this sweeping emotion? Relief. It was relief. It was only when she rose to fetch her book that she realized she hadn't left him her number.

CHAPTER 4

ASH WEDNESDAY

ST. PETER'S was everything she'd imagined from Marie's lively description. Now, five weeks after that first evening with Marie, Maggie sat within it's bright airy confines, waiting for the Ash Wednesday service to begin. She'd deliberately come early to give herself this silent hour before the church began filling with its astonishing range of parishioners. Everyone from the island's wealthiest developer (or so Marie claimed), to the poorest Cuban immigrants worshipped here. Maggie had come to treasure her time in their midst, but today, she needed this time alone.

Reflection, she'd always believed, was the whole point of Lent, and so much had happened since she'd arrived, she wasn't sure she could take it all in. She wasn't really sure she wanted to. For eight months she'd done nothing but analyze and agonize and question every word and action of every person in her life from Harry to Dr. Toser. She'd only gradually realized how sick she was of living that way, with such doubt. Now, for the first time, she was learning to react to her life as it happened—"in the moment," according to Glendalynn, who was an intriguing cross between a Baptist and a New Age Spiritualist. But today was Ash Wednesday, and she craved quiet time to take stock. She wondered if this change in her, this unlikely willingness to embrace what might come, was a result of Key West? Or of cancer? She suspected both.

January had passed with incredible swiftness. In Connecticut it was the longest month of the year, dragging on interminably as slate gray seas mirrored cold, bleak skies. Here, the sunlit days passed sweetly, and Maggie was endlessly amused when Key Westers whined about the cold if the temperature dropped below 75. Even the days seemed longer here, though she knew they were in the same time zone. How could time not fly in such a place?

Although she never fell into what one would call a routine—the very word routine was anathema here—her days had taken on a certain shape, even perhaps a substance. Although she made a point of cultivating the tentative bond with Lily and spent a great deal of time with Marie, through whom she met other islanders, Maggie remained essentially alone. It was not necessarily a deliberate choice, but having spent her entire life as a quiet, unintrusive observer, she fell naturally into the role.

There surely was plenty to observe! She'd spent many hours on Duval Street, sometimes with Marie or Glendalynn and a few times even with Lily, but more often alone, exploring new restaurants or shops. Those first few days, she'd walk about for awhile and then buy a take-out meal and scurry home, but each day brought increasing confidence, and soon she was dining out alone when none of her companions were available. Mangoes, where the staff associated her with

Marie and consequently treated her kindly, became her favorite spot. Though Robert always led her to a coveted street-side table, she would occasionally bring a book and sit at the bar so as not to tie up a table during their busiest hours.

She soon discovered that no one was alone for long in Key West, at least not in public. Carl, the Mangoes bartender, with his long blond ponytail, emerald stud earring, and broad open face, was an avid reader. Not only did he make her feel welcome and comfortable, they were soon exchanging books and reviews. Carl had "heard wonderful things" about *Tuesdays with Morrie,* so when Maggie confided she was having a problem getting into the book, he offered to trade her one of his Anne Perry mysteries for it. Soon they were discussing plots and even the authors' personal lives. From there it was a short leap to exchanging their own personal histories. Maggie was continually amazed at how easily Key Westers volunteered what she thought was extremely—and sometimes, excruciatingly—personal information.

Carl's was simply a happy story. He and his partner, also a bartender in a swanky Continental cafe on Williams Street, had just purchased a two-bedroom, two bath, stucco ranch— "sort of a rosy, shell color," he explained. They'd found what they clearly considered the perfect home in a residential part of the island, far enough away from the hustle and bustle of Duval to provide a haven. "Let me tell you, Mag, when the two of us finally get home from work at 2 or 3 in the morning, that old peace and quiet is worth the price of admission," Carl had declared one night as Maggie was making her way through a barbecued chicken, avocado, sun-dried tomato and fresh mozzarella pizza.

"It's got the perfect layout, sort of that circular thing going for it. The realtor called it an 'open floor plan.' Whatever. Tile floors. Tough to keep clean, but beautiful.

And skylights! Mags, you should see our skylights! All that exposure makes it absolutely sweltering, but the place just shimmers with light. We could grow a rain forest in there. We've already got one outside. The place is just smothered with bougainvillea. Scarlet and purple. Gorgeous. The half bath is brand new and basic, but the master bath is really elegant. Double sinks, huge tub, amazing. Of course the kitchen needs help. Desperately. Everything's olive green and old, old, old. Not even a microwave. So fifties. Of course most people in Key West never eat in anyway, but the last thing we want to do when we have time off is go out. So we're having it all redone. The decorator's coming tomorrow. Stay tuned for details."

Carl's excitement was contagious. Maggie, who'd put her book aside to give him her full attention, couldn't help wondering why her son-in-law Tom—about the same age as this effusive young man—never displayed even a hint of such joy. Even after Caroline had announced her pregnancy, he'd balked at buying a small cape in Hartford's southend. "How can I even think of owning my own home in a nice, safe neighborhood when so many of my clients are homeless and hungry?" he'd asked sanctimoniously. Remembering the disappointed tears glinting in Caro's eyes, Maggie felt a rush of anger. At the time, she'd been in the middle of chemo treatments and numbed by her own situation. She'd never even asked Caro how she felt about giving up the new house. Now recalling the scene as one of so many fragments that had barely touched her over those eight months, she deeply regretted her silence.

And when she turned back to Carl, who'd just brought her another iced tea on the house, she felt not one whit of guilt over her traitorous comparison between this kind man and her cold son-in-law. Setting the glass on a fresh napkin and removing the one that had been practically dissolved by condensation in the hot Key West night, Carl looked at her directly and observed, "You know, you're a great listener, Mags. But you don't say much about yourself."

Maggie had quickly looked away, chastising herself even as she did so, I'm acting like Lily! Carl was right, she still guarded her history—her pain—as if it were something precious to be protected from all who might seek it. Carl was courteous enough to avoid a direct question, but Maggie knew she'd not been forthcoming with anyone except Marie. With her stoic "Missoura" spirit, Marie apparently felt no need to go over the same fragile ground again and again, and Maggie, appreciating this discretion, had gratefully lapsed into characteristic silence. Indeed after her first slip with Lily, she'd carefully monitored her speech, preferring to settle safely into the familiar role of listener. Mark, whatever Lily had told him, never pressed Maggie for information. In fact he kept a careful distance as if afraid to disrupt whatever circumscribed friendship might grow between her and his wife. Although clearly suspecting there was much more to Maggie's story than she'd blurted at that first breakfast, Lily never overtly pushed the subject beyond installing the phone. Maggie felt safe on that account: Lily's own limitations would keep her curiosity unspoken.

Maggie's own reticence was only partly because she was still taken aback at how easily people here poured forth their woes and joys. The first night she'd dined with Glendalynn and Marie, following a LEAST meeting at the vine-covered Baptist church, Glendalynn had spoken easily in her slow, deep voice of the life she'd left behind. "I lived in D.C. for almost twenty years before I found Jesus," she drawled, "And when I say I lived, I mean L-I-V-E-D. Big government lawyer. I ran with a crowd up there that was so high on itself, sex and cocaine were just the trappings. Can't believe the things I did. Can't believe the things I thought were important.

"But I'd sworn I'd never go back to Georgia where I was born. The way I was raised? Never. Never spend all Sunday in church, moaning and groaning and waiting for the Lord to save me. I wasn't going to be like my mother. No way. No how. I was going to save myself. Then one Sunday morning, right after sunrise, I was walking home from some all night party the firm partners had given. I shouldn't have been out there in that neighborhood, but I was too tired and out of it and sick of myself to care. I'm about a block from my town-house, and I hear the strains of Amazing Grace. Ringing out like a crystal bell. Calling me. I hadn't murmured the words in decades but I knew them by heart. I followed that sound to a small storefront church. I walked down those steps and inside like I was in a daze. So many people inside, they could hardly move. Mostly poor. Mostly Black. And they were singing and swaying and raising their hands. Importuning the Lord. Beseeching the Lord.

"That day I found the Lord again. Except He hadn't been lost, I'd been the lost one. Two years later I came down here for vacation. And stayed. I was home."

They'd been eating at an outdoor Mexican restaurant called Gato Gordo. Glendalynn, with her extraordinary looks, had drawn many glances, both admiring and envious, when they'd first come in. Now having finished her tale, she began eating her pulled pork burrito with a delicacy that would have passed muster at a four star restaurant. Maggie, immensely impressed, had watched the striking woman for signs of embarrassment or at least awareness of the impression she made. But Glendalynn betrayed no such sign, and Maggie had marveled at this typical Key West attitude. In fact after her initial shock, she rather enjoyed these fascinating revelations and admired the bravery that allowed such candor. Perhaps she even wished she possessed such courage.

But she didn't. At least not yet.

Raising her eyes to meet Carl's frank, concerned gaze, she swallowed some tea and said softly, "My life changed in ways I'd never imagined possible last year. I'm trying to figure out what I really have. Or had. And what I want to have. I'm trying to get back in touch with God." Then she took a deep breath and smiled, "Stay tuned for details."

His face had creased with a wide, kind delighted smile, and he'd put his large soft hand over hers and squeezed slightly before turning to an irate man in a flowered shirt who was loudly demanding a Heineken.

Now, sitting in the still church awaiting the start of the noon Ash Wednesday service, she pondered whether she would ever be able to spill the personal details that seemed the mainstay of Key West relationships. Would she ever be able to tell the sweet, open-hearted Carl about the terror of cancer—had he guessed?—or the confusion she felt about her life and family in Connecticut? About Harry? These were emotions she'd not even confided in Marie, perhaps because she couldn't fully admit or define them herself.

Over the past weeks, Harry had astounded her by defying history. After she'd called and left that stammering message on her second day in Key West, she'd been making a liverwurst, mustard, sundried tomato and red onion pumpernickel sandwich from ingredients she'd purchased at the little grocery store. She was taking a great deal of time over it, remembering how unified Harry and her daughters had always been in scorning her weakness for this combination. Their teasing was so merciless, she'd not bothered to make it for some time and had forgotten her craving. Tonight, she'd even bought chips and spicy V-8 juice to go with her masterpiece. And she intended to eat it in front of the TV. Whether it was her hilarious encounter with the stranger, Patrick, or just the relief of feeling she'd done her duty—whatever that might be at this stage—toward Harry, she felt like this first solitary meal in her own cottage was a celebration. She felt like a teenager whose parents had left her the house, the credit cards *and* the car keys.

She had the television remote in her hand when the phone rang. Rather, it trilled, and at first she thought she'd pressed the wrong button and done something to the TV. Even after she realized it was the phone, it took her a moment to react. Only when it occurred to her that it must be a wrong number or a solicitation—who knew she was here?—did she move to answer it. Her voice cracked a little when she said hello.

"Margaret?"

When a rush of conflicting emotions kept her silent, Harry sped on, uncharacteristically offering an explanation. "I just got home and got your message. I figured I'd work late since . . . well, as I said, I just got home. But you didn't leave a number. I thought you might be calling from a pay phone? Well, you'd left Caroline the number of the people who own the cottage. Your landlords? So I called her and got it. Well, actually Tom gave it to me after making it clear he had better things to do then keep track of us."

Us. It struck her how few times Harry used the word. Us. We. Ours.

"Well, after he gave it to me, I called the number. Your landlords? And the man answered. He didn't want to give it to me at first. Probably figured I should have had it if I was who I said I was. But then I heard him saying something to his wife, and afterwards he told me the number."

Maggie had a sudden flashing image of Lily's small, secret smile, but she had no time to nurse this small aggravation. Poor Harry was winding down.

"And so, I figured I should call. Um. So, your refrigerator's new?"

She had to adjust to his questioning tone before she could answer. If she didn't know better, she would have said he sounded worried, or maybe even uncertain. But she dismissed such an unlikely notion, telling herself he was probably just tired. Drawing a long breath, she answered, "Yes. It is. Really clean and spacious. I just filled it. There's a little store around the corner, and I just got back. They've got just about everything I need. You wouldn't believe what I'm about to eat ..."

They'd talked in this manner for about ten minutes, their voices strained and discomfited but glad for neutral conversational territory. She offered him a few selected facts, telling him about meeting Marie, but not how. She didn't think he'd particularly care that she was wandering around the city dehydrated and exhausted, but she didn't want to give him any ammunition to use against a venture he'd already all but forbidden. Besides, she knew he'd never be able to keep such information from Caroline, and she could just imagine her daughter's violent reaction to the image of her mother collapsed on the Episcopal Church steps. She also described Fort Zachary Taylor in great detail, but omitted her daring plunge into the ocean as well as meeting a strange man and the sloppy cheese dog she'd consumed at the snack shop. She'd no real reason to avoid these details, but there was no point in testing Harry's patience. She didn't mention the termites either.

Harry, after his initial monologue, had little to add. He spoke tentatively of the weekend sales at the store, as if anticipating her lack of interest but having nothing more exciting to offer. He started to report on the girls, but then realized he knew as little about his daughters' lives as he now did about his wife's. But even when a long silence stretched, one she couldn't think how to fill, he'd stayed on the line. She'd smiled a little to herself then, thinking that even in her absence he craved her silence.

She asked him to give her number to the girls, knowing full well he might forget if she didn't mention it. To her surprise, he answered, "Already have. I e-mailed it to them right after I hung up with your, um, landlord." She'd forgotten that. Harry and the girls e-mailed each other regularly. At least he had that.

Finally, mercifully, he cleared his throat as if preparing to ring off. She held her breath, wanting them both to be released from this now. He asked, "Could I call you again? Tomorrow?"

"Tomorrow?" she repeated too quickly to hide the strain in her voice.

"Well," he said, and she detected a touch of raw hope in his voice, "Well, it's Sunday."

Sudden, unexpected tears burned her eyes. *Well, it's Sunday.* His day off. The only day he couldn't burrow into his safe routine at the store. Sunday. The first day he'd really be alone. Without thinking, she replied, "Of course. Tomorrow." And her stomach contracted at the eagerness in his response, "OK, then. Same time? I'll call you. Love you."

He hung up so fast she didn't have a chance to say it back. And then, when she realized he'd done it deliberately in case she didn't respond, a few of the scalding tears fell.

They'd talked in the same guarded fashion the next night, and thereafter, he'd called her two or three times a week and always on Sundays. Bemused, she often thought that he'd not spoken as much with her in a year—*the* year she most needed to hear his voice—as he had in the past five weeks. Lord, she prayed silently huddled in the back pew as a few Ash Wednesday celebrants filtered into St. Peters, I truly am an empty slate. Write something that I can understand. Because right now, everything's in a different language.

The church was growing crowded. Today's mid-day service was to be a gathering of the faithful from every corner of the island, the first of several ecumenical events Marie, Glendalynn and other members of LEAST had planned. St. Peter's had been chosen because it was the largest church, but it was clear that every faith community was well-represented. A group of veiled women, bent with age and clad in long black dresses, complete with hose and sturdy black shoes despite the heat, filed slowly in, settling in a pew they obviously considered their personal territory. Tall, ebony-colored men and women in vivid African garb were not far behind. Well-coifed older white women in pastel suits and matching pumps were among the crowd, some clinging to balding gentlemen who might have been first or second spouses. Or perhaps simply companions. Tourists, dressed in every style from amaryllis-splashed sundress and pale twill trousers to bathing suit tops and cut-offs, strode in, a few impatiently checking their watches as if resenting every lost moment of vacation.

There were others, Catholics that Maggie recognized from attending Mass here, who craned their necks about as if awed and a little perplexed to see their sanctuary filled with strange penitents. Children of every race and color darted among the adults and in and out of the floor to ceiling windows that lent St. Peter's its unique open-air character. The priests kept chickens and roosters that frequently wandered into the church through these window-doors, startling Maggie every time she saw them strut in with their distinctive, jerky gait, stretching their scrawny necks and bobbing their shrunken heads. But today they were nowhere to be seen, their domain disturbed by this mass of humanity. The crush of heat from close bodies threatened to overwhelm the air conditioning, but no one moved to close the windows. Indeed, people were already gathering in the side yards to participate as best they could in this extraordinary service.

As a Eucharistic Minister, Marie would be part of the procession that included ministers and members from Congregational, Lutheran, Baptist, Seventh Day Adventist, and Eastern Orthodox congregations among others. Glendalynn would also march up the center aisle, tall and proud, representing her church as choir director. Thanks to Marie, LEAST's greatest triumph thus far this year, was securing the participation of a retired rabbi and an Imam, both from Miami.

"For Ash Wednesday?" Maggie had asked incredulously when Marie told her.

"For Ash Wednesday in *Key West*," Marie had answered emphatically with her now familiar flapping hand.

This diverse group of clerics and lay assistants was to gather in the wide boulevard in front of the church. Traffic police were already assembling when Maggie had come in an hour ago; apparently this annual service had garnered something of a reputation for crowds. The Key West police obligingly kept drivers, sometimes irate, at bay to allow celebrants easy access to St. Peter's. A wailing dirge sounded from the massive organ to signal the start of the procession.

Maggie had selected her usual half-concealed spot in the back pew on the left, but now she regretted her customary reticence. A very large woman had seated herself with great ceremony and much huffing and puffing next to her, effectively blocking much of her view. The woman, freely perspiring in defiance of the church's laboring air conditioner, was pressed uncomfortably against Maggie, making it difficult for her to lean forward to see the parade of celebrants. She caught only a glimpse of Marie and Fr. Dominick, and then, Glendalynn beside a small, dignified man with an embroidered yarmulke.

Her perspective hardly improved when they reached the altar, as she struggled to see over a forest of people, most of whom somehow seemed taller than she. The celebrants had filed off into two rows on the left and right of the main altar, leaving only the clerics in the direct line of vision behind the altar. Marie, Glendalynn and the other lay participants were only partially visible as they took their seats for the various readings and prayers.

The sound system, at least, was adequate. The traditional Catholic liturgy had been liberally expanded to incorporate all the assembled traditions. Each cleric read a passage about renewal and the need for penance from his or her holy book, and the entire congregation was mesmerized when the Imam, a handsome, ascetic-looking man rose to read from the Koran. Likewise when the rabbi followed, his voice ringing out Isaiah in a way few here had ever heard.

Maggie found herself tremendously moved as she listened to the reverent words spoken out openly in this unlikely community. She dropped her face into her hands, not to hide tears, but to draw the words close and hold them within. It was a universal message. Repent. Change. Hope. For the Lord will come to save His people. And yet, in the midst of this promise, both somber and joyous, her spirit cried out.

But what does it mean for me? Was cancer a punishment? What must I repent of? Is this, coming here, is this the change I am to make? What should I do? Where is my hope? Have You come to save me, too?

And even as her heart poured forth these rending questions, a small, dark, strangling thing from within castigated her. How dare she question the Lord? How dare she consider Him accessible? How dare she consider Him her *Friend?* Look what had come of that!

But she recoiled from that sibilant voice, knowing with an instinct as true as the Lord's presence in this place, that this voice was an enemy; granted, an enemy within her, but an enemy nonetheless. She had come here to rediscover God, and this thing most surely wanted her to fail. God had never left her, but this tiny monster had raised a clamor to deafen and muddle her. Ridding herself of it would take all her strength, and she understood abruptly that even that would not be enough. She'd been shown repeatedly over the past year just how puny all her strength was.

She needed God's help. She needed His strength. She needed to open herself to Him and let His power flow through her, combine with her pitiful human will to banish this tenacious villain. It would not be easy. Even here, immersed in God's presence in a way she'd never known, it shrieked with all its evil might to keep her from hearing and feeling God.

It cannot keep you from Me. My grace is enough for you. All you need do is let it go, and when your grip on it loosens, I will take it from you. I am the Lord Your God, Who loves you.

The words formed in her mind, written large and clear, overpowering the thing she now knew was of her own making. Taking her hands from her face, now soaked with unabashed tears, she drew a sweet, deep breath of incense and grace. Then, ordering her cruel creature into her lungs, she blew out forcefully. A gesture of body and soul, she knew it was just a start, and when the large woman beside her, hearing it as a sob, patted her shoulder comfortingly, Maggie smiled.

The service continued, and though it threatened to be the longest Ash Wednesday rite in Key West's history, the crowd was rapt. There was no fidgeting or sighing, and even the tourists who'd entered with one eye on their watches were becalmed. Maggie, now attentive again, thought perhaps she was not the only one who'd come here with shadowed anguish and a deep hunger for healing.

Glendalynn's minister, a slender, silver-haired Black man provided an unexpected sense of release. Starting in a sonorous, low timbre, he spoke of sin and repentance, humility and forgiveness, his voice rising in a crescendo as members of his own church sang out, "Amen," and "Yes, brother," by way of encouragement. Soon, he had most of the congregants crying out and swaying, clapping their hands and raising their arms in the air. Maggie, who'd always thought this kind of thing a bit put on, was surprised to feel a genuine surge of excitement as she joined in.

It was probably appropriate that he was the last speaker, for the crowd lapsed into a humid, panting exhaustion. Holy Communion would come next, followed by the distribution of ashes for those who wished them. Priests, deacons and eucharistic ministers stood at the front of the church in four separate stations. Just before the shuffling line of communicants blocked her view, Maggie was comforted to glimpse Marie turning to the left aisle where she would distribute the host while a colleague stood behind her with the cup. The line was long, but the hot press of bodies was somehow, here, not unpleasant.

Pleased to receive Communion from Marie, Maggie came forward slowly, her hands carefully cupped before her. "Maggie, this is the Body of Christ," Marie declared, and Maggie gently took it. She briefly closed her eyes in thanksgiving and started down the long aisle.

One of the last to receive, she felt many eyes upon her as she made what now seemed an endless trek back to her seat. Wishing again that she'd had the forethought to sit closer to the altar, she raised her eyes to the organ loft, knowing there would be no choir today to follow her progress. There was only the organist who'd blasted out the sweet, mournful dirge that had started the service. And he was looking right at her.

Patrick.

She barely made it to her seat, all but stumbling into the arms of the matronly woman who had been watching her closely and now reached out to grasp her, all but hauling her into the pew. Maggie could feel her face, white as sand a moment before, suffused with hot color. He had been there all that time! Had he been watching her? Had he seen her own wrenching epiphany? Of course not, she told herself sternly, don't be an idiot. He would have had to be hanging over the balcony like a chimpanzee to have seen her. He could not have spotted her until she joined the line for Communion.

Then a horrifying through struck her. What if he'd been there the whole time she'd been sitting in church before the service, overwhelmed with thoughts and emotions? Didn't organists often come early to make sure all was tuned and ready? Had she heard any rustling above during her meditation? But what if he'd just stood there watching her? She wouldn't have heard that, would she? Mortified, she groaned softly, prompting her ever-sympathetic neighbor to give her a crushing one-armed hug.

Stop being such a fool, she upbraided herself. As if he'd be interested enough to stand and watch you for an hour! Don't flatter yourself! He probably wouldn't even recognize you as the same mustard-stained, bedraggled mess who climbed out of the ocean that day.

Then why, in the split second her eyes met his as she returned to the pew, had he broken into that infuriating, knowing grin?

There was a rustling through the church as the lines reformed for ashes. She was not moving. There was no way she would walk back down that aisle again only to find him watching her with insolent amusement. Then, as her large neighbor lumbered to her feet and made room for Maggie to go forward, a languorous, melancholy music filled the church. Maggie squeezed her eyes shut. On this, of all Ash Wednesdays, she desperately yearned for the humbling cross of ashes. If he was playing the organ, he wouldn't be watching her. She rose.

On the way back, after Father Dominick had gently pressed the cross onto her forehead, she kept her eyes riveted to the carpeted floor. Although the organ played on, she would not risk glancing up.

Following the evident tradition here, she filed out with the rest of the crowd directly after receiving ashes. Once she reached the street, she kept going, darting quickly onto the small side street that would lead her past the tiny cemetery with its eerie raised graves and back to her cottage. As she practically raced around the corner, she heard Marie's voice booming out after her, but she didn't turn back. She would tell Marie she didn't hear her. Anything to avoid what was sure to be a humiliating encounter. As the strains of a somber melody trailed behind her, she didn't know whether to feel relieved or mocked.

She hadn't seen him since that first day at Fort Zachary Taylor. She'd returned to the beach several times, always cajoling Lily or Glendalynn to come along, thus providing herself an excuse to politely avoid him. Or so she told herself. Each time she'd managed to ignore the small twinge of disappointment at his absence. Increasing her pace as she passed the vine-covered graveyard, she flushed hotter just at the thought of her aberrant behavior.

Disconcerted by her own overreaction, she recalled a lunch she'd had with Macy over a year ago. It had been the previous Christmas; having finished shopping early, they'd decided to treat themselves to an expensive meal. Leaving the suburban Hartford mall, they'd driven to Max's in the city, a restaurant known for its upscale business clientele, especially at mid-day. Macy, always dressed to the maximum advantage, was wearing a red wool dress, well-fitted and clinging. She paraded seductively after the maitre-d' to their table, evidently delighted that he'd selected one at the far end of the restaurant. Margaret, cringing behind her, couldn't help but notice the many admiring glances directed at her bold friend.

"What was that all about?" Margaret, uncharacteristically annoyed, had asked once they were seated and the maitre-d' had moved away.

"What?" Macy had asked innocently, casually inspecting her red manicured nails.

"Macy!" Margaret had insisted still embarrassed, "You had half the men in here drooling, and not over their food."

Macy had observed her coolly for a moment and then leaned forward intently. "Listen, there's nothing wrong with a little bit of harmless flirting," she'd said unapologetically, "In fact, *your* marriage might benefit from a little strutting every once in awhile."

Margaret had looked at her aghast, and sighing in exasperation at her naiveté, Macy had continued, "Let's be honest. We've both been married long enough to know that after those first few years, or those first few kids, things cool down a bit in the bedroom. Passion takes a little effort. It's a matter of feeling good about yourself, of feeling attractive. Of making *him* think you're still attractive. And if I feel I'm attractive to someone besides my beloved husband, well, that can only spice things up with him. Right? It's not like I plan to actually do anything.

"Come on. You're not going to tell me that things in the intimacy department are as good between you and Harry as they were 25 years ago, are you?"

Margaret, feeling uncomfortable and prudish, had demurred and managed to change the subject. Though she'd never discuss it with anyone, much less Macy, the truth was that things *had* always been good between her and Harry when it came to the "intimacy department," as Macy had so quaintly put it. At least when it came to physical intimacy. Indeed, what she and Harry had always lacked in emotional closeness, they made up for physically. Even when she knew that other couples their age had a fading sexual life, hers and Harry's had remained strong.

Now, finally slowing her pace as she neared the cottage, Maggie admitted something she'd never allowed herself to acknowledge before: she'd managed to accept Harry's emotional inaccessibility by telling herself that he expressed all his love in the privacy of their bedroom. She'd told herself that his strength and commitment there reflected what he couldn't communicate in any other way.

But was it true? Or had she convinced herself that sexual intimacy was enough for their marriage so that she wouldn't have to consider the truth? Or the alternative?

Lowering herself gingerly into the wooden chair on her porch with a dry mouth and racing pulse, she confronted the questions she'd avoided for most of her married life. They'd become more pressing over the last eight months. She and Harry had not made love once since the diagnosis. After three decades of passionate sex, they'd barely touched each other. And of course, their long-standing routine of showing affection only in private had made it all but impossible for them to resort to casual affection. The sweet, quick kisses and lingering touches she'd seen pass between Lily and Mark were achingly unfamiliar, and she felt a sharp pang of loss every time she glimpsed these displays.

To be fair to Harry, she'd shown no signs of desire. At first, she'd been simply horrified about the cancer, and after chemo started, she was often too sick and exhausted to care. But had he been responding—or not responding!—in what seemed to him a patient, loving way to her illness, or was he repulsed by the disease? Had he been hopefully awaiting some signal from her, or had he been relieved to avoid sex in the new world of cancer?

Now that she'd cracked the window for such disturbing questions, they whirled in with a turbulence that left her reeling. But she would not back away. If this time was to account for anything in her life, she *could* not back away. If her marriage was little more than an empty shell, she had to admit it and face the future.

But if it were true, why had Harry been so angry about this retreat to Key West? Wouldn't he have simply been relieved to be free of her? Why had he hunted down her telephone number and persisted in calling her every few days? Was he calling merely because his routine had been disturbed, and he was rattled? Or was it because he'd admitted the prospect of a profound loss that he'd not faced, much less communicated, during last year's ordeal?

And now that some compelling instinct had driven her away from him, would they each be able to find answers in separation? What if each came to a different conclusion? What if the answer *was* the separation?

In the midst of all this, how was she to resolve the conflict she felt at the sight—let's face it—the very idea of Patrick? Was it only because he embarrassed her, that she was so discomfited by his presence? Or was it as Macy had said?

Did she sense in him someone who would find her attractive, and therefore, make her feel attractive again? Did she think his attention would wipe away her scar, smooth out her burns, erase the gaping wound of cancer?

Besieged and frightened, she flung herself from the chair and fled inside. The wet heat of the closed cottage crept around her, but she didn't stop to switch on the air. She could not hesitate now. Striding into the bathroom, she closed the door and faced the full length mirror she'd effectively ignored from the day she'd arrived. The perspiration beaded on her forehead and ran through the cross of ashes, leaving smudged trickles on her face.

Slowly, forcing herself, she peeled off the white peasant blouse Christine had given her last Mother's Day. She stripped off the soft cotton camisole she'd taken to wearing because it felt soothing against the burns and covered the whole mess more completely. She watched the camisole drop to the floor, and then with tremendous effort, raised her eyes.

The scar had grown elongated and smoother, nothing special were it not for where it was. If it had been along her leg or arm, it might have been from knee surgery or a childhood accident. The burned skin had nearly healed, though it was tight and shiny. She touched the area tentatively; there was no pain. Not there anyway.

And then she knew. No man—not Harry, not Patrick, no man—would reject her because of this. Rather it was the unmended, burning gash in her spirit from which they would recoil.

Who wouldn't?

Wrapping the blouse about herself, she sunk to the cool tile floor, and for the second time in as many hours, a plaintive cry rose from her heart: *I can't do this alone. Where are You?*

And for the second time, blessedly, the words came to her, writ bold and strong: "Be still and know that I am God."

She felt her pulse slow and her ragged breathing ease, and then smiling wryly, she whispered, "Easy for You to say."

Chapter 5

Valentine's Day at Mangoes

She couldn't remember the last time she'd actually dressed with any care for Valentine's Day. But it was also Marie's birthday, and Maggie wanted to honor the spirit of the occasion. A number of LEAST committee members would attend the party in Marie's honor—at Mangoes, of course—and Maggie was determined to make a good showing for Marie's sake, if not for the day's.

She slipped on a dark rose colored, sleeveless, raw silk dress. If fell like a smooth, sophisticated sheath, one she would have never given a second glance if Lily hadn't insisted. They'd stopped in at Chico's yesterday on their way to Fort Zachary Taylor so Maggie could get details of the birthday party from Glendalynn. As Maggie chatted with Glendalynn, Lily had typically shied away to the racks of clothes. She was holding the dress firmly when Maggie turned back to her.

"This is perfect for the party," she said in her soft, breathy way. Glendalynn immediately weighed in with her approval, moving straight to Lily's side in a show of solidarity. Maggie, surprised and distracted by the intuitive gentleness Glendalynn showed Lily, had been hustled toward the dressing room. Her half-hearted protests were ignored as Glendalynn, ever the brilliant saleswoman, had pronounced, "She's right. It *is* perfect. Just try it on, for heaven's sake. Don't be such a priss. It's not exactly a slinky, sequined, spaghetti strap black dress, is it? Not that you couldn't use one of *those*, too!"

Maggie had paused to look at the price and turned right around to put the dress back on the rack, but Glendalynn would have none of it. "Don't you poor-mouth me," she declared, "Besides, I'll give you my discount. For a dress like that, it's as good as stealing!"

Maggie, shooting them an exasperated look, had disappeared inside the cubicle and examined the dress carefully. It was a little short for her taste, but the arms were cut high and would provide the coverage she required. Still. She didn't need a new dress, even if it was Marie's birthday. Knowing there was no way out but to try it on, she began undressing, certain the chic dress would look ridiculous on her. Lily, and even Glendalynn, would take one look, and then she'd be off the hook.

Problem was, when *she'd* taken one look in the mirror, she'd fallen in love with the dress. Glendalynn had been smug when she'd bought it without further protest. Though it was probably not so much the dress, she thought now, feeling the silk fall softly around her, as it was how she looked in it. Like someone else. The dress made her look like someone else entirely, and for the first time since last May, the person in the mirror looked not exactly familiar but, well, whole.

Over eight agonizing months she'd been forced to shed Margaret with her curly, dark hair and plump hourglass figure. More accurately, Margaret had been ripped away from her. Yet she'd never become truly comfortable with her replacement and had often been startled by the thin, ascetic woman staring back at her in store windows and mirrors. With her short, thick white hair, haunted eyes and hollowed cheeks, this replacement was hard to fathom and a little frightening. She looked like an impostor wearing Margaret's clothes, which hung limply on her. But she'd developed no style of her own; clothes purchased specifically for her were simply a smaller version of what Margaret would have bought. On the replacement, they'd looked commonplace, boring and unremarkable.

Until now. This dress made Maggie real, brought her to life in a way that had not seemed likely, or even possible. It was like turning on an old black and white TV set and finding that it now projected in full color. She couldn't remember the last time she'd felt so extraordinary in clothes, but she knew it had been long before last May. Perhaps this was the way most women felt in their wedding dress, a piece of clothing that signified a new start, a new life. Hers, however, had been selected more with an eye to expense than elegance, and in it she'd felt only pale, nervous and relieved to have the wedding about to be over.

Now shaking her head briskly, Maggie rolled her eyes. She was standing here, mooning at her own reflection as if she'd never seen it before. She quickly smoothed on wine shaded lipstick, also purchased yesterday at Lily's unrelenting insistence, and ran her fingers through her hair. A comb was useless with this thick mop, but tonight it seemed to fall into a softer shape. Maybe it was growing longer. Starting to turn away, she couldn't resist one more shy glance at the woman in the dress before she quit the bathroom.

She emerged to the sound of knocking, and saw Mark
and Lily standing on her porch in the twilight. She'd not yet
switched on the outside light and didn't at first recognize the
large parcel Mark carried. Flipping on the porch light, she
opened the door and stopped short. Beaming with uncon-
cealed delight, Mark held a huge spray of flowers in an expensive cut glass vase. Roses were artfully arranged with baby's
breath and graceful ivy.

Mark, the nonchalance in his voice belied by an irrepressible grin, said, "Just came for you. Thought I'd bring 'em
right over. Lily came along for the show."

He was lit up like a young boy, and Maggie, despite
herself, had a flashing insight: his pleasure in delivering this
intriguing gift was sharply enhanced by his wife's radiant
participation. Lily glowed with warm anticipation, and
Maggie realized that Mark enjoyed few such happy, normal
occasions. The mundane act of bringing flowers around
back had become a cause for celebration simply because
his wife had willingly joined him. He'd not had to prompt
or cajole her. She'd come along easily, happily, as any wife
might have to watch their friend receive this bounty. But
Lily was not any wife, and so for Mark, this was a joyful
event.

But not necessarily for Maggie.

Her feelings were decidedly more mixed as she trailed
behind Lily and Mark, who'd placed the flowers on the table
and was urging the sealed card on her. "Well, come on," he
teased, "Let's see who the secret admirer is!" Lily went along
with the pretense, her eyes brimming with excitement, probably at the knowledge that it was she who'd had the phone
installed and who'd instructed Mark to give Harry the number weeks ago.

Maggie hesitated. What was wrong with her? They all
knew Harry'd sent the flowers—roses!—but it was so

uncharacteristic, she could not manage the enthusiasm she knew they expected. The arrangement was gorgeous, no question, and the vase itself must have set her thrifty husband back several hundred dollars. She smiled a little at the thought. She could just imagine him agonizing over the less expensive alternatives the florist probably offered him.

But when Harry had finally selected the exorbitant vase and signed off on the costly roses, had he meant to send them to the bland, undemanding woman he'd married ... or to the woman in the dress who was changing daily, before her very eyes?

Summoning up as bright a smile as she could manage, Maggie motioned Mark and Lily into seats and taking one herself, ceremoniously reached for the card. But as she slipped a fingernail under the flap, she abruptly froze. What if the roses *weren't* from Harry?

You are pathetic, she mocked herself harshly. Surely you're not thinking of *Patrick! Patrick,* who doesn't even know where you live? *Patrick,* who played on at the service Wednesday while you fled like a schoolgirl? *Patrick,* who probably thinks you're a wanton slob who can't even finish lunch without wearing half of it?

Lily, misreading her paralysis, said anxiously, "You want privacy, don't you? Mark, let's go."

"No," Maggie said quickly, "Of course I don't want privacy. I'm glad you're here. Both of you." She smiled reassuringly at them and opened the card.

HAPPY VALENTINE'S DAY, MARGARET. I'LL CALL YOU AT 7. H.

Mark and Lily, watching her closely, took the color that rushed prettily into her neck and face as a flush of pleasure. It wasn't.

Oh great, she fumed silently. Marie's party started at 7. It was already after six, and she'd intended to offer Mark and

Lily a cold drink and then walk out with them. And now she was stuck here doing penance for an exhausted marriage and a $500 flower arrangement.

Almost immediately she was ashamed of herself. Was this petty resentment because the flowers *hadn't* been from Patrick? Her stomach plunged at the incipient admission and her flush faded as the color drained from her face.

Alarmed, Lily reached for her hand. "Is everything all right? We thought you'd be pleased. I know whenever Mark gives me flowers, I'm thrilled ... "

And that's just it, isn't it, Maggie thought: Mark gives you flowers. Regularly. Often. Not just to make up for 30 years of lost opportunities.

Again, she knew this was unfair. She could not ascribe motives to Harry without truly knowing what was in his heart. Not that either of them excelled in reading each other's hearts. And after all, why would her husband expect she'd have plans on Valentine's Day? They hadn't gone out together on Valentine's Day for decades.

Lily and Mark were waiting anxiously. She smiled weakly and offered them at least part of the truth. "I guess I'm overcome. This is just not like Harry."

"What is 'like' Harry?" Mark asked quietly.

She looked up at him swiftly to see whether he was judging her. She couldn't have blamed him. What did he know of her, really, other than she'd apparently left her husband for an indefinite time with no particular plan and no other apparent source of income than the man she'd abandoned? Mark knew nothing of the cancer despite her persistent fear that it was somehow evident to everyone. Whatever Lily might have suspected from the still-guarded conversations they'd had, she didn't know much more than Mark, certainly not enough to explain Maggie's presence or her situation.

But she herself would not do so now. She wasn't sure she could. And she *was* sure she didn't want to. Instead, she gave Mark an answer that was part truth, part rueful irony. "Harry," she said deliberately with a humorless smile, "is like a rock. He's the Chevrolet of men."

Thinking vaguely that she'd have never said such a thing a few months ago, she ignored the continuing question in Mark's raised eyebrows and added without a surfeit of courtesy, "I'm afraid you'll have to excuse me. Harry will be calling shortly, and then I really do have to go to Marie's party."

Her landlords rose in consternation, not sure how what should have been a warm, happy occasion had turned cold. Maggie saw anger brewing on Mark's brow, but she would not worry about it now. She had her own worries. Following them to the door, she had the grace to observe Lily's distressed confusion and with a stab of remorse, she said, "Thanks for bringing the flowers. I think I'm just tired and grouchy. I should probably skip the party and take a nap!" She reached out and gave Lily's limp hand a quick squeeze. "We'll talk tomorrow. How about breakfast on the porch?"

But Lily merely shrugged without looking at her. Great. She'd managed to hurt the one person who would be most damaged by her temper. Mark shot her a dark backward glance to confirm her guilt.

She closed the door, disgusted with herself and in a miserable mood. The prospect of a joyful, lighthearted evening had evaporated. She looked sourly at the flowers, wanting to blame them and Harry. Or was it the woman in the dress? Maybe this new creature wasn't quite as desirable and exciting as she'd thought.

She thought about calling Marie to say she'd be late, but abandoned the notion. No one in Key West bothered with such things. Nor did anyone worry particularly about being on time. Or even showing up for that matter. She remembered how annoyed she'd been a few weeks ago after waiting over an hour for Glendalynn when they'd made dinner plans. Maggie had sat at The Hard Rock Cafe feeling like a fool as she nursed a white wine spritzer and watched the street, hoping to see Glendalynn striding in her direction. When she finally stalked home she was even more irritated to find no message waiting for her on the machine. There was no answer when she called her friend's home. By the time she'd gone to bed, she'd still had no word and her aggravation had turned to concern. Glendalynn must have gotten sick or, worse, been in an accident; what else could have kept her from their carefully laid plans without so much as a message?

Maggie, unable to sleep for worry, was up and dressed well before Chico's opened, hoping to learn something from Glendalynn's boss. She was waiting outside the store when Glendalynn strolled up the street, spiffily dressed as usual. Outraged, Maggie demanded, "Where were you?"

Glendalynn, a blank look on her face, responded, "When?"

"Last night!" Maggie cried, now truly angry.

"Oh!" said Glendalynn, realization dawning in her eyes and voice. "Oh that. Well, I was having a visit with my friends Rich and Suzanne, and one of my favorite movies came on the tube—you know, on the American Movie Classics channel? *Guess Who's Coming to Dinner?* I never miss it. I probably catch it three or four times a year. So I just stayed at their place and we ordered take-out. Had such a good time, I just fell asleep on their couch. Didn't get home until an hour ago. Sorry." She waved her hand dismissively and sauntered into the store. Then, as if it was a second thought, she called over her shoulder, "Maybe we can hit the cafe for dinner tonight." Without waiting for an answer from Maggie, who was standing in the street, mouth gaping and hands in the air like a supplicant, Glendalynn disappeared inside Chico's.

Looking back on the incident, Maggie couldn't suppress a smile. Key West and its people were, as Caroline would say, "a learning experience." And what she'd learned so far was that it was about as far from New England as possible while remaining on the same planet. She'd discovered that many Key Westers had come here expressly to escape the norms and routines that governed the rest of the world. Glendalynn, it turned out, had meant no harm and was frankly amazed at Maggie's hurt irritation.

Maggie, in turn, had learned to relax once she understood that expectations here were not the same as at home. She still couldn't imagine skipping a dinner date, but she'd begun to worry less about punctuality—something she was renowned for at home. The nurses at St. Francis had told her she was the only patient they'd ever known who was always early for chemo. That's me, she thought now, the only cancer victim who primly showed up early for her weekly dose of poison.

Maybe these Key West-inspired changes were what caused her to chafe so at Harry's presumption. It wasn't Harry who was technically wrong for expecting her to wait for his call. That was the woman he knew. But after only a few weeks in this unencumbered new place, Maggie was more accustomed to making her own schedule. And keeping it at her convenience. She hardly wore her watch at all anymore. Poor Harry, she thought suddenly, he doesn't have a clue.

The phone rang, startling her out of this disturbing reverie. Pausing to look at the clock hands poised precisely at seven o'clock, she smiled a little and reached for the phone. "Hi, thanks for the beautiful roses," she said into the phone.

"You're welcome, I'm sure. I wish I'd sent them."

Maggie froze. She'd only heard the voice once, but she recognized it immediately. As her mind began to race, her first thought, surprisingly distressing, was that Harry wouldn't be able to get through.

Patrick spoke into the charged silence. "Sorry. Again. I don't seem to do anything but upset you."

"Not at all," Maggie murmured, thinking, he's got that right.

"Then why did you take off so fast after church Wednesday?" he asked outright. "Marie was hoping to introduce us, but you were long gone by the time I finished the recessional. I've really scared you off, haven't I?"

Maggie, feeling herself grow warm, said more forcefully, "Of course not. I just had to get home that day. I'd made plans." There, she told herself, at least you can get a generic lie out without stumbling all over yourself.

A brief silence suggested Patrick's opinion of her unoriginal excuse. Whether too polite to express it, or whether he simply wished to avoid further offense, he merely said, "I wanted to let you know that Marie invited me tonight. I'm not officially a member of LEAST, but I'll be playing at some of the events, so I know everyone on the committee. Anyway, I asked Marie for your number so I could let you know I'd be willing to stay home if my presence would make you uncomfortable."

Even as the protest was forming on her lips, Maggie couldn't help thinking that he'd certainly waited until the last minute to express concern for her sensibilities. Had he put off the call until the appointed time of the party in the hope that she'd already be on her way? Then he could merely pretend to be sorry, yet again, for disconcerting her. She finally managed, "Don't stay away for my sake. Marie would be disappointed. Besides, I'll probably be late. I'm expecting a call from my husband."

Now, what had made her say *that?* Surely Marie had explained at least the rudimentaries of her situation to him. The silence stretched a bit, and she found herself curious to hear how this unflappable man would respond.

"Ah," he said with no inflection, "And it is Valentine's Day, isn't it? Marie mentioned that you were separated."

Perfect, she thought in annoyance, that certainly clarifies the thing. Before she could censor herself, she added archly, "Geographically."

"Well," he commented, the niggling humor in his voice reminiscent of his mustard observation over a month ago. "I hope you'll be able to make it. I'll tell the assemblage about the delay. It is, I assume, unexpected." Before she could think of a suitably cool reply, he'd bid her a cheerful farewell and rung off.

She'd barely had time to digest the fact that she'd been bested again before the phone rang. She glanced up. Seven-o-eight. Oh boy. "Hello?" she ventured cautiously.

"I've been trying you for almost ten minutes."

Actually, eight, she thought taking in the mildly aggriev-ed tone that was as close as Harry came to expressing anger. Before she could make her excuses—*you wouldn't believe the number of telemarketing calls I get down here!*—he drew a deep breath and went on rapidly, "Sorry. That's not how I meant to start. I wanted to start with Happy Valentine's Day."

He paused and she took her cue, "The roses are lovely. And the vase! It's just extraordinary. Waterford, isn't it?" She babbled on, describing the arrangement in excruciating detail and ending lamely, "You should really see it."

"OK."

"Um, OK what?"

"OK, I'll come see the arrangement. I could get a flight down tomorrow. I already checked. I'd fly into Miami and rent a car. I'd be there by two. I figured it would be better to rent a car since you turned yours in. That way we could take a ride up to explore some of the other Keys. Maybe even stay overnight at a Bed & Breakfast somewhere."

NO! Her mind shrieked. I didn't mean it! I don't want to explore other Keys. I've just begun exploring *this* one! I don't want to drive anywhere. I love walking. I don't want to stay overnight at a B&B. That was so typical of him! B&Bs are New England, not Key West.

She asked weakly, "What about the President's Day sale?" Every year, Harry held a huge mid-winter computer sale on President's Day weekend to boost sales during the winter doldrums.

"I postponed it until next weekend. That'd give us a good six days together," he said eagerly, having thought it all out ahead of time. More tentatively, he added, "I thought maybe you'd come home with me."

Silence. There it is, she thought. After a moment, she took a shaky breath and said, "Harry, I'm not ready to see you. I'm not ready to come home."

More silence. Her heart ached at the pain she was causing him. But she knew she was right. It was not time. She was not finished yet. She was not finished becoming who she would be. And what if this dear, strangled man whom she'd dutifully loved all her adult life didn't want that woman?

Finally he said in a low, bruised tone, "Please. Margaret. I miss you. I'm all out of sorts. There's nothing here without you."

Her tears spilled over at the anguish in his voice. She let him hear them in her own when she replied, "Harry, I miss you, too. But it seems to me we've been missing each other for years now. I don't want to come together until we can really find each other again—not just find our old habits and our old routine. And that's what it would be if you came here now, or if I came home. Just a return to what we had."

"Was that so very bad?" he asked plaintively. Then, as if afraid of her answer, he plunged on, "Look, I'll sign us up for Retrouvaille. They're offering classes at Caro's church as one of their Lenten programs. We could drive up together. I'll take the time off. Maybe we could even meet Caro and Tom for dinner once in awhile after the course." While Maggie envisioned the long, silent car trips to and from Hartford, punctuated by a tedious dinner—Thai, since that's all Tom would eat, or pay for—with her grating son-in-law and feverish daughter, Harry added hopefully, "Look, I've learned a lot about Retrouvaille. I think maybe we could get something out of it. I've even been talking to Macy. She thinks it's a great idea."

I bet she does, thought Margaret, recalling in a brand new light Macy's impassioned defense of flirting. She put aside this fascinating bit of information, and her own rather surprising reaction to it, for later review. With Harry depleted and waiting, she considered her words carefully. Perhaps for the first time in 30 years, she must be honest. He deserved at least that. They both did.

"I think you're right about Retrouvaille. I think we could benefit from it. But Harry, that's partly because we don't have much to start with. We've shared a bed and three decades of tradition and routine. And maybe if it hadn't been for cancer, that would have been enough. Maybe I'd have never wanted more. Or needed more. But I do. Now I do.

"I've discovered that when people say so offhandedly, 'life is short,' they mean it. It's not just that life is short; it's that *my* life is short. Maybe very short. Hopefully, not. But the length is not so much the point. The point is that God gave us this extraordinary gift—this life! And you and I, we agreed to share that precious gift. And we haven't shared it. We haven't embraced it. We haven't celebrated it. We've just slogged through it.

"Down here, I'm learning to do more than slog. I'm learning to savor. To take my time. To examine and learn and experience. And Harry. My darling. I want to memorize how to cherish the gift of life before I come back. I want to be able to teach you. If I do that, maybe Retrouvaille really will work. Maybe *we* really will work."

Her sobs were soft in the lingering silence as she fought the tendency of many years to retract and soothe and reassure. This was another thing she'd learned over the past year: sometimes there is no way around pain but through it.

Harry asked quietly, "Do you remember that Valentine's Day at Valle's?"

She hadn't thought about it for years. It had been their first married Valentine's Day, a real occasion in those bygone days where such anniversaries were tenderly noted. She had still been uncertain about whether he'd truly forgiven her for ruining the Hawaiian honeymoon when he came home one day early in February. He told her that Valle's, then a renowned steak house in Hartford, was offering a special Valentine's Day menu. He knew she'd been disappointed when dual cases of the flu had decimated their first New Year's Eve, and so he'd made the Valle's reservations. When she worried aloud about the cost of such an extravagance, he'd told her he'd been saving since New Year's.

They'd worn their intended New Year's finery, garb that would be considered shabbily old fashioned by today's standards: a ruffled ivory blouse and floor-length, velvet scarlet skirt for her, and a heavy charcoal wool suit with a blazing white shirt and skinny black tie for him. Valle's had employed parking valets for the evening, and Harry reluctantly handed over the keys, grumbling a little. But he'd seen her face and recovered himself admirably, taking her arm and escorting her up the steps. They were greeted by a red-velvet clad hostess, who smilingly handed Margaret a single red rose. Thrilled, she accepted it graciously and proudly followed the woman to their table, convinced that everyone in the restaurant watched she and her handsome young husband with boundless admiration.

The memorable dinner, concocted long before anyone had even heard of cholesterol, had been served with a flourish by a young man who turned out to be an ambitious student putting himself through college. They'd held hands during the meal, as they had, for that matter, during the entire drive from Old Saybrook. They'd indulged in the restaurant's famous dense loaf spread with butter, a hearty salad soaked in the creamy house dressing, filet mignon glistening with sautéed mushrooms and onions and huge baked potatoes smothered in sour cream. Dessert was a luscious chocolate mousse cake gilded with bittersweet chocolate hearts. Today, the chef would be imprisoned for attempted murder just for conceiving such a menu. Margaret, anticipating this bounty, had shyly tempted Harry to bed that afternoon, knowing full well she would not want to reveal her bulging belly in an after dinner lovemaking session. They'd made love again anyway when they got home, eventually growing silly as they patted each others' rounded stomachs.

They'd been so young.

"I do remember," she answered softly.

"Well then, don't forget." he said. And he was gone.

Maggie held the receiver for a long moment. Harry, against all odds, had managed to surprise her.

It was some time before she wandered out the door and headed for Mangoes. She no longer particularly cared about being late. Indeed, were it not for Marie, she would not have stirred from her cottage at all this night. The street was thickly dark, and she nearly collided with her wild-eyed neighbor before seeing the rail-thin woman. Elvira, as it turned out, really *was* her name, and a broom had turned out to be her favorite weapon. Maggie had seen her frequently wield it, sometimes waving it in the fashion of a saber, but more often obsessively sweeping the sidewalks surrounding her house. She was out there at all hours, chattering to herself and sweeping like an automaton as if determined to clean any renegade cars away from her curb.

Despite the reluctant tolerance with which most of Elvira's neighbors, including Mark and Lily, viewed her, Maggie was still leery. She stepped off the curb and circled into the street as she approached the woman, who was muttering imprecations as she swept frantically. Her eyes flickered toward Maggie, who gave her an even wider berth. Passing quickly, Maggie couldn't avoid the crawling sensation that the woman was right behind her, raising her broom like a club. It was all she could do not to sprint ahead to the sprightly glow spilling onto Southard from Duval Street.

She slowed her pace when she rounded the corner into the electric flow of life. Duval was alive with Valentine revelers; clearly the wild 48-hour celebration of Mardigras—concluded just a few days past—had done nothing to slake Key West's appetite for celebration. The street was vibrant with people, strolling in and out of stores and cafes, some hurrying to see the next best thing and some meandering as though the night would never end.

Maggie focused her attention on one particularly joyful group. The party was well underway as she watched from the shadow of a store awning across the busy street. Robert had seated Marie and her guests, including Carl who'd taken the evening off just for this occasion, in a fairly secluded corner of the large cafe; they had a good view of the living street theater while maintaining a bit of privacy. Not that they especially needed it. Their pleasure in the event and each other was apparent even at a distance.

Although she couldn't hear their actual words, Maggie saw faces creased with laughter, glasses poised for toasts, hands gesturing to accompany elaborate tales, and plates passed to and fro so everyone could taste everything. Marie was naturally at the head of the table, surrounded by her guests and a number of others who stopped periodically to greet her happily and join the amiable circle for a moment or two. It occurred to Maggie that this must be a landmark birthday, but which one? Sixty? Seventy? Eighty? Surely not, and yet one could not even make a credible guess merely from observing Marie. Did anyone at the table really know?

She recognized most of them. Father Dominick was there, relaxed in jeans and an embroidered shirt. Carl was taking it all in, probably glad to be in the role of celebrant instead of servant, and Glendalynn sat next to her latest companion, a hardware merchant named Bill. Her pastor was also there, as was, to Maggie's surprise, the little Jewish rabbi who'd spoken so eloquently two days ago on Ash Wednesday. Of course, Patrick was at the center of things, and now he raised his voice in a delighted guffaw at some comment of Carl's, bending from the waist in a surfeit of glee. It made Maggie smile to see him.

It was a golden group, softened and blurred at the edges, like a small, intimate party out of *The Great Gatsby.* Watching them from her distant vantage point, she was overcome with a loneliness so desolate it stopped her breath. Would she always be on the periphery, the child at the window, looking inside, waiting, hoping? Would she ever find her place again, whether it be back in Connecticut with Harry or here in Key West? Or anywhere? The desolation became a gaping chasm as she wondered if she'd ever truly had a place in the world at all.

Choking, unable to breathe, she turned to flee back to her one small haven and all but fell into the huge arms that extended to embrace her. Arthur. She knew it was him even before she looked up, even as she stared into the T-shirt that said: HANG WITH JESUS; HE HUNG FOR YOU.

Dizzy with relief and gratitude, she wept in his arms, and he held her quietly, stoically, like a banyan tree with an all-knowing soul. Finally she looked up and said, "I was just going home." Without missing a beat, he answered, "I was just going to wish Marie a happy birthday. You come with me."

Without protesting, she took his arm and as he led her across the street, she whispered, "Do you know how old ...?"

Giving her a mock ferocious look, he growled, "Don't even think of asking."

They were greeted with shouts of welcome and quickly drawn into the circle. Marie received Arthur's bear hug with a proprietary air as though graciously accepting her due. Maggie sat between Arthur and Father Dominick, and though she felt Patrick's eyes follow her, his gaze had surprisingly little impact on her. She'd thought to leave after a few minutes, but the evening passed swiftly. She learned to her delight that Arthur, though not a technical member of LEAST, would reprise the role of Jesus on Good Friday. As he had in previous years, he would carry a cross through Key West neighborhoods, both rich and poor, and to various churches. This, it seemed, was not a great tourist attraction, but this year the LEAST committee was already wrangling with the mayor and city council to be allowed to walk on Duval Street for at least a block or two. "They give the whole street to Mardigras before Lent even begins; they can certainly give us a few yards to show everyone how Lent ends," declared Father Dominick. The procession would end at the Congregational Church, the starkest on the island by all accounts and thus most suitable for that day's silent conclusion.

Arthur, it turned out, was as the Baptist minister averred, "A preacher powerful in word and deed." Though not a member of any particular church, he led several AA groups in Key West and was known as a faith-filled and faithful counselor. He was rumored to rise from his bed at 4 a.m. to meet a fallen brother or sister who'd waited until the bars closed to call him.

Glendalynn abruptly turned to Marie and, utterly changing the subject as was her wont, she asked, "What's your best birthday memory?"

Maggie, who was disappointed that the question hadn't been about Marie's actual age—since only Glendalynn would dare—was nonetheless intrigued. But when she turned to Marie, her breath caught. The older woman's eyes, sharp and bright a moment before, had glazed with memory and a wash of unshed tears. The table was hushed by the time she answered.

"We were in California, Cal and I. We'd not yet discovered Key West then, and we spent two weeks every February in Sausalito, just north of San Francisco over the Golden Gate bridge. There was a ferry that ran almost from the door of our inn, which just about hung over the bay, directly to San Francisco. Occasionally Cal would take the ferry over to spend a morning meeting with potential clients. He always tried to line up at least a couple of meetings; that was how he justified the trip to himself. He was a typical mid-westerner, my Cal.

"During this particular year, he had a meeting set up on my birthday; it was the only day this client could meet him. He'd be back by noon, but I felt mighty sorry for myself and let him know how selfish I thought he was. He said little by way of reply, but on the morning of my birthday, he rose earlier than usual, dressed carefully in the one suit he always packed for these meetings, kissed me gently and told me to go back to sleep, he'd be back even before I awoke. I was furious, having convinced myself he would cancel the business, and barely let him kiss me.

"Now our room had a massive window, facing the bay. We could watch the huge three-deck ferries come and go. I listened to his footsteps echoing down the hall, and determinedly turned my back to the window. I decided to lay there and fume for the entire morning and be in a real state by the time he returned. Except, of course, I fell asleep! When I finally woke, it was near on noon, and the fog had flowed down, as it does, onto the bay. I was immediately a little anxious, though I know those ferrymen are accustomed to such conditions, and went over to the window. I sat there nervously watching the clock and thickening fog.

"Then I saw two things simultaneously: the ferry steaming along solidly, seeming to materialize out of nowhere, still a quarter mile off-shore; and Calvin, alone on the top deck exposed to the damp while the rest of the passengers huddled sensibly below. He was waving. For the whole time it took for the ferry to arrive and dock, he waved his arm in a long sweep, back and forth. He was a tall, lone, gangling man, and he stood there with his hat off. He couldn't even see me, but he had faith that I was there watching for him, worrying. And he just stayed up there, waving.

"That was my best memory."

Maggie felt the tears fill her eyes, and she was relieved to see Carl crying openly as the gentle dignified rabbi put his hand over Marie's and murmured, "You were both blessed."

"Yes. We were." Marie said softly. After a moment, she asked, "Where's my cake?"

They made short work of it, and Maggie, two hours later than she'd planned, rose to leave. She firmly declined Patrick's offer to walk her home, but stopped short at Marie's imperious, "Wait."

"I'm going with you," she announced, and then responded to the round of groans at her desertion, "Listen, I'm old, and it's my prerogative to leave my party when I want to. I'm old enough to make a grand exit." And then, taking Maggie's arm dramatically, she did indeed make a grand exit, earning applause and catcalls as they crossed the street.

The walked slowly, leaving the lights of Duval behind them and merging with the night. "How old are you?" Maggie asked.

"None of your business," Marie answered, following with her own blunt question, "What's wrong with you?"

Swallowing her wan denial, Maggie answered shortly, "Harry called before. I think I might have really hurt him. I don't know what I'm doing. I don't know what I'm doing here!"

After a moment, Marie asked incongruently, "Did you have a good time tonight?"

"Of course," Maggie answered with a touch of impatience.

"That's what you're doing here."

Maggie, a bit annoyed at this facile answer, demanded, "Did you tell Patrick I was separated from Harry?"

"I did."

"Why?"

"You're here. He's there. That's separated, my dear. Whatever else you're calling it, that's separated."

They parted at their respective corners, and Maggie watched her friend's angular form disappear into the close darkness. She paused at her own gate, her eyes drawn to her cottage. The fan light was glowing, spilling soft light onto the spray of roses which shone with their own beauty, a welcoming beacon. Had she left that light on? No. Her eyes flicked over to the dark house looming above the cottage.

There was no light, and she sensed more than saw a stirring in one of the windows.

Lily.

Maggie smiled faintly. It was clear whose side her landlady was on. And yet Maggie knew instinctively that Lily was not necessarily taking Harry's part. Instead, she had the distinct impression that the lovely, fragile woman upstairs wanted the best for her. And somehow Lily had come to believe that *was* Harry. But was it?

Maggie let herself in and walked slowly over to the roses, absorbing the vision they made in the ambient light. As she reached up to switch off the light, she saw that a small gecko had managed to scale the Waterford vase and was resting on the thick-cut rim. He cocked his tiny head, as though questioning her.

"Don't look at me," she told him, "I don't have any answers," and then went to bed.

Chapter 6

One Long, Hard Day

She woke, rather astonished that she'd actually slept at all, and her first thought in the early morning light was that she must make it up with her landlords. Her petty rudeness last night had been inexcusable, particularly in how she'd wounded Lily. Mark, she knew, hadn't shot her that wrathful look for himself, and she couldn't erase from her memory his angry disappointment on behalf of his wife.

Rising quickly, she dressed and walked rapidly down the street to Dunkin' Donuts. She purchased an assortment of muffins and coffee; it wasn't exactly croissants, prosciutto-wrapped melon and English tea, but it would have to do. Bearing these gifts, which she hoped would at least get her through the door, she climbed the front steps to the big house. Mark, on his way out, almost bowled her over. His glowering stare was only somewhat mollified by a quick glance at her offerings. Still, he couldn't resist a small, mean jab.

"Did you tell everyone at the party last night about your roses? Or were gifts from lonely husbands not a fitting topic?"

Her face darkened, but she would not be baited. It was she, after all, who'd brought this on. Forcing a smile, she answered, "It was really Marie's night. I didn't say much at all."

"There's something new," he muttered and passed her brusquely, slamming the truck door and taking off with a short screech of tires. The sound brought Lily to the front door, where she hovered uncertainly upon seeing Maggie. Maggie rushed into the breech. "I brought breakfast. It's not nearly as elegant as what you're accustomed to, but . . . " she trailed off, hoping Lily would come to her assistance.

She didn't. Instead, she stood, silently rooted and wide-eyed, until Maggie finally realized that Lily was actually paralyzed, uncertain herself how to react. Sighing inwardly, Maggie plunged on, "Look, I acted like a real jerk last night, and I'm sorry. You've been nothing but kind to me, and I blew the perfect opportunity to show how much I value your friendship. What I said last night was entirely true. I'm overcome by everything right now; maybe overwhelmed is more accurate. Whatever. I don't feel very comfortable talking about it, but I'm trying to figure out what comes next for me, and last night was particularly confusing. I took it out on you and Mark and I shouldn't have. Will you forgive me? Friends again?"

Lily was still staring, her mouth slightly agape. "You mean you're not mad?" she asked in her breathy whisper.

"Mad?" returned Maggie quizzically. "At you? Why would I be mad at you?"

"For having the phone installed? For leaving the light on the roses last night? For not minding my own business?"

She posed each possibility as if it were an excruciating question whose answer she dreaded. Her voice rose perilously on the last, and Maggie hastened to reassure her. "Lily, I'm not mad at you. You're the one who should be mad. I behaved like an ungrateful brat last night, but not because I'm mad at you. If anything, I'm mad at myself."

Lily looked at her in consternation, and when she finally spoke again, Maggie knew just how deep the misunderstanding between them had become. Her voice quavering, Lily asked, "Did you leave him because he abused you?"

Too stunned to consider her reaction, Maggie burst into laughter. "Abuse me?! *Harry?!*" she exclaimed, and then seeing Lily blush furiously and look down, she quickly recovered herself. "Oh Lily, I'm so sorry. I've given you an utterly wrong impression. And it's all my fault. I show up here mysteriously; I act like I don't want to talk to anyone from home; and then I pitch a fit when my husband sends me a marvelous bouquet of roses and calls me on Valentine's Day. No wonder you're confused. Believe me, it's not your fault."

Somewhat comforted if still perplexed, Lily murmured, "I thought maybe you were trying to hide from him, run away or something. That girl, Abby, she's the one who made all the arrangements for you to rent the cottage. I started to wonder if maybe you didn't want your husband to know where you were. And then last night when you got so upset about the roses and the phone call, I thought I must have really messed up to put the phone in and make Mark give him your number. I thought maybe I put you at risk, and that you were furious with me."

Without stopping to think Maggie left the food on the porch table and put her arms around Lily. The slender, fragile woman froze at first, and then slowly, like a river melting in the spring, relaxed in Maggie's embrace. Maggie, certain she could feel every bone in Lily's delicate frame, eventually stepped back and looked directly into her friend's eyes.

"Listen. You did *not* do anything wrong. You have to believe that. My reluctance to talk about what's really going on has been confusing and upsetting for you, and I'm so sorry about that. But I'm not on the run, Lily. At least not in the way you imagine. Last May, I found out I had cancer. Breast cancer. I've been through treatment; they think it's gone, but it's hard to know with cancer. The whole experience turned me inside out. I don't know how else to say it in just a few words.

"It is like my whole life—my calm, ordered life—became a screaming vortex and everything I thought I valued got tossed into the maelstrom. That's exactly what it became: a clamoring, intense, indescribable, private vortex. I couldn't explain to anyone what was happening. Not to my kind, dull, unemotional husband; not to my needy, frantic daughters; not to my best friend; and at first not even to my sweet, smart assistant Abby who did, indeed, make these arrangements for me when she finally figured out what I was going through.

"But what scared me the most, what really scared me into listening to Abby and getting on a plane for the first time in my life was that I felt I couldn't talk to God. Or that He couldn't hear me. Or something like that. This terrified me. So I came here to try to find Him again, to try to find my life again. To understand what it should be—what I should do—in this new context."

Lily, in an unexpected show of warmth, took Maggie's hands in hers. She asked softly, "And have you found what you came for?"

Maggie breathed out a sound that was half-sob, half-laugh. "I wish I had a clear answer. I have found God again, though I have more questions of Him then I've ever had. But I know He's there, and that is a relief so blessed I can't even describe it. About the rest of it, I'm not so sure. Harry, my daughters, my work, my life are all still whirling around in the vortex. I feel like I'm outside of it now, I've come at least that far with God, but it's like I'm looking in at all the people and parts of my old life and trying to pick what's important. I know that sounds cold. That's what you saw in me last night, that ability to remove myself from everything and just observe. In one way it feels right, necessary in order to have some sort of perspective, and it's so much better than the pure panic I had been feeling. But in another way, it is really frightening. For the first time in my life, it seems like everything is tenuous, uncertain. I really don't know what's going to happen, what I'm going to do.

"I worry, what if I can't bring myself to want my marriage again? What if I can't forgive Harry for leaving me on my own to face the past year?"

Lily interposed quietly, "Does Harry know you need to forgive him? Does he know why?"

"How could he *not* know?" Maggie snapped, refusing at first to consider Lily's suggestion. She'd nurtured her hurt too carefully, held it too closely to entertain the notion that Harry might himself have been paralyzed and stymied by cancer's brutal intrusion into their well-ordered life. After all, she'd told herself many times, if he didn't know how utterly he'd abandoned her, then what was such a stale, uncommunicative marriage worth anyway? But Lily's observation had raised another question: When had she become so resentful? Had it been just now, as she'd had time to think about the past year, or had it been building the entire time?

Reading the conflicting emotions crossing Maggie's features, Lily wisely kept silent. Maggie continued her litany in a more subdued voice, "What if I fall in love with Key West the way so many people obviously have? I've listened to their stories—even your story. What if this starts to seem like home to me?"

Lily regarded her gravely for a long moment before a hint of a smile dispelled her somber expression. "Maggie," she said, still grasping her hands, "Key West doesn't 'start to seem like home' to people. It either is, or it isn't. And if you don't know yet, it isn't. The real question for you is, what will you do when you leave here?"

Maggie felt the breath had been knocked out of her. Lily, using just a few words, had crystallized her worst fear. Yes, she was infatuated with Key West, but no, she had not experienced the extraordinary sense of belonging she'd heard described by so many including Marie and Glendalynn. So what would happen next? What if she didn't belong here *or* there? What if she couldn't fall in love with this new life, and yet, couldn't bring herself to love her old life again? Would she spend the remainder of her days aimlessly searching?

Leading her gently to the wrought iron table where their coffee was growing cold, Lily said, "You need to give it more time. You're trying to distill a lifetime of experience and recover emotionally from cancer. You can't do all that in a couple of weeks." When Maggie looked at her doubtfully, Lily added mildly, "Let's have breakfast."

But an hour later as she returned to the cottage, the food hadn't filled the emptiness in her. The phone rang as she entered, but she ignored it. It was unlikely to be Harry at this hour—he'd be at work, and besides he probably wouldn't call so soon after last night's wrenching conversation—but she was taking no chances.

She'd promised to accompany Marie on her round of Meals on Wheels deliveries, so she headed for the shower, hoping the afternoon's experience would ease some of her own despair. Her mother, who'd been a dedicated volunteer, had always chirped, "There's no better way to forget your own problems than to help someone else with theirs." As with most of her mother's little adages, she'd dismissed this one with an indulgent nod of superficial agreement, but now she wondered about what problems had plagued her unfailingly cheerful mother. If her mother had been troubled, why had she never noticed? Was it that we all want to think our parents are perfectly happy all the time? Or had she been that dismissive, that self-absorbed?

Maggie was beginning to think she'd been absent for most of her own life. Certainly, she'd managed to avoid any exposure to real emotion or pain. Maybe she wasn't all that different from poor Harry after all. The thought left her feeling strangely bereft, but whether for Harry or for her own lost chances she could not tell.

The phone was ringing again when she got out of the shower. Groaning, she wrapped herself in a towel and went to answer it. It wasn't like the day could get any worse, right?

Wrong.

Caroline was in full, wrathful voice before Maggie had even said hello. "What is *wrong* with you, Mom? Well? Can you just tell me that? If not, maybe you can tell me why you *devastated* Dad last night? Do you know what it took for him to send those roses, to make that call? Do you know how hard it would be for him to drop everything and get on a plane and come down there? Do you? No. Of course not, because everything's all about you all of a sudden! Forget Dad. Forget what he's going through. Forget his shock and confusion. And, *of course,* forget us. Forget me and Christine. Don't even give us a second thought!"

Maggie listened silently to this diatribe, calculating in her mind how long before Caroline was to give birth. The doctors had said on or about April 4, the day after Easter, which would make Caroline very pregnant right now; in that horrible stage where her whole body and way of life was under siege, but the end was still not close enough for comfort. Still, Maggie thought wryly, it was not like this kind of outburst was unusual for her eldest daughter. Caro, as Harry used to say, shot first and asked questions later.

When she heard nothing but heavy breathing on the other end of the phone, Maggie asked quietly, "How are you feeling, Caro?"

"Yeah, like you care!" came the reply, more sob than sneer. "Some mother you turned out to be!" she added, lest Maggie miss the point.

Keeping her own temper with surprising ease, Maggie answered, "You know I care, and you will find out in a decade or two yourself that being a mother doesn't mean doing everything for your children all the time. I can't have the baby for you, Caro."

"No, but you could *be here,* couldn't you? Is that so much to ask?" her daughter all but screeched.

Abruptly overcome with weariness, Maggie nearly gave in. Yes, of course I'll be there, she came close to saying. Just to end the conversation. Just to have it over with. Just to have a definable, razor cut role. But one small spark still glowed in a spirit that suddenly seemed weighted by lead, and instead, she answered patiently, "Caro. Listen. I don't know when I'll be home. *You* don't know when you'll have the baby. But I promise you, honey, you'll do it whether I'm there or not. And Tom will be there with you."

Her daughter expelled something between a moan and a frustrated shriek, a familiar sound that told Maggie the worst was over. She waited silently, and after a few seconds, Caroline had collected herself enough to mount a more subtle attack. "OK, never mind me and the baby," she said, her voice now low and intense, persuading, "What about Dad? How could you abandon him like that?"

Maggie didn't know whether to laugh or cry at the irony of her daughter's question. *She* had abandoned *him?* And yet, she knew she could never explain to Caro that it was utterly the reverse situation that had driven her to Key West. To her daughter, she *had* abandoned Harry, and there would be no two ways about it. After all, for all their lives, her daughters had seen her protect, nurture and compensate for their father. The fact that he hadn't managed to do any of that for *her* would be unremarkable to them. Why, she wondered, had it become so remarkable to her?

"Caroline," she said, exhaustion dragging her voice, "I did not abandon your father—or either of you, for that matter. And honestly, I think you know that. When I've worked through the things I need to work through, I'll come home. But it won't be before that." She didn't tell Caroline that her father had been the one who'd abdicated their marriage. She didn't say how deeply she'd longed for Harry's help, his touch, his *participation* for all those long months. She didn't say that even if she came back, it might not be to Harry.

There were some things, it seemed to Maggie, that mothers should not tell their daughters. Even in self-defense.

Caroline was drawing a long breath to launch the next salvo when Maggie said softly, "I love you, Caro," and gently hung up the phone.

It rang twice again as she dressed, and was burring away as she walked out the door on her way to meet Marie. Quickly covering the two short blocks to Marie's bungalow, she found the older woman waiting in her rugged little jeep. Maggie always had to repress a double-take when she saw her friend in this decidedly unlikely vehicle. Marie was not someone who paid much attention to convention, and her choice of transportation certainly reflected that.

The jeep was idling; Marie, one of the few Key Westers who actually owned a garage, did not like to leave it parked outside for very long. Elvira would have loved her. Maggie opened the passenger's door to find a stack of covered trays on her seat. As she looked around for another place to stow them in the rather inconvenient jeep, Marie looked at her impatiently and said, "Just hold them on your lap, for goodness' sake. They won't hurt you! Get in and buckle up. I'm already behind schedule."

Maggie, well beyond having her feelings hurt any more today and also accustomed to Marie's lack of tact, smiled grimly and lifted the trays, sliding under them. "Sorry I'm late," she said, "Caroline called."

"That why you look like something the cat dragged in?"

"Thanks for noticing," Maggie said with a grimace, and Marie, in her typical gruff, kind way, reached over and briefly covered Maggie's hand with her own age-freckled fingers. "Didn't mean anything by it," she commented.

"I know," Maggie replied, "it's just that I feel like one of those huge, balloon-like punching bags that kids whale away at. You know the kind. The ones that have some kind of weight at the bottom so that they keep bouncing back up no matter how many times they're punched into submission. Between Caro and Lily, I feel like I should have stayed down after the first punch."

By the time she'd finished recounting the events of her morning, they'd reached their first stop. But before climbing out of the jeep, Marie looked directly at her. "When Cal died, all our friends and family assumed I'd sell our place down here," she said, "We'd just bought it and intended to grow old here together. They gave me all kinds of reasons to sell: stay close to the family; go back to work to take my mind off things; save money. You name it. I had no intention of selling. I knew this is where I wanted to be, and I certainly didn't want to be back there without Cal. They weren't thinking about what I wanted, though. There's something I learned long ago, my dear. Everyone has their own agenda. You'll be fine as long as you make sure you have yours and stick to it."

With that she picked up one of the meals along with a large paper sack she'd put in the back of the jeep and strode into the first house, a small run-down cottage on Thomas Street. Maggie followed, smiling genuinely for the first time since she'd awakened. Once at the screen door, Marie called out loudly, "Here I am, Maude, and I've brought a friend," before entering.

The darkness in the house was stunning after the bright sun, and Maggie needed a moment to orient herself. The house that gradually materialized before her eyes had the cracked ceilings, worn carpets and faded walls of an ancient dwelling, but it was very tidy. Marie, clearly familiar with the interior, made a brief stop in a kitchen that was no bigger than a closet and then proceeded down a short hallway and into a tiny bedroom. Even here the shades were drawn against the sun; a small, frosted globe table lamp provided the only light. Against one wall was a carefully made single bed with a white, pilled spread that might have been for a child, and a dark mahogany bedside table holding a half-full glass of water and a small, gold-plated, old-fashioned clock. The water and clock rested on an ancient crocheted doily that, once white, had faded to ivory. There was a rubber tipped walker at the foot of the bed beside a covered commode. A matching four-drawer dresser doubled as a TV table, and a tiny black and white television placed precisely in the center of a larger version of the bedside table doily droned tonelessly. A sturdy floor fan whirred audibly, blowing around tepid air.

Everything in the room was neat and small, including the wizened, little woman seated in a high-backed Queen Ann chair covered in what had once been bright floral fabric. Her chocolate colored skin had taken on a grey cast suggesting great age and a near end to her journey, but she sat ramrod straight and watched them with sharp black eyes. She wore a clean, shapeless, sleeveless black house-dress with a tiny white collar. Maggie was reminded of an imperious, watchful starling as the old woman nodded brightly at Marie and motioned impatiently toward the TV.

Anticipating her, Marie had already moved to switch it off, and now dropped inelegantly to her hands and knees to retrieve a prettily-painted, folded table-tray from under the bed. There were no other chairs, and Maggie, not daring to disturb the well-made bed, stood silently in a corner. The tiny woman's eyes darted back and forth between her and Marie. "Now, Maude, don't be rude," Marie directed, as she opened the tray and placed it firmly on the woman's lap. "Say hello to my friend Maggie."

"Hello, friend Maggie," repeated the little woman, and Maggie wasn't sure if Maude was greeting her or mocking Marie. Her bright, winking eyes offered no hint, but Marie chuckled and patted her knee, saying, "It's a wonder anyone comes to visit you at all, you scamp!" Maude's eyes grew truly merry at this affectionate rebuke, and as Marie placed the carton of food in front of her, she reached her frail thin arms up and circled Marie's neck. For a brief moment, they held the fragile embrace, Maude's dark wrinkled face pressed against Marie's own creased cheek. Maggie's throat ached at the sight, and she realized that fewer years than she might have imagined, or hoped, separated the two women.

"Now, now," Marie said briskly, "Time to eat. We'll visit with you while you have your dinner. At least we'll be more interesting than that old television of yours." Maude, her sharp humor back in place, raised her eyebrows quizzically as if withholding judgment on Marie's claim of superiority over the television, and Marie again laughed dryly at her expression.

Sitting unceremoniously on the bed, Marie did most of the talking, telling Maude about her birthday party and then moving onto various tidbits of local news. Maude listened closely, grunting assent and nodding periodically as she ate delicately, peering up at Marie between tiny, lady-like bites. She seemed to concentrate as carefully on Marie's words as she did on the food, and so Maggie was surprised to see that she'd completely polished off her dinner. Not even a crust of the requisite bread slice or a smear of the butter pat remained.

Crossing her plastic fork and knife carefully over her empty plate, Maude looked up at Marie expectantly. Maggie, curious, also looked to her friend, who dragged the paper sack out of the corner where she'd left it when they'd come in. Staring into the bag solemnly for some time, Marie returned Maude's waiting glance and asked, "Chocolate chocolate chip or peanut butter fudge?"

"Peanut butter fudge," Maude crowed excitedly, and Marie removed a plastic-wrapped cookie, the diameter of which nearly out-sized Maude's little face. With great ceremony, Marie swept away the empty food carton and placed the massive cookie directly in the center of Maude's tray. Eyes shining, Maude observed the treat with unsurpassing delight, and gently, without actually touching it, placed her wasted hands with fingers splayed on either side of it, treasuring it.

Maggie, pierced with a pain both sharp and exquisite, looked away. But Marie simply asked Maude, "Will you save it for later?"

Maude, removing her gaze from the cookie with some difficulty, nodded wordlessly, and Marie said, "Well, your milk is in the fridge. Will you be able to get it when you're ready?"

"I do believe I will," Maude affirmed, adding, "This is a pretty good day."

A pretty good day, Marie told Maggie as they returned to the jeep, meant that Maude would be able to make what for her was an excruciating long journey down the hall and into her kitchen. On a pretty good day, she could make it to the half-bath off the hallway to use the toilet and wash up at the sink. On a pretty good day, she managed to dress herself and make her bed, though the two tasks might take well over an hour.

On a bad day, Maude would be so crippled by arthritis that she'd not get out of bed at all except to crawl painfully to the commode. She would have to drag herself to the end of the bed and lower herself onto it. On a bad day, the powerful medication that she seldom took because it wreaked havoc on her stomach, would barely take the edge off her brutal pain. On a bad day, Marie would find her in an antiquated lace nightgown humming *Amazing Grace* through gritted teeth, unable to even watch television for the agony.

"Doesn't she have any other help at all?" Maggie asked in a voice strained with distress.

"Of course she has help, but do you think anything would be enough?" Marie replied. "She has a daughter and grandchildren who are torn between love, guilt and grueling frustration because she refuses to go into a home, or even to allow an aide to come and stay with her. It was only last year after a bad fall and a stay in the hospital, that she accepted the need for a home health aide to come in twice a week. And that was only because the admitting doctor at the hospital refused to let her come home until she agreed. Even at that, she flatly refused to work with the physical therapist the doctor sent. When the poor woman showed up, Maude screeched a blue streak and kept it up until her neighbors called the police. That pitiable therapist was nearly hysterical when the police led her out of the house; Maude had told them she was trying to rob her, and it took all afternoon to straighten it out. Needless to say, no one tried to force more help on her. Her church sends in a maid to clean once a week, but we had to tell her she was a volunteer. If she knew they were paying the woman, she'd put a swift end to that."

"Can't her family do anything?" Maggie asked plaintively.

"What do you want them to do?" Marie responded pragmatically. "It's not like she makes it easy on them, and believe me, that sweet old lady has one razor-sharp tongue. I've heard her lash out once or twice, and the blood does flow. They do their best. At least one of her grandkids checks in every day, and her daughter cooks her meals on weekends. But all of them work, and a couple of the granddaughters have kids of their own. There's only so much they can do. Everyone would feel better if she'd go into a home. Everyone, that is, except for Maude."

Marie chuckled, but Maggie was outraged. "Can't you help them talk her into it?"

"Can't *I* help them talk her into it?" Marie repeated. "I couldn't even get her to accept the cookies that are the highlight of her day if I didn't tell her they were part of a surplus program offered by the government. I'm just lucky her thrifty existence kept her from the bakery near Mallory Square where I buy them.

"And besides, I'm not sure I would help them talk her into it if I could."

"How can you say that?" Maggie asked incredulously. "You know how she lives!"

"I do. And I also know it's her choice to live that way. Just like it may be my choice some day," Marie declared, and then, looking sideways at Maggie's unrelenting profile, she added, "And frankly I'm surprised that you, of all people, would suggest that a person's most vital decisions should be made by her family."

Effectively silenced, Maggie stared out the window until their next stop. Marie, in typical fashion, acted as though her pointed reprimand was merely part of the conversation, and ignoring Maggie's sullen silence, cheerfully explained that members of LEAST shared this particular Meals on Wheels route. Mondays and Fridays were her days; Arthur filled in on weekends when there were fewer meals to deliver; Glendalynn took over on Tuesdays, her day off; and Patrick covered Wednesdays and Thursdays.

"He's been asking about you, you know," she told Maggie blandly.

"So I understand," Maggie answered sardonically, refusing to revisit their testy conversation on the subject last night.

"His wife died of cancer four years ago."

Groaning audibly, Maggie buried her face in her hands and then immediately raised it again, demanding, "You didn't tell him, did you?"

"Of course I didn't." Marie answered primly, but before Maggie could exhale in relief, she added, "But you should."

"What?!" Maggie cried, her voice high with encroaching hysteria. Turning in her seat to look directly at Marie, she continued, "You're kidding, right?? Why in the world would I ever do that? I don't even know the man. I've barely exchanged two sentences with him. I can't even decide what I'm going to do about the next five minutes of my life, and you want me to tell some perfect stranger that I'm only two months past my last radiation treatment? You want me to dredge up all his bad memories and mix them up with mine? Boy wouldn't that be fun!

"Are you out of your mind, or what?"

Unperturbed, Marie answered, "Not so far as I know." Then, waiting a beat, she said, "It's not some dirty little secret, you know."

"What isn't?" Maggie asked, exasperated.

"Cancer."

Maggie, deflated and perilously near tears, went back to looking out the window. Marie, however, was not finished. "I don't dwell on it myself, but when I do talk about cancer, I talk to him. He understands. All of it. He was there with her right to the end, and there's a peace in him because of it. It's rather extraordinary, really. For a man, that is.

"I'm not saying you have to tell him. You don't have to talk to him at all. Those are your decisions. But you should make them and make them consciously. You can only float in one direction or another for so long without hurting people. Or at least misleading them."

Maggie did not reply. Despite the truth of Marie's observation, she felt raw and betrayed. She was not accustomed to such harsh declarations. If words could sting so deeply, perhaps Harry was right to employ stoic silence in the face of any conflict. Her stomach twisted at the thought that she was getting exactly what she'd claimed she wanted. Emotion and honesty. They aren't, she thought, all they're cracked up to be.

They made four more stops, and each time, Marie toted the much anticipated bakery sack along with her. Larry, a 77-year-old diabetic, happily received a giant, sugar-free carrot raisin muffin; Clara, a rail thin Cuban immigrant with MS, barely spoke or touched her meal but her eyes glowed when Marie handed her a massive chocolate-chocolate chip and macadamia nut cookie; and Melanie, a 90-year-old who talked incessantly of the days when "the real Conchs ran this island," greedily snatched her brownie, saying, "No nuts, right?"

At their final stop, a picturesque ranch house with well-tended, lovely gardens on Leon Street, Marie left the paper sack in the jeep. When Maggie reminded her about it, Marie said, "It's empty. Jake can't eat sweets. He can't eat much of anything. We come here mostly to visit and keep his sister, Lorene, company."

Maggie followed her up the flagstone walk with trepidation. With all they'd seen, how could this be worse? Expecting to see two pitiful, ancient, dying siblings, she was nonplused when a pretty woman of about 35 answered the door. She wore black slacks with a simple white tunic, and Maggie took her for a nurse's aide until Marie embraced her, saying, "Lorene, how are you both today?"

The lovely, even features trembled and crumpled for just a moment before she collected herself. "It's not a great day," she said softly in a pronounced Southern accent, "but I know he'll be pleased to see you." Then, assuming the role of courteous hostess, she offered Maggie her hand, saying, "I'm sorry to be so pathetic. I'm Lorene. Welcome to our home."

Maggie took her slim, strong hand as Marie said, "Maggie's making the rounds with me. She's here for the season."

"Well, aren't you kind to come," Lorene said, "My brother is always happy to see a new face. Now, can I get you all some iced tea, or should we go right in?"

Oddly, her hospitable warmth filled Maggie all the more with dread. There was something unnerving about Lorene's almost desperate determination to maintain social proprieties. The house was beautiful, expensively appointed and absolutely spotless. Everything was carefully in its place including a collection of elongated Lladro statues and a grouping of elaborately decorated Tiffany Easter Eggs. An artfully arranged vase of lilies and irises graced a marble-tiled dining room table. Maggie wondered if they were a Valentine's Day offering for Lorene, but then discarded the idea. She had the sense that this elegant woman had long since abandoned the prospect of romance, or had it taken from her. The perfection of the gardens, the house and Lorene herself seemed to clash precariously with an invisible, clinging malady that pervaded every room.

Marie suggested, "How about Jake first, tea afterwards?"

"Why that would be just fine," Lorene said gratefully, and Maggie remembered Marie remarking that the visit was as much for Lorene as it was Jake. Steeling herself against the overwhelming reluctance that had possessed her, Maggie trailed the other two women as they proceeded down a hallway to a slightly open door. "You've got visitors, darlin'," Lorene sang out as they walked in.

The room was breathtaking, so full of light, plants and flowers it might have been a greenhouse. The room comprised a corner of the house and two walls boasted huge bay windows looking out into the gardens. The walls were painted a cheerful, textured lemon yellow, the ceiling was stippled white, and all the furniture was white with green accents. Everything was simple, suggesting well-selected quality; no expense had been spared here. There was a wide, white table holding what appeared to be a brand new PC, complete with printer and a file of shining disks. Flowering plants were everywhere, on the matching bureau, the side tables, and resting on a variety of wrought iron holders placed directly on the blond wood floors. A long Captain's table held what appeared to be an indoor vegetable garden complete with flourishing pots of herbs and hothouse tomatoes.

To enhance the spectacular lighting, there were two skylights, though the bed was scrupulously positioned so as to avoid any direct sun. The man lying atop it, who lived in this realm of light, looked as if the sun had never touched him. Propped up by bright yellow pillows that made his sallow skin appear even more sickly, he also looked incapable of enjoying the view, using the computer, or even eating one of the tomatoes growing beside him. He'd been carefully dressed, probably by Lorene, in jeans and a blue polo shirt, but the clothes hung on him. His dark, limp hair, deeply circled eyes and hollowed cheeks combined with the oxygen tubes in his nose, meant a wasting illness. Maggie had a hard time imagining that this man, nearly a corpse already, could ever recover.

And then he grinned. It was just the shadow of a smile, really, offering a mere hint of the beauty he must have possessed not so very long ago. His would have been a delicate handsomeness, much like that seen in so many of today's slender, intense-looking young stars. Maggie's trepidation dissipated, and she watched with growing comprehension as Marie sat comfortably at his bedside. She herself pulled a chair close to the bed, while Lorene sat at the foot.

They spoke for just a few minutes, until it was clear that Jake was exhausted. He barely spoke at all, occasionally chuckling in a hoarse gasp as his sister and Marie traded bits of gossip and island news. His hand, held fast by Marie, was skeletal, and it relaxed completely as he fell into slumber. They crept out quietly; it was obvious that such gentle sleep came seldom to Jake.

They spent another half hour with Lorene, but the sharp, forced humor of the sickroom could not hold up in Lorene's spacious, well-appointed kitchen. After a few attempts at light conversation, she merely sat silently, her back straight against the high-backed Italian bar seat. With the smile—a mere gaping grimace frozen on her face, tears rolled down her cheeks. She did not sob or tremble or drop her face into her hands. She simply sat there, the steady tears tracking through expertly applied make-up, leaving dark mascara streaks.

Maggie had never seen such utter despair. As Marie rose to embrace her, Maggie realized that Lorene was grieving for her brother every day of her life . . . and his.

It was mid-afternoon by the time Marie dropped her off at the cottage. Maggie, wrung out and in a morbid stupor, started to silently climb out of the jeep when Marie's firm hand gripped her arm. "It's not always like that," she said.

Maggie stared at her unbelieving. "How could it not be?" she asked, mournfully, "None of them are going to get any better, or any younger, are they?"

"No," Marie admitted, "but after a while, you'll see their courage and dignity more clearly than their age and disease."

"I don't think I can. I don't think I will," Maggie answered wearily, unsure herself whether she meant perceiving them differently or visiting them again.

"I think you can." answered Marie. "You decide if you will."

Maggie had collapsed on the couch before she noticed the oversized envelope on the computer table. Mail. Each week, Abby forwarded her mail, and Lily brought it around to the cottage. Maggie felt incapable of even opening the envelope, but some need for normalcy, even banality, brought her to her feet. She sat heavily in the computer chair and lifted the envelope. Only then did she notice that it was not from Abby. The return address was The University of Hartford, scrawled in Christine's childish hand. Her heart lifting, Maggie opened the flap.

She pulled out a large wall calendar featuring photos from various famous ballets. Christine had scribbled a few words on a square yellow post-it stuck to the front of the calendar: *Happy VD, Mom! xoxoxoxo Chrissie.* Maggie smiled: how typical of her unfocused child to send her a calendar two months after the New Year. Maggie had always given both her daughters a new wall calendar every Christmas, sentimentally circling family days, anniversaries and birthdays. In the few months when there was no special occasion, she would make up a ridiculous non-event for a particular day and write something silly. It only occurred to her now that she'd forgotten the girls' calendars this past Christmas.

Idly, she began paging through the months, thinking that Christine had selected the calendar for the dance photos. But as she went, she noticed that certain days had been marked with large red hearts. Valentine's Day was the first, and the heart contained the initials *M + D + Ca + Ch.* Her eyes misted; this is what she used to write when the girls were little: *Mom + Dad + Caro + Chrissie.* St. Patrick's Day was marked with a heart that said, *Corned Beef and Cabbage—YUK!* Maggie laughed aloud. She'd always made the traditional meal even though the kids and Harry had detested it, or at least pretended to, sending up a chorus of *YUK!* when she served up the boiled dinner.

Her emotions high, she continued on, noting the Easter heart that exclaimed, *"HE IS RISEN!";* the heart on April 4 that read hilariously, *Caroline POPS;* and the May first heart that proclaimed, Flower Day. The heart on May 12 was larger and had a clear message: *Mother's Day + Ch's recital/graduation = Mom home?*

Maggie studied this heart. It was the only one with an arrow through it.

CHAPTER 7

LIFE'S A BEACH . . . CONCERT

MAGGIE DID ACCOMPANY MARIE ON HER VISITS THE NEXT WEEK. And the week after that, and the week after that, and the week after that. At first she simply told herself it was a Lenten sacrifice. She'd always given up something for Lent, usually chocolate or desserts. But somehow this year, the first year of her new, post-cancer (she prayed) life, refraining from sweets seemed ludicrous, a childish gesture that had lost its meaning.

She'd always admired people who said, "Instead of giving something up for Lent, I'm going to try to do something that matters, make a contribution." This had always seemed to her to be more in keeping with Christ's courageous, agonizing journey. To give something back, in honor of Jesus, Who'd given all, was surely the more fitting Lenten offering. Yet, she'd never bothered; it was simpler just to stay away from her favorite treats. This year, however, was different;

this year called for something more meaningful, even more difficult.

And at the end of that first day with Marie, she could think of nothing more difficult than to continue with these visits. It was the last thing she wanted to do. It was also the one thing she could do to truly give thanks for the gift of healing she'd been given.And yet even as she determined to make this wrenching offer of thanksgiving, she questioned herself. Was she offering herself this way as a form of gratitude or as a hedge against a recurrence? Was she making an act of faith, or was she making a deal with God: Look at me! Look how good I am! Look what I'm doing to prove myself worthy! Look how I'm doing your work! Keep me healthy!

Such self-examination, which in Key West had become a way of life for her, only led to more painful speculation. Did she really believe she was healed? Did she really believe that God would support her, no matter what? If she did, why was she plagued by what Dr. Toser had called the Five Year Fear: that tenacious voice constantly reminding her that cancer was not considered fully vanquished until it had been eradicated for five years. If her faith was what it should be, why was she obsessed with this fear—despite Dr. Toser's warning against it?

She'd come here to reestablish her relationship with God, to reassert her faith, but in the process, she'd generated more questions than answers. She knew now that she had been at fault, that she'd slipped her hand out of God's clasp, and that God had waited faithfully for her to return. Indeed, she could once again feel His presence, and that was a blessed relief. Yet she continued to stumble, questioning, afraid. The revelation that disturbed her most was the realization that her faith, her pre-cancer faith, had not been as rock-solid as she'd thought. It had been an unchallenged faith, easy and perhaps even infantile. This new faith was more of a struggle, an agony, a journey whose destination she could not discern. This required the kind of trust she wasn't certain she possessed. Through it all, she kept returning to the one question that still left her breathless with terror: Was she worthy of the kind of healing, physical and spiritual, that she craved?

And so, a month after her first Meals on Wheels delivery with Marie, she sat at the computer wondering if her Lenten commitment was an act of generosity or expiation.

Accompanying Marie was not the only Lenten task she'd undertaken, but surprisingly it had turned out in many ways to be the easiest. Marie had been right; she'd come to appreciate the grace, wisdom and even beauty of those they visited. Maude had become her favorite. Her outrage at the old woman's insistence on independence, such as it was, had been transformed into first, admiration, and then real advocacy. She'd come to realize that without the little dignity Maude fiercely protected, the old woman would surely shrivel and die. And Maggie, testing true independence probably for the first time in her life, had come to appreciate its value.

That was the reason her other Lenten commitment, and truly it was a sacrifice, had been more difficult. She'd resolved to do it that very same day when she'd finally looked away from Christine's questioning, pierced heart. She'd been seated then at the computer table as well, and her eyes had fallen on the keyboard. The PC was much like the one she used at work. Mark had left instructions taped to the desk about using e-mail. Without giving herself time to reconsider, she'd turned it on, and as the gentle whirring of technology coming alive filled the room, she'd plugged in the modem and read the instructions. She had to look up Chrissie's e-mail address; she'd never communicated this way with her daughters. That had always been Harry's realm.

Dear Christine, began her first e-mail to her youngest child, *I don't know the answer to your May 12 heart equation. I guess I've just begun to realize how much I don't know.*

Christine had written back by nightfall, and Maggie had made her second Lenten decision by the time she'd crawled into bed on that terrible, auspicious day. She would send regular notes to Chrissie, maybe even to Caroline. It had turned out to be both, but it was to Christine that she poured out her large fears and small triumphs. She'd discovered in her daughter's responses a level of comprehension and sensitivity that she'd never imagined. Certainly, she'd never observed it before in the quirky, quiet child. But the endearing, watchful girl had become an adult whose depth left Maggie wondering how she'd missed the transformation. Or had Chrissie always been this way, and she'd just never looked hard enough?

Aside from exacerbating her growing fear that she'd not been the discerning, observant mother and wife she'd thought herself, the ongoing exchange between her and Christine had forced her, sometimes painfully, to acknowledge her thoughts and experiences. Writing them provided a clarity that, while falling far short of providing answers, nonetheless gave her an odd sense of progress, though there was no other concrete sign of it.

Even so, she'd never have written more than her first uncertain note, were it not for her daughter's extraordinary receptiveness. Christine's innate ability to understand her mother's confusion and even fear had astonished Maggie. At first she'd censored herself, leaving out details and emotions she thought might disturb Christine. But Christine's capacity for honesty soon became evident in her responses. She had relentlessly, if compassionately, probed Maggie's most superficial statements, demanding more truth from her mother. It was as if Christine knew that Maggie's anguish was sharper then she was willing to reveal.

For her part, Maggie could not avoid the disconcerting thought that Christine must have sensed her distress and unhappiness long before their first exchange. How long? Maggie wondered. Had Christine seen the silent chasm in her parents' marriage, in their life, before Maggie herself had been able to identify it? And if so, how had this knowledge impacted her child? Had Christine avoided all serious attachments because she feared the kind of emptiness she'd seen in her home? Certainly there had been enough interested boys and, now, young men. Yet Chrissie remained studiously uninvolved, forming loose and easy friendships that went no further.

And what about Caroline? Had she really been attracted to Tom because of his community-minded, socially responsible lifestyle, or had she been drawn to someone who spoke his opinions and emotions regardless of consequence? Had she sentenced herself to a lifetime of pompous proclamations and subtle bullying because she craved passion, regardless of its price?

These were not questions Maggie had dared broach with Christine, despite their new found openness. Christine's willingness to embrace her mother's experience may not extend to intrusive questions about her own life. Besides, this was a discussion they must, someday have face-to-face. E-mail, Maggie thought, was not adequate for probing how much damage you'd done your daughters through your own blind complacency.

But it had opened a door between her and her children, and thus she perched perspiring at the computer on this hot St. Patrick's Day. She started a long note to Caroline, trying to assuage her growing fears about the birth. All signs were good, but Caro had always been a worrier, and Tom was not helping by continually dismissing her fears and reminding her that the birth process was a natural one that women with far fewer resources than she regularly endured. He was of the opinion, too often expressed by Maggie's way of thinking, that Caroline need only accept that a certain amount of pain would, of course, be inevitable and stop worrying about it. Then he would leave for work, impatiently noting that he was very much needed by his clients, and, after all, someone had to work. Caro had stopped working in her seventh month, and he was determined not to let her forget it. His incipient resentment was only making Caro's state of mind worse.

There were times, more now than ever, when Maggie would have cheerfully choked the life out of her sanctimonious son-in-law. But as it was, she could only do her best to comfort Caro long-distance, and even that might only be done with limited success. It was Tom's attention and support that she truly needed, and Maggie could only hope some of the empathy he displayed toward his clients would eventually come shining through for his wife. The sooner the better.

Meanwhile, she started what she hoped would be a consoling note to her daughter.

Dear Caro, I do understand how you feel. Believe me, this is the hardest time, the weeks before the baby is born. I spent the last four weeks of my pregnancy with you crying. About everything. I can remember I cried all night when your father mentioned he liked the iceberg lettuce in his salad torn instead of chopped. I'd been chopping it. I thought it was the end of the world that I had made such a glaring mistake! What was wrong with me that I didn't know how my husband—the father of my child!—liked his lettuce?? What else was I completely ignorant about?? What other vital things had I missed? And if I couldn't manage to care properly for my husband, how would I ever care for my newborn child?? If I couldn't manage to anticipate the needs of an adult man, how would I ever meet the needs of a helpless infant??

Caro, I tortured myself for hours that night. I never even touched my dinner; never mind the misbegotten chopped salad. Your father gave up trying to comfort me and just went to bed. Of course, he couldn't begin to imagine my true fears; probably I couldn't have even named them myself at that point. It probably all sounds silly to you now, but it may be a little bit of what you are going through, though you are so much more sophisticated and capable than I was.

But maybe Tom is not so different from Dad. Maybe he really doesn't understand what you're going through, just as Dad didn't with me. After all, how could a man truly comprehend the extent of what we experience in pregnancy, never mind motherhood? And looking back over the years, I imagine your father was as scared in his own way as I was in mine. It's just that his fears were less about the changes in his body and emotions and more about his new role as a father. Knowing your father, I can just imagine the questions that must have been eating at him during those last months. Would he be able to provide for a child as well as a wife? Would he be able to take care of both of us physically and financially? Would he be able to keep us safe? Would he continue to progress in his career and would he have to trade family time for a better salary?

Do you think the same questions might be plaguing Tom? He seems so sure of himself and competent, and yet his whole life is about to change in ways he can only begin to imagine. I believe that he will come around and, of course, that you will be a wonderful mother! You'll both do fine. Here, Maggie hesitated for just a moment before adding,

Dad and I ended up doing fine—you and your sister are the living proof!

Maggie read her words over before sending them to Caroline. Though she'd been unduly kind to her arrogant son-in-law, she didn't change a word. He probably *was* hiding his own fear—apparently most men did—and besides, Caroline needed something to hold on to; some sense of solidarity with her mother and every other mother and mother-to-be. Satisfied that she'd provided at least that, Maggie hit the send button and checked her electronic mailbox before powering down.

There were no new messages. She'd stopped anticipating an e-mail from Harry, though when she'd first started her tentative web conversations with her daughters, she fully expected to receive a note from him. Surely Caro, if not Christine, would give her e-mail address to Harry, who would naturally welcome the opportunity to communicate in the technological arena most comfortable to him. At first she dreaded seeing his address pop up in her mailbox, knowing he would likely dredge up their bruising Valentine's Day conversation. Their talk had left her more discomfitted than she wished to admit, and the last thing she wanted to confront was an e-mail version of the same confusion.

But Harry hadn't sent that e-mail. Or any other. Not that first week and not in any of the days and weeks that had followed. He'd continued to call, but never once mentioned her fledgling internet skills. Maggie sensed that he was deliberately avoiding computer communication as though sensing it would put her at a disadvantage. Did he somehow understand that the technology that had so often taken him from her would not restore them to each other now? In the midst of her own uncertainty, she was warmed by his unspoken sensitivity. But then, Harry had always been chivalrous and respectful. When had those quiet strengths lost their power to please her? Or had she simply stopped noticing them?

Though he never directly referred to their painful Valentine's Day confrontation, something had changed in their conversations. There was a freedom that had not existed before, a sense that something elusive had been named and, though not resolved, was no longer to be avoided. Or feared.

She knew he'd be spending tonight with the girls. He'd offered to cook them a St. Patrick's Day boiled dinner, a dubious and hilarious thought for all of them, including Maggie. Harry's idea of cooking a boiled dinner would be to throw hot dogs into a pot of boiling water and warm canned baked beans. Tom, of course, would use the opportunity to work, too dour to appreciate the silly joy of such an occasion. So it would just be Harry and the girls gathering in their warm kitchen, doors and windows cozily closed against the March cold wave that was cruelly staving off New England's delicate spring. Maggie, who'd been amusing herself with visions of the evening and Harry's unintentional culinary antics, was surprised to find herself vaguely bereft. She turned away from the computer and rose abruptly, intent on her own plans for the evening.

It was time to get ready. The sun was still high, and the days were growing longer. At home, that process had always seemed to drag out over an excruciatingly long period, but here the lengthening days seemed natural.

She still didn't know what to expect from this evening's outing. The event itself was not all that extraordinary: a concert on the beach by the Pier House on the sunset side of the island. And while the musician *was* Leon Redbone, an outdoor concert by such a living legend was not an unheard of occasion in Key West. Few Conchs would attend; it was, for all its touted local flavor, still an event of The Season, aimed mostly at tourists or the baby-boomer residents who were still dismissed as "newcomers" by the old-timers.

What made this evening unusual and, thought Maggie a bit anxiously, unpredictable, was the company she would join for the show. Marie, enthusiastically backed by Glendalynn, Patrick, and Arthur had hatched a plan to take their Meals on Wheels clients to the concert. All of them. From irascible, nearly crippled Maude and grouchy Melanie, to Jake who could hardly lift himself from the bed anymore and Lorene, whose obliterating grief was becoming harder and harder to conceal; they were all to come.

With great pomp and circumstance, Marie had formally invited each of them during last week's visit, and Maggie had been surprised when none of them refused or even demurred. Indeed, they'd all responded with breezy acceptance as though fully expecting the invitation, as though their attendance at the concert on the edge of the island would be an easy thing. Clara, the vainest, was more concerned about what she would wear than whether her thin, trembling limbs would carry her to the beach or through the long, humid evening. Only Lorene raised concerns.

She'd waited until after they left Jake, who'd happily accepted Marie's invitation and was snoring gently in the torpor to which he blessedly retreated to escape the pain. Then Lorene had turned on Marie, her southern manners barely concealing her anger. "Don't you think that's a bit unfair?" she asked in brittle, tight voice. They hadn't even reached the kitchen; Lorene faced Marie in the hallway right outside Jake's door. No iced tea was in the offing today.

Marie had asked mildly, "How is it unfair?"

Lorene, barely able to control herself, responded, "Well, take a look at him, won't you? He can barely move, can't take himself to the bathroom without help, and now you've got him all excited about a concert he'll never see. And a picnic he'll never eat. What in the world were you thinking?"

"I was thinking of him," Marie answered unperturbed. "And you." Lorene opened her mouth, but nothing came out, so she closed it again, blinking furiously. Marie continued, "I would have never asked him if I didn't know we could arrange for him to go. Arthur's flirted his way into getting us a van for the evening, one of those poor girls at the airport rental is just smitten with him. He and Patrick will do all the lifting and hard work. Jake's just a feather these days; he'll be nothing for them. They're gentle as they are strong so he'll feel no pain, or no more than usual. As to the picnic, we'll see. Seems to me, he just might be able to take a mouthful or two of something out there in the open air surrounded by great music and good friends."

Lorene started to interrupt, but Marie continued as though she hadn't noticed. "And what about you? When's the last time you've been outside this house? You're even having the groceries delivered, for goodness sake! If it weren't for that garden, conveniently right outside his window, you'd never feel the warmth of the sun on your face! You think you've created a little oasis here, but the trouble with an oasis is that you can forget there's a whole other world out there. And like it or not, child, in a shorter time than any of us want to admit, you're going to need to be part of that world again."

She took Lorene's quavering chin in her hand and raised her ravaged face. Looking directly into her eyes, Marie said, "Jake is going to the concert. You are going to the concert. We are all going together. And we're going to have a marvelous time!"

That had been a week ago, and Maggie, donning jeans and a sweatshirt for the big night, fervently hoped so. She really had no reason to be nervous; she'd not had to do anything. The others had made all the arrangements, buying the food, securing transportation, gathering chairs and blankets, getting permission from family members. All she had to do was show up at Marie's where Arthur and Patrick would pick them up after fetching Glendalynn and the elderly partiers. Patrick had called her last night to ask if they should swing by her cottage and save her the walk to Marie's, but she'd rejected his invitation with a scorn that bordered on cruel.

"In case you haven't noticed, I'm one of the ones who *isn't* disabled," she'd told him rudely, and now she blushed furiously at her disdainful words. He'd answered in his usual jocular manner, noting dryly, "Actually, I had noticed."

Why did she feel the need to be so discourteous to the man? Her confusion when it came to Patrick had only intensified after Marie's revelation that his wife had died of cancer. She'd done her best to avoid him, exchanging nothing but superficial niceties when they did happen to meet at church or a gathering of mutual friends. On the rare occasions when he thought of some plausible excuse to call, she'd rung off as soon as possible, though never with the degree of rudeness that she'd employed last night. Had she felt compelled to make so petty a remark because she knew she'd see him tonight? Had that been her pathetically childish way of warning him off, of making sure he knew she wasn't coming tonight for *his* sake?

Honestly, sometimes she disgusted herself. He was a perfectly nice man who made no attempt to hide his desire for friendship and perhaps something more. Yet, she responded like an inexperienced, surly, frightened virgin who'd never met a man before. It was appalling. He was a kind, sensitive, gentle man. A widowed musician, for pity's sake! She had nothing whatsoever to fear from him. She didn't have to do anything she didn't want to do. And maybe that's what disturbed her so violently.

She didn't know what she wanted to do. Or what she might do.

She also couldn't help feeling that he somehow knew about her cancer, though she believed Marie hadn't told him. She knew Marie well enough to know that she'd have had no qualms admitting it if she *had* told him! But Maggie still couldn't shake the sense that he knew, and she resented how vulnerable that left her feeling. She was troubled by the thought that something showed in her; that against her will, something revealed what she'd been through. Was it obvious to everyone? Or as she suspected, was it Patrick's own experience that allowed him to recognize it, that indelible stamp that cancer leaves even when it's gone?

Had it left its mark on him?

She couldn't continue to act like a petulant child in his company. Tonight was supposed to be about the old folks; it was as good a time as any for her to start growing up a little herself.

She grabbed a sweater—more for one of their guests who might grow chilled during the evening than for herself—and locked the door behind her, leaving the porch light on. She imagined it would be a late night. Elvira was obsessively sweeping her porch, but Maggie had ceased to fear the frantic, pitiable creature. She called out, "Hello," as she had taken to doing, though she had little hope of a reply. As usual, she got none, though Elvira had progressed to where she could briefly hold Maggie's gaze before her frenzied eyes turned back to the inward madness that held her so in thrall. Maggie thought fleetingly that Elvira might fit right in with tonight's group; certainly a match between her and Maude would be worth the cost of admission. But of course it was impossible. Elvira never left her yard, and besides, Marie would not be thrilled to see Maggie leading the neighborhood scourge down the street to their little group.

They were waiting for her. It seemed she was the only one in the least nervous about the night's ambitious adventure. Everyone was in high spirits and clearly anxious to be on the way. It took a moment for Maggie to join the enthusiasm; she was most immediately struck by how bizarre a picture they made. Despite their barely repressed collective excitement, at first glance they looked like a group of hastily patched dolls come to life just in time to play with their strange warped toys. The inside of the van, open at the back so they could watch for Maggie coming down the street, was littered with a disconcerting collection of canes, walkers, wheelchairs, not to mention an oxygen machine and infusion apparatus for Jake.

The occupants themselves made an odd and endearing contrast to the accouterments they required for just this simple outing. Melanie was dressed in the same severe black house dress she wore each time they visited. It was, Marie had explained after their first visit, typical garb for an elderly Conch, and Melanie wore the unrelieved black proudly as a sign of her heritage. For tonight only, she had donned fresh-water pearls that looked as old as she.

Larry, who remained suspiciously stout despite the strict regimen meant to keep his diabetes at bay and significantly reduce his bulk, looked like a Midwestern farmer in oversized denim coveralls, complete with metal buckles in the front. His T-shirt had a rather extensive message that was mercifully obscured by the front of his overalls. Arthur was no doubt the culprit who'd secured the bright yellow shirt covered with black writing, and Maggie thought it better for all involved—including other unwitting concert-goers—that the words were concealed.

Clara, who'd fretted endlessly about her outfit, had settled on a chic pair of black capri pants with tiny embroidered rosebuds paired with a sleeveless, cropped black tunic and black sandals. Clara, in her day, had evidently been quite the fashion plate. Problem was her day was long since past: she now carried about 85 pounds on her five-and-a-half foot frame, and thus, resembled nothing more than a well-dressed scarecrow.

Maude was spry in an unlikely combination of a straw hat and navy sweat pants with a sky-blue sweatshirt that read: Welcome to Key West. Drink Up! Maggie glanced ominously at Arthur who was grinning hugely as he watched her response to his artistry. Sometimes, she thought, he had a slightly twisted sense of humor.

Cranky as usual, Melanie signaled the start of the evening, shouting at Maggie, "Hey, you're late! We're not going to get the best seats! I want to be close enough to touch Leon! Let's go!"

Her sentiment was vociferously echoed by the other five and even Jake, supported by Lorene and reclining on one long seat in the van, gave a weak thumbs up sign. Arthur laughed aloud, a great, deep laugh that emerged from the soles of his feet; Glendalynn rolled her eyes; and Marie chuckled indulgently as she carefully balanced a stacked collection of picnic baskets and coolers on the floor of the front seat. Patrick smiled tentatively at her, and Maggie, remembering her resolution, smiled warmly in return.

She climbed in and they eased onto the street. Key West's narrow streets were not exactly made for large, disabled-accessible vans, but Patrick was apparently accustomed to maneuvering the lumbering vehicle, and they arrived without incident. Marie had arranged for parking with the hotel's manager; his mother in Miami was a very satisfied recipient of Meals on Wheels, and he was happy to help. Not that any sane man who wanted to continue to do business in Key West would have refused Marie.

Their prime parking place—Maggie doubted the band had a better spot—allowed them extremely good access. They had only a few yards to travel to reach the beach, and the same hotel manager had reserved one of the few pavilions on the site for them. Still the journey was arduous; it took them nearly 30 minutes to traverse the distance and settle themselves.

Maggie dreaded the curious and probably annoyed looks they must have been attracting, but her concern for their charges was obviously unfounded. They glanced neither right nor left as they made their way unhurriedly to the pavilion they evidently thought belonged to them. Chattering among themselves, they took no notice of the hordes around them. When Maggie finally dared look around to gauge just how much untoward attention they were earning, she was surprised to find that very few concert-goers had given them a second glance. And those who had were nodding pleasantly, happy to share the evening's joy with such a dignified group. There was no sign of resentment or discomfort. Maggie, returning a number of smiling glances, finally relaxed.

The evening turned out to be more enjoyable than she'd imagined. The pavilion provided a perfect venue. It was dry with comfortable benches along the inner circumference as well as around a spacious table on which Marie and Patrick arranged the copious picnic. They'd brought old-fashioned fare somewhat modified to meet the needs of dentures, food allergies, dietary limitations, and weight considerations: homemade lemonade that had been perfectly sweetened by Lorene, faux fried chicken (oven-baked in a brave attempt to maintain the pretense of Larry's diet), low-fat red potato salad with a yogurt based dressing, three bean salad with its sweet tangy liquid purchased directly from the deli, huge whole grain rolls, sliced fresh fruit, and an assortment of the huge cookies so highly-favored by these diners. Marie kindly looked in the other direction when Larry broke off half a cookie. When she glimpsed Maggie watching her feigned ignorance, she merely lifted her angular shoulders in an eloquent shrug: why deprive him of this small treat on such a special night? Maggie couldn't have agreed more.

Marie was rewarded for her kindness when Lorene sent her a tearful look brimming with unspoken gratitude. Jake had a plate in front of him and every once in awhile, with Lorene supporting his head, he managed to swallow a bite of potato salad or beans. Maggie thought it might be the most wondrous sight in an evening filled with miracles.

They were still eating when the band took the outdoor stage, and although Melanie was not close enough to touch the debonair Leon with his signature panama hat, they had an unimpeded view of the blues legend and his very capable band. They sent their particular brand of crooning blues into an indigo night sky glimmering with star pinpricks of light over the sea. Song after song wafted into the moist night: *Ain't Misbehaving, Nobody's Sweetheart, One Rose That's Left in My Heart, Are You Lonesome Tonight, When You Wish Upon a Star.* Maggie closed her eyes, seeing God breathe in the gift of this achingly sweet music, pleased to savor the talent He'd created.

The high point of the first set came when Leon Redbone graciously performed Melanie's request, *Champagne Charlie,* blowing her an elaborate kiss when he finished. Maggie thought the old woman might faint for sheer excitement.

The band took an intermission and Maggie and Glendalynn began gathering up the detritus of their picnic dinner. But no sooner had they started then a chorus went up from their sprightly guests: they were not ready to depart. "They're going to play a whole 'nother set," Larry observed

knowingly as though he were a regular beach and blues affi-
cionado.

"Yeah," chimed in Clara, "It's too early to go home now.
The night is young!"

Maude and Melanie merely glared around menacingly as
if daring anyone to try to forcibly remove them . . . since that
was the only way they intended to go. Indeed, Maggie
thought, repressing a yawn, it was the party-givers and not the
party-goers who were ready for bed. But a glance at Jake soon
sobered her. While the food and excitement had added some
color to his waxen face, he looked exhausted. The outing had
been a good idea for him, but it was time for it to come to a
close.

Marie had also noticed, and so they compromised.
Patrick would drive Lorene and Jake home, help them get settled and return for the rest of them. Melanie started to
protest, but Marie would brook no dissent. "Listen," she
declared sternly, "You're all getting an extra hour, and if I hear
one more complaint we're all getting in that van right now
with Jake. And Melanie, the first stop will be your house."
Melanie clamped her mouth shut and squinted up at Marie
from between thunderous eyebrows. However, she knew
when she was outflanked, and she wisely made no further
comment.

Arthur lifted Jake as if he were no more than a small
child and carried him gently toward the van with Lorene
hovering anxiously. Patrick, who had started after them,
paused as if debating something with himself. Then he
turned abruptly as though not wanting to give himself a
chance to reconsider and asked Maggie, "Will you come
with us? Lorene and I might need some help getting him
settled."

Maggie doubted it, but she nodded a little too quickly, as
if afraid she might issue a denial she did not mean. She felt

Marie and Glendalynn watching her, but she studiously ignored them as she quickly joined him and walked toward the parking lot. She would not give her speculating friends the satisfaction of a backward glance.

She sat in the back with Lorene and Jake, though they were oblivious to her presence. Indeed, she felt like a voyeur to an intimate family tableau that wanted no witness. The back of the van was dark; brother and sister were backlit only by street lamps and the headlights of passing cars. It was only in profile that Maggie could see Lorene cradling her brother's wobbling head, too large for his wasted body, in her arms. She must have been searching his face for signs of distress or pain, but she apparently saw none for some of the tension flowed out of her body and she slumped a little over him.

Jake's voice was so hoarse, Maggie could barely hear it; she knew Patrick, driving in the front, would not even know he'd spoken. But his words were meant only for Lorene, and so it did not matter.

"Don't worry, Sis," he whispered, "I'm fine."

"Why darlin', I'm not worried! What in the world do I have to worry about?" she warbled, perilously close to breaking down.

"Lor?" he asked rawly.

"Yes, darlin?"

"I just wanted to tell you. This is the best night of my life. The best."

His voice faded into silence, and it was only by the rise and fall of his chest in profile that Maggie knew he was still breathing. It was only when they pulled into the well-lit driveway and Patrick opened the van's back doors that Maggie saw Jake's face wet with Lorene's silent tears.

Asleep, Jake was heavier, so Patrick gently strapped him into a wheelchair and used the van's lift to lower it to the ground. He never woke but Lorene stayed at his side, holding his hand as they wheeled up the walk and into the house. Maggie trailed after them, toting the oxygen. She realized that Jake had not needed it all night. It was the first time she'd known him to be comfortable for more than a few minutes without it.

It took less time than she thought to get Jake settled; he was as pliant as a rag doll and Lorene was well accustomed to his care routine. She'd refused to have an aide in, though Marie had argued for hours with her about it. In the end Marie had given up, later telling Maggie,"I think she needs to keep busy every second. She needs to do all the dirty work. It's the only thing she *can* do, after all."

Patrick kindly refused Lorene's offer of coffee, and instead of the relief she must have felt to have the evening over, Maggie was slightly surprised to see a quick flicker of disappointment shadow Lorene's face. It was gone as swiftly as it had come, and Lorene was all Southern charm in the next instant, but Maggie noticed how reluctantly she stepped out of Patrick's farewell embrace. It was not really all that astonishing that Lorene would yearn for comfort from a man like Patrick. And surely it was not shocking that Patrick might use his considerable experience and warmth to provide such consolation.

What was surprising was her own discomfiture at the thought.

They drove for several minutes in silence, but the tension in the van was palpable. On the other hand, Maggie told herself wryly, it was all emanating from her. Patrick, typically, was completely at ease. He remarked,"I think that was worth it for Jake—the evening out. It might have cost him something in energy, but it had to be good for him."

Maggie agreed, and before she could stop herself, added, "Is Lorene in love with you?"

Patrick gave a brief laugh, saying, "For weeks you won't discuss anything other than the pretty flowers and the hot sun, and now you want to know about my love life?"

Embarrassed, Maggie nonetheless persisted, "Is she?"

"I might suggest that your attitude toward me makes it surprising that you want to know," he said ironically.

"And I might suggest that you're working mighty hard to avoid answering."

"Touché," he said with a small flourish, "Well, how should I answer? I think, no. She's not in love with me, but she needs so much—comfort, help, warmth, affection, understanding—and I guess she believes I can provide at least some it."

"Can you? Will you?"

"Am I going to get my own chance at Twenty Questions when you're done?" he asked with a hint of exasperation. When she didn't answer, he said, "No, I didn't think so. Nevertheless, since it seems that I'm the one in our barely existent relationship who must do all the giving, I'll try to answer you.

"Can I? Yes, of course. I'm something of an expert in comforting distraught people, as I know you've heard. Will I? I don't know. That's the simple answer. I don't know."

"Why?"

He sighed deeply, but she wasn't sure whether it was at her brazen persistence or at the complexity of the question. Finally, he said, "I need to be careful to be nothing more than a good friend to her now, because I'm not sure I feel any more than that. I might. Someday. But I don't know right now. And Lorene is very vulnerable at present. I don't want to mislead her. I don't want her to ever think I took advantage of her."

"Like you're not trying to take advantage of my vulnerability?"

Patrick pulled the van over and turned to look directly at her. "Do you consider yourself vulnerable?"

Maggie took some time answering. "I think the truth is I've been excruciatingly vulnerable all my life; it's just that I've never known it. The really odd thing is that I'm probably stronger now than I've ever been, and yet I've never felt weaker. Or more vulnerable."

Patrick looked out the window and said carefully, "I think that's natural, given what you've been through."

Maggie breathed in slowly. He did know. He had recognized it. Working to keep her voice steady, she asked, "Is it that obvious?"

"Not to others," he answered quickly, sensing her need for reassurance. "Not at all. It's just that for me . . . well, whether it's a man or woman; a victim, a survivor or a loved one, I just know. Someone once told me that God marks all who've suffered with or through cancer so that we can recognize each other. And help."

Maggie smiled in the dark, but her voice was skeptical. "And you think you can help me?"

"I don't know," he answered slowly, all banter drained from his voice, "Maybe I think you can help me."

CHAPTER 8

LOSS AND GAIN

JAKE died the next morning. Right at dawn, according to Lorene, who recounted it with a serenity that spoke of how gentle his passing had been. There were no signs in her placid face or steady voice of the brutal grief and anxiety Maggie had noticed in the days and the night before.

Marie had wakened Maggie shortly after receiving Lorene's call, and now the three women were sitting quietly in Lorene's immaculate kitchen. The silence was not disturbing; Lorene herself seemed so peaceful. Maggie couldn't help wondering whether Lorene was in shock. She'd been so devoted to Jake, so devastated by anticipating the event which had now overtaken them. Was this serenity an unlikely reality, or an escape from it?

Lorene had stayed in Jake's room after they'd returned from the concert. He'd been sleeping when Patrick and Maggie left, and Lorene said he never woke as she sat in the comfortable chair by his bed, holding his limp hand. As the first sliver of sun gleamed over the ocean, Jake had suddenly grasped her hand tightly, "not like he was in pain, or anything like that at all," insisted Lorene, "but more like he wanted me to know he knew I was there. It was him saying good-bye. Then he sighed and was gone."

Her eyes were bright and dry as she recounted this parting. Maggie saw no ruinous signs to suggest the uncontrolled weeping she might have expected Lorene had done in private before they arrived. She merely looked exhausted, but not in the agitated way that meant fear or anxiety was driving away sleep. Instead, she projected the simple weariness of someone who had worked hard and long and was finally ready to sleep.

Yet by the time they'd arrived, she'd ground and brewed hazelnut coffee and set the table with china cups and plates. The comforting pungent aroma of coffee floated through the house as she greeted them and softly told Marie to go and bid Jake good-bye. Maggie followed Lorene back into the kitchen as Marie disappeared inside the lovely room that had been Jake's entire world. There were strawberries and cream with croissants and plum jam on the table when Marie returned, looking more ravaged than Lorene. She was stooped over and trembling, her entire aspect so damaged, that Maggie rose in alarm to go to her. She had aged frighteningly during the few minutes she'd spent in Jake's room, but she held up a hand to warn Maggie off. She shuffled to the wide paned kitchen window and stood for several minutes leaning on the counter.

Lorene waited several minutes and then, as if knowing it was the right time, rose gracefully and embraced her friend. For the second time in less than 12 hours, Maggie knew she was witnessing something so private her very presence felt intrusive. Embarrassed and isolated, she was ready to slip out of the room when the two women, arms around each others' waists turned back to her. They walked slowly to the table, Lorene supporting Marie until she'd lowered herself painfully into a chair.

After serving Marie a heaping plate of berries and cream with a jam laden croissant, Lorene poured coffee and gestured for Maggie to serve herself. Only when all three had before them a breakfast so elegant it seemed inappropriate, did Lorene describe Jake's final hours. When she reached the part about Jake squeezing her hand, Marie looked up, a spark of pleasure lighting haggard features.

Seeing this fleeting hope, Lorene must have understood that Marie was blaming herself. Lorene said urgently, "I tell you truly, Marie, it was last night that made these final days worth living for him. He did nothing but look ahead to that concert from the moment you mentioned it. He spoke more in the last week—and always about the upcoming outing—than he had in the whole month before. He ate more, and enjoyed the taste more, last night than he had in as long as I can remember.

"You were *right* to invite him, and I was wrong to resist. I know in my heart that the promise of last night kept him alive for precious days. I'll thank God for your perseverance every day of my life."

By the time she'd finished, some color had returned to Marie's pallid face, and her eyes were sharp and bright again. But it was only when Marie spoke that Maggie knew she'd been restored to her usual pragmatic, Mid-western self. "Have you thought about arrangements?" she asked Lorene, adding tentatively, "Will you take him home?"

Lorene's pretty face hardened swiftly, and she answered decisively, "We are home. This is the place that has made us welcome, and this is where he will stay. Where I will stay."

Marie agreed to meet her later so that they could talk to Father Dominick about the service, and when Lorene assured them she'd be fine alone and would perhaps even get some sleep, they left. As soon as they'd climbed into the jeep, Maggie asked, "What did she mean about Key West being home? She seemed angry all of a sudden."

"Not all of a sudden," Marie answered, "My guess is that's been building for a lifetime. She and Jake moved here from Mississippi a couple of years ago. Jake had lost his job as a master chef in some big hotel there when the owners found out he had AIDS. When he threatened to go to court, they beat him to it. They made sure everyone—including other hotel and restaurant owners who might've hired him—knew about his illness. Not only could he not get a job, he ended up with no health insurance and no friends. Their parents are conservative Christians—so-called—and they rejected him out of hand. Only Lorene stood by him.

"She'd left Mississippi years before—the great escape, she calls it—and moved to New York. By the time Jake became ill, she'd made quite a bit of money at a Wall Street banking firm. She negotiated a good severance package for herself, sold her Manhattan apartment, and came to Mississippi. She stayed there just long enough to pack Jake up and move down here. Told me she never once spoke to her parents, never once visited the church that she'd grown up in and that had abandoned him. She just rented a car and drove until they reached 'the end of the world!' Can't you just hear her saying that with her pretty southern accent?

"Don't be fooled by Lorene's southern belle act; she's tough as steel. She drove that car straight through, with Jake sleeping off and on in the back. Can you imagine what she must have thought about on that long drive? She'd given up everything without so much as blinking, and she didn't hesitate for a moment once they arrived. She'd purchased the house within weeks, furnished it in days, found him specialists and naturopathic physicians; you name it, she did it. I met her shortly after they arrived, and let me tell you, watching her, it was surely easy to imagine her taking Wall Street by storm. What she couldn't charm her way into getting, she simply bought.

"After awhile, they started attending Mass, it was mostly Jake at first. Lorene came periodically, but anyone could see it was just to please him. Her anger at the church back home that had turned her brother out was unassailable. What she felt spilled over to any church, any religion. I remember we talked a lot about faith being something felt toward God and not toward a church or religion. That seemed to comfort her a little, and she started to accompany Jake more often. They went to the Episcopal church occasionally, too; I think Lorene didn't want them to feel committed to any one particular denomination or parish after what had happened.

"Meanwhile, Jake started to do well on the 'cocktail,' and for awhile was even able to work. He built a good reputation as a substitute chef at a number of the better restaurants on the island. And in case you haven't noticed, the Key West work ethic focuses as much on leisure as on work, so there was plenty of demand for him. Then about six months ago, the virus reasserted itself; it does that sometimes: sort of outsmarts the 'cocktail,' is how Lorene puts it.

"Despite all he'd been through, Jake remained sweet-natured as could be; no bitterness whatsoever. It was Lorene who arrived here filled with fury, and as time passed, it did not lessen in the least; rather, it simply crystallized into diamond-hard resentment. It's so pitiful really: Jake was the one who always sent their parents anniversary and Christmas cards, and they never once acknowledged these gestures. On the other hand, they would have loved to hear from Lorene, and she never once considered contacting them. My guess is she'll not even let them know he's passed, unless, of course, she thinks it might wound them. In that case, she's probably on the phone as we speak."

Such a violent rage was hard for Maggie to imagine, particularly in someone as pleasant and courteous as Lorene. When Marie left her off at the cottage, she was still wondering about it. Did she have the capacity for such consuming fury? She doubted it, and that somehow made her feel diminished. She feared that she lacked the passion necessary for either great rage or great joy, perhaps even for great love. And though Lorene should have been the last person she would trade places with at that moment, Maggie envied her passion nonetheless.

The wake was the next night, Saturday, and the funeral Mass, on Sunday afternoon at St. Peter's. Father Dominick had made no objection to Jake being cremated; indeed, the burial space on the island was severely limited, and a number of graves were already situated above ground. Maggie never knew whether Lorene had told her parents; they did not attend either the wake or the Mass.

Lorene had invited all those attending the service back to her home, and the party—for indeed, it was more a celebration of Jake's life than a mourning of his death—lasted well into the night. In the magic way of Key West, Leon Redbone had somehow learned that the hallow-eyed young man who'd listened to him with such deep pleasure at the beach concert, had died the next day. The musician, his face half-shaded as always by an impeccable panama hat, showed up at the party. After gallantly greeting Lorene, he sang a beautiful rendition of *If We Never Meet Again This Side of Heaven,* moving everyone present to tears. Even Marie had dashed a hand across her eyes by the time he finished.

Some of the island's best chefs had prepared a repast fit for the passing of a king, and Redbone stayed long enough to happily polish off a heaping plate. Arthur told

Maggie that he'd not had such good food and music at a funeral for as long as he could remember. Patrick, who'd played an extraordinarily lovely rendition of *Amazing Grace* at the Mass, stayed busy helping Lorene serve and greet guests. He glanced several times at Maggie, but there was none of the cheerful teasing she'd become accustomed to. His demeanor was thoughtful as though he'd not forgotten, or resolved, their conversation the night of the concert. They did not speak, and if Lorene, visibly grateful for his presence, noticed that his attention was somewhat divided, she gave no sign.

Maggie was inexplicably restless the next day. She'd not gotten to bed until well after midnight, but despite feeling spent and exhausted, still had slept poorly. She was up shortly after sunrise; it came surprisingly early these days, a sign that time was passing more swiftly than she wanted to admit.

Borrowing Lily's bike, she rode to the beach at Fort Zachary Taylor, noting how quiet Key West was first thing in the morning. Just a few hours ago, there would have been lights and action and every kind of personal drama being played out, but as if by special dispensation, the lightening skies brought with them silence and consolation, if just for a few hours.

The city itself looked sad and worn in the early light, like a playground grieving for the raucous children who had gone home. The streets were bleak and littered, the storefronts garish and untempting. Maggie rode steadily, listening to the silence that reigned only for an hour or two here; a sense of loneliness followed her up the long, deserted stretch leading to the beach. She knew vaguely that riding out here alone this early in the morning was not the wisest course, but she felt no fear. She even smiled a little, knowing Margaret would never even consider such an outing, and thinking that on some things, Margaret was probably in the right. But now she was driven by something stronger than any sense of danger.

She needed to make some decisions. The most important one, she thought ruefully as she walked the bike along the beach, would be how much of sane, unemotive Margaret should be incorporated into who she'd become, into Maggie. For she'd come to realize, slowly and maybe even against her will, that neither Maggie nor Margaret could thrive separately. If she'd managed to fall blindly in love with Key West, to recognize it irrevocably as home, as had so many others, then she could have been only Maggie forever. But as it was, her love for this island was different. She was not consumed by Key West, though she'd been vastly comforted by it. And no matter how much she may wish it otherwise, Key West had not offered her the answer; it had merely freed her to raise the questions.

She spoke all this to God as she watched the magnificent waves rolling toward the shore and then dissipating a little before crashing upon it. While she knew the difficult decisions were hers to make, she was grateful to have at least found her way back to prayer. If she couldn't now see the end to her story, she was back in contact with the One Who could.

"Anytime You want to clue me in . . .?" she asked aloud on the deserted beach, and then chuckling a little, she turned her face into the breeze and wheeled the bike back onto the road.

Back at the cottage, she switched on the computer. She'd been writing Caroline daily since last week when her obstetrician had made the distressing prediction that the baby would be late, probably by at least a week or two. Caro had called her mother with the news, wailing and eventually bursting into tears. The doctor might as well have sentenced her to another month in jail, her daughter had moaned. The tears came when Caro confided that Tom's immediate reaction had been to tell her she'd quit work too soon. Maggie had ground her teeth together, wondering if her son-in-law was becoming more of a jerk every day, or if she herself had just been too adept at ignoring him.

She'd considered calling Tom as soon as she'd rung off with Caroline. When she'd finally rejected the idea, it was not because of the oblivious reticence that had neutralized her so often in the past. She was no longer concerned about avoiding confrontation or even soothing her son-in-law's distemper. In fact, she was tempted to call him just to make him as miserable as possible, or at least as miserable as Caroline. What stopped her in the end was the searing knowledge, born of newfound clarity, that she must not interfere in this. Caroline, for all her heat and light, was very much like a child when it came to communicating with her husband, and he was quite content to treat her as such. And while Maggie could do everything in her power to encourage Caro to change this pattern before it became entrenched, she could not do it for her.

Now, she wrote a short note to Caro, and then checked her own e-mail box. Pleased to see Christine's address, she opened the note and read the few lines swiftly. She went back and read them again, this time more slowly.

Mom, my graduation recital plan has been accepted by the department and my professor so I have a few days off before I start serious rehearsals. Can I spend them with you?

C

Maggie sat, her heart pounding, waiting for resentment and resistance to flow through her. But instead, she had a sudden vision of Lorene cradling her brother in her arms in the van after the concert, anticipating the soon-to-come parting. Maggie wrote one line back.

When do you arrive?

Plans were quickly made, and nearly a week later on Palm Sunday afternoon, Maggie borrowed Mark's truck—gruffly offered, "since I don't need it for work," to drive to the airport. Maggie watched the sky anxiously, fearful that her daughter's plane would touch down only to take to the skies again in the same unnerving way hers had nearly three months ago. When she'd warned Chrissie about it, her fey child had merely laughed and said, "Oh Mom! I thought you were over your fear of flying!"

For myself maybe, Maggie now thought as she waited nervously for Christine's plane, but not for you. Did mothers ever stop worrying over their children? she wondered. Her worrying gene had gone dormant last year when her own disaster struck, but it was certainly reasserting itself now. Twenty years from now would Caroline be pacing some airport terminal, terrified that something, anything, might go wrong on the plane carrying her child?

Of course, she had no way of knowing which of the small planes was Christine's, and it was only when the scratchy public address system announced the flight number that she relaxed. Her daughter, looking tinier than ever in the distance, was dressed in jeans and a sweater which she quickly stripped off when the heat hit her, revealing a sleeveless black body suit underneath. Toting one canvas bag, she descended the plane's steps onto the sizzling tarmac and floated toward the terminal with that extraordinary grace that still amazed Maggie. Where did she get it? Surely she'd not inherited such style and balance from Harry or her. They were both renowned klutzes, the affable joke of every dance floor. Macy had once observed, "If Chrissie didn't look so much like Harry, I'd think she got switched with some other kid in the hospital nursery." Remembering the comment now, Maggie thought it cruel.

At the time, she hadn't thought anything of it all.

It seemed forever before Christine passed through the check point and walked into Maggie's waiting arms. Holding her tightly, Maggie felt tears squeezing out of her closed eyes, and when she drew back to look at her daughter, Christine noticed and asked in surprise, "Mom? You OK?"

Maggie closed her eyes briefly, regretting whatever she'd done—or more accurately not done—to leave Christine surprised that her mother was overcome with emotion at the very sight of her. The moment passed; Maggie nodded briskly, "Of course I'm OK. I'm fine. It's just so good to see you."

Christine looked at her with a touch of skepticism, as if to say, Gee Mom, you could have seen me every day if you hadn't left us! But her daughter's glance was tempered by a quick grin and the same understanding that had characterized her e-mail notes. She answered mildly, "It's good to see you, too. Really good, Mom."

On the drive back to the cottage, they talked constantly, easily picking up where their last e-mail exchange had left off. Maggie breathed a silent prayer, *"Thank You!"* for that precious communication that had begun as a Lenten sacrifice. She was just beginning to realize how much those five weeks of notes had altered her relationship with both girls. Another secret of Harry's that she'd never appreciated. Or even recognized.

Christine's break from college would last until Easter, but they'd agreed that she should return on an early morning flight on Good Friday. She wanted to be close by in case the obstetrician had been wrong about Caroline's late date. "It's not like Tom is going to be much good," Christine had told her mother darkly, "I might as well be in the delivery room with her; I'd probably do her more good."

Maggie had been privately relieved that Chrissie planned to leave before the Good Friday and Easter weekend services so carefully planned by LEAST. She'd anticipated this weekend for months, and though she welcomed her daughter with a full heart, she still cherished the thought of keeping those three sacred days for herself. But now, as she parked Mark's truck precisely in front of their rambling house, Maggie was already aware of how sharply she would miss Christine; five days suddenly didn't seem like enough.

They weren't. And yet again, they were. Christine had come for more than a tour of Key West, and in her gently determined way, she used the time to promote her agenda. Though she never once balked at any of Maggie's plans, from joining Marie for the Meals on Wheels route to sharing a midnight goat cheese, chorizo and asparagus pizza with Maggie and Carl at Mangoes, Chrissie was on a campaign to bring her mother home. Not right away, necessarily, and not without seeking to herself experience what Maggie had found in Key West, but Christine nevertheless intended to say those things that could not be adequately expressed over the internet.

She began shortly after she'd admired her mother's cottage and unpacked her few belongings. Maggie, eager to show Christine Key West's vibrancy, suggested they go to the island's famous sunset celebration. Maggie had gone several times with Lily, but she was still astonished and delighted every time she passed through Mallory Square and onto Sunset Pier. Every day in the late afternoon, a collection of amateur and not so amateur entertainers gathered on the long boardwalk that overlooked the Gulf of Mexico and a small island known as Sunset Key.

Every inch of the long, interconnected esplanade boasted its own specialty. The sunset performers hailed from all over the world, and some simply arrived before Christmas and stayed for The Season. Others, like the ageless acrobat with a long gray ponytail who rigged up his own tightrope, had stayed forever, making Key West their home base. Maggie had seen him and several other Sunset actors shooting pool one night in a local diner. Just like anyone else, she'd thought in surprise, having that very afternoon seen him somersault off his tightrope after pacing confidently across the wire as he juggled fire.

The acrobat was one of the most talented to grace the boardwalk. Others were simply unique. There was the utterly motionless, white-painted man who many passers-by simply ignored, thinking he was a statue. During particularly crowded weekends, he posed within a roped-off space so that people would know he was alive. Those paying particular attention could watch him move, almost imperceptibly, over a long period of time until his original pose had been altered so slightly most would not notice. Some nights, no one even noticed him. On others, there were hundreds pushing and jockeying for a position to watch.

Maggie led Christine to one of the most popular shows: a couple with faux French accents who had trained cats. But these cats were not trained simply to lie down or offer their paws in a cute handshake. They would prance through a series of complicated tricks, ending with the show-stopper when several would jump through a burning hoop. All the while, the scantily clad lady trainer would howl in pidgin French, brandish a whip that never once came near one of the animals, and urge her trained pets on to greater feats. The crowd always roared in excitement at the fire trick, and though this was not Maggie's favorite show—she rather liked the acrobat—she and Christine maneuvered their way into the crowd to watch for a moment or two.

Chrissie naturally gravitated toward a dance performance that had just recently come to the pier. Maggie had never seen it and was surprised at how much she enjoyed the dancer's silent, modern interpretations. They were "dancing sunset," according to the announcer who introduced them; and their graceful, arching movements, enhanced by umber, orange and red full body-stockings, indeed mirrored what was even now occurring on the horizon. Maggie noticed Christine watching the program with an intensity she'd never seen before in her daughter. Perhaps dance wasn't simply a major she'd "stumbled onto," as Tom disdainfully contended.

They wandered through the huge combination arts and crafts/flea market that clogged the public entrance to the pier. Christine stopped to admire a pair of beaded earrings, and Maggie bought them for her, happy to be able to do a normal mother-type thing. They settled at one of the many waterside cafes to watch the actual event that drew thousands daily to this teeming square. Maggie, excited as she was every time she came here, waited for the hush that inevitably fell over the surging mob at the moment the sun sank below the horizon, seemingly into the endless sea. This silence, so unlikely in such a mass of humanity, was to Maggie as much a phenomenon as the sight of the fiery, shimmering orb dropping abruptly out of sight.

The speed of it always fascinated her; she'd thought during her first time here that the crowd was completely ignoring the sun as it seemed to hang forever in the western sky, barely moving. Then there was a perceptible increase in excitement as people turned from the entertainers and their drinks to rush toward the railings and hang themselves over the sea, riveted on the sun that had stopped crawling and was now plunging toward the sea. Maggie could never stop herself from expecting to hear a sizzling sound as if the earth's hot star might extinguish itself in the ocean.

Tonight, as always, there was one sacred second of utter silence after the last curving bit of red disappeared sending spectacular streaks of red, rose, orange and indigo into the sky; and then: applause. The clapping started gently, a respectful expression of universal awe, and then surged into a wild ovation for one of the most spectacular sights in the world. And just as Lily had turned to her after her very first sunset, Maggie now turned to Chrissie and said, "And it happens all over again in 24 hours."

Christine's eyes were brimming as she clutched her mother's hand across the table. Maggie was secretly thrilled that Chrissie instinctively comprehended the blessing of this moment, until she breathed, "I wish Dad were here."

Maggie looked at her, at first stunned and then wary. Was the whole week going to be a yearning for Harry? Or even a defense? And yet Christine, who'd never been a dissembler, looked perfectly sincere in her wish. Maggie couldn't imagine why; it was not like Harry could ever begin to appreciate this ordinary miracle. He'd probably just say he could reproduce a more geometrically accurate rendition of sunset at this latitude on his computer. Given the right software, of course.

"Why?" she demanded bluntly, annoyed that the precious moment was over if not, in fact, ruined.

Christine looked at her blankly, and so she repeated irritably, "Why do you wish your father was here?"

"Mom!" Chrissie exclaimed incredulously as though Maggie had just asked the sum of one and one, "Dad loves winter sunsets! Don't you remember? How he used to rush home on every sunny day in January and pile us all into the car? How we used to rush down to the beach so we'd make it in time to see the sun go down into Long Island sound? How if there were the right kinds of clouds, he would make us wait for a few minutes after sunset, so we could see the light diffused in all the colors over the sky?"

Disgruntled, Maggie started to say she hardly thought that watching a freezing, cloud-obscured sunset over steel gray waters from the inside of a cluttered old Chevy was the equivalent of what they'd just witnessed. But then she looked at her daughter's face and swallowed her words.

Chrissie, searching her face, asked, "Mom, don't you remember how excited you used to get?"

Now, it was Maggie's turn to look blank, and Christine continued urgently, almost pleading as if, suddenly, the most important thing in the world was to make her mother remember. "How you used to get us all dressed in our coats and earmuffs and mittens even before Dad pulled into the driveway? How we would all wait on the couch, watching for him through the bay window? It was the only time you used to let me stand on the couch—'just so you can see Daddy coming,' you used to say. And then Caro would get jealous, and you had to let her stand on the couch, too?

"Mom, don't you remember?"

She did, distantly. But the memory seemed buried under layers and layers of silt that had slowly, inexorably sifted over such memories, cooling their warmth and silencing the joyful noise they still clearly made for Chrissie. And in her befuddlement, Maggie was abruptly grateful for at least that: she had not given her daughters a completely barren childhood.

And then her stomach twisted with the realization that Christine's memory had featured Harry as the bearer of joy, the bringer of color.

Blinking hard, Maggie squeezed her daughter's hand. "I do remember," she said, "It's just that I hadn't thought about it for a long time."

A wave of relief passed over Chrissie's intense, elfin features, and she offered her mother easy absolution, "Well, of course not. It's so exotic and exciting here, I can't imagine how you could think about anything else!"

This facile dispensation struck Maggie with the force of a blow. Her purpose in coming to Key West had been to heal, broaden and clarify; had she instead created a narrow place of escape where she could nurture her scars until they became hardened and impenetrable?

Chrissie was watching her mother, blissfully unaware of the chaos she'd unleashed in Maggie's spirit. Or was she? Maggie studied her daughter. Christine had never been a manipulative child, and indeed, she'd done no more just now than recall a lovely memory and speak the truth. Yet Christine had come as much to remind her mother of her old life as to celebrate her new one; that much Maggie knew. And maybe this, then, was true clarification. Albeit, thought Maggie smiling wryly, by fire.

"What's so funny?" Christine asked.

"You are," Maggie replied, "I think you're here for more than just a break before your senior recital."

Christine's gaze faltered, and Maggie was achingly reminded of the hesitant child she'd been. But then Christine looked up and held her mother's gaze. "Mom, it's great here. I knew that from your notes. You're a great writer, you know? The way you described this place, yourself here, it was like I could just see it. And it scared me. I thought, 'Why would she come home? Why would she ever leave there?'

"And then I started thinking of all the reasons for you to come home. Of everything you'd left behind. Not just cancer. As big as it was, it was just a little part of what you left back home. And really, Mom, you can't leave that anywhere. It's going to be with you wherever you are, regardless. Hopefully, only as something you endured in your past, but with you, nonetheless. You didn't get rid of cancer by coming down here, Mom, you know? But you did leave a lot of other great stuff behind—like the winter sunsets and a million memories like that. I didn't want you to forget all that. All of us.

"But now I'm here, and I can see what you love so much. It's totally different. I can't even describe it, but I understand. I want to say you should leave this behind, but I can't. I want to make the decision for you, but I don't know if I could leave here if I were you." She looked away again, and this time her eyes stayed riveted on some distant spot on the darkening ocean. She said softly, "I just don't want to lose you. Not to cancer. Not to Key West."

Maggie wanted to tell her she wouldn't. She wanted to tell her that Key West was not home, but that *home* was also not yet home. She wanted to say, "Chrissie, you've made me feel closer to home than I have in years." But she didn't. Instead she raised her daughter's small hand to her lips and kissed it as she used to when either of her girls had a scrape or bruise. Then she said, "So has anything interesting been happening in good old Connecticut for the past few months?"

Chrissie's mouth twisted into an ironic grin. She began, "Well, I've been meaning to tell you about Macy . . . "

Macy was only one of many topics they discussed over the next few days, yet Maggie returned to what Chrissie had said again and again as if Macy had become an annoying mosquito bite that required repeated scratching. Making no attempt to hide her amusement, Christine reported that shortly after Maggie'd left, Macy had invited Harry to "unload on me anytime" he wanted. "I presume she meant unload his *feelings,"* Chrissie had grinned, "but she didn't specify."

When Harry had all but run in the opposite direction— the very apt description of his likely reaction brought an unwitting smile to Maggie's face—Macy had taken a different tack. She'd taken to inviting the three of them, Harry and the girls, to various events and meals. After Harry had responded with mumbled apologies to the offering of several Sunday dinners—"she probably thought Dad wouldn't be so scared if her husband was at the table!" Christine had chortled— Macy took the somewhat desperate measure of inviting Caroline and Tom to a "home cooked" St. Patrick's Day dinner, suggesting that she "of course!" bring along her father and sister. Macy apparently thought Caro was the most approachable of the three, and normally she'd have been right. But Caroline was very pregnant and very irritable. She all but bit Macy's head off answering that she and her *sister* would be dining with their *father* at home. That, by the way, *he* would be preparing their home cooked dinner.

Macy, not one to surrender without a bruising battle, eventually snared Harry by offering to explain Retrouvaille. "She must have sensed that Dad would do anything to get you back," Chrissie had slipped in, slyly watching her mother from under her eyelashes. When Maggie gave her a look, she grinned good-naturedly and told her mother that Harry had still managed to outsmart Macy. After she went on and on about how Retrouvaille had saved her and Mike's marriage, she could hardly refuse when Harry innocently told her he'd pick up a bottle of Mike's favorite wine so that they could all three relax together as they discussed it. Christine couldn't keep herself from laughing in delight at her father's dubious naiveté.

Whatever hopes Macy had had about getting Harry alone evaporated. Not only was Mike present that evening, he'd invited another couple they'd met at Retrouvaille. Whatever Macy had hoped for, Harry's visit turned into a rather serious night of discussion. Still, Maggie had the prickling sense that Macy was seeking to practice her self-described innocent flirting. On Harry. She'd had a brief notion about it over a month ago when Harry had mentioned Retrouvaille, apparently well before Macy's failed attempt at a little tete-a-tete. Even then, though, she'd evidently been trying.

Maggie felt no jealousy, but she realized with some surprise that it was not because she didn't care about losing Harry. It was simply because she knew he would always be faithful. Not once in over three decades had she ever doubt-ed him, or, for that matter, even wondered about his fidelity. Even now, having not seen or touched her husband in nearly three months, she and Chrissie could sit around laughing at the idea of any woman trying to tempt him. Even today, after all that had happened over the past year, she could take her husband's faithfulness for granted.

And it occurred to Maggie that this ordinary thing was very precious indeed.

Macy was another matter altogether. Christine, however, believed Macy had done her parents a favor. She shared this rather unlikely opinion with her mother on Thursday after-noon, before she was to leave the next morning. Maggie had taken her, finally, to Fort Zachary Taylor Beach, saving this beautiful place for last. They were seated on a large blanket Lily had dug up for them to take along. Borrowing Marie's jeep, they'd packed fresh fruit and lemonade which they were just finishing when Christine's bland statement about Macy caused Maggie to stare at her incredulously.

"You're kidding, right?" Maggie asked.

"No, I'm not," Christine insisted stubbornly. "That night they finally got together to talk about Retrouvaille was a big-ger night for Dad than it was for Macy. He told me and Caro that, for once, Macy didn't do all of the talking. Dad probably didn't notice but I'm guessing that was because Macy was pouting and hoping one of the men, at least, would notice. Obviously, they didn't, and the other couple spent much of the evening talking about Retrouvaille. I figure Mike probably invited them because he can't be so sure about the stability of his own marriage and might not feel too comfortable counseling Dad.

"The other guy—Paul, I think was his name—told Dad how Retrouvaille isn't some bizarre touchy-feely weekend thing; how it's all about communication and learning to actually listen to your spouse without worrying about how you're going to immediately answer back. It's about not being defensive. It helps couples learn how to talk to each other and really empathize with each other. It's supposed to help you move toward feeling the kind of unconditional understanding and love for each other that God always feels for us."

"How do you know all this?" Maggie asked, taken aback by the idea of Harry sharing such details with his daughters.

"I already said: Dad told us," Christine answered matter-of-factly, adding in the next breath, "Mom you really don't know what he's going through. It's not only that he misses you; it's that he's starting to understand something's been missing all along. And he's gotten a lot more open with Caro and me, admitting how hard your leaving has been and how much he wants to 'rebuild things.' His words."

Then anticipating Maggie's skeptical look, she hurried on, "Mom, he did *not* tell us these things so that we would tell you. Come on! You know Dad. He's just not that devious, and he really is struggling with all this. Can you imagine him actually opening up and telling us this stuff? Dad, actually talking about how he feels?? I'm not saying he's great at it, but he's trying at least. He's trying *hard,* Mom." She trailed off, fresh out of words. It was this, they both knew, that Christine had come to say.

"Chrissie," Maggie said quietly, "Why are you telling me all this? What do you want me to do?"

Chrissie's face crumpled. "Oh, Mom," she groaned softly, "I don't know. I want you to come home! But I know you have to want it, or it won't work. I just thought if I told you about Retrouvaille and how hard Dad is trying to understand—*to change!*—then maybe you would want it. To come home."

Maggie pulled her daughter close and held her. Finally she said the only thing she could: the truth. "I'm not ready to make any promises. But you've surprised me and reminded me of things I'd forgotten. Or maybe ignored. You've given me a lot to think about, sweetie, and you probably don't know how important that is right now."

Patrick found them like this, their arms draped around each other's shoulders. Watching them from the edge of the beach, he hesitated. He was reluctant to interrupt, but he knew Christine was leaving tomorrow, and he couldn't help wondering if Maggie would be going with her. He needed to know.

He'd already met Chrissie on Tuesday night when Marie threw a pizza party in her honor. As they'd walked home that night, Christine had told her mother flatly, "He likes you." Maggie had swallowed and said, "Yes, I think he does," to which Chrissie, somewhat disarmed by her mother's honesty, answered, "He seems nice. He's hard not to like . . . but I'm definitely going to try!"

Now as they saw him walking slowly toward them, letting them finish what they'd started, she told her mother, "OK, I like him. I just don't want you to!"

They were laughing when Patrick reached them. "Was it a good joke?" he asked, smiling.

"Well, it sort of depends on the punch line," Chrissie answered, "And we don't know it, yet." She gave her mother a brief, affectionate look and then rose, saying, "Why don't you guys take a walk. I'm still hungry, and I'm not leaving Key West without trying one of those famous Chili Dogs."

As she left them to climb up the knoll to the snack shop, Patrick called after her, "Try not to get any on you!"

"No promises," Christine called back, having heard how Patrick first met her mother on this beach, "Like mother, like daughter, you know!"

Maggie rolled her eyes at him as he reached a hand down to haul her up. She took it, knowing she never would have before, and wondering why she did now. Was it because they both knew it now signaled the easy comfort of friendship, and no more?

They walked awhile in silence. When Patrick spoke, it was a statement.

"You're going home with her."

"Everyone seems to know what I'm doing except me," Maggie answered sharply, and then added in a more subdued voice, "I'm not going back with her."

"But you are going back." Again, he was definitive.

"If you say so."

"Maggie, I'm asking, OK?" he said, exasperated.

"It sure didn't sound like a question to me."

"Sorry. I meant it to be."

"Are you in that much of a hurry to get rid of me?" she asked.

"You know I'm not," he said, again at a loss, "But I can see how much Christine wants you to go home with her."

"Patrick," she said in a slightly irritated tone, "Everyone wants me to do something. It's always been that way, and it probably always will be that way. I'm learning that the trick is to figure out what I want. And do it."

"And do you want to go home?"

She stopped, forcing him to turn to her. "Do you want me to?"

He gazed at her frankly. "No, I don't," he said, not touching her, "but it's as you say, if you stay, it has to be what you want. You shouldn't stay because I want you to, and you shouldn't stay because your family wants you *not* to." She smiled at that as he paused, considering something and then drew a deep breath and continued, "But you need to know something. I need you to decide. They need you to decide. All of us . . . we have lives, Maggie. And the break you've taken from yours has brought ours to a grinding halt. You need to write the end of the story. Or at least the end of this chapter."

She looked at him sadly, struck for the first time by the full force of what she'd done. And what she must do. She smiled wanly and, raising a hand briefly to his face, said, "To be continued. Soon."

CHAPTER 9

RISE!

CHRISTINE boarded the plane for Hartford's Bradley International Airport at seven-fifteen the next morning, Good Friday. She never told her mother how stunned she was the day before when she'd looked up from her chili dog to see that painfully tender moment on the beach. Stunned and worried. But she'd said all she could, and to make her mother regret whatever it was she'd found in Key West would be wrong. Maybe even cruel. Christine's only comfort was that when embracing her before she boarded the plane, Maggie whispered, "Soon."

"Soon, *what?*" Christine wanted to cry out, but she knew she'd have to be content with that one word.

Maggie left her and drove home to change her clothes for the Good Friday pageant. While she missed Christine, at the same time she welcomed this time alone with her friends and in her new place. She'd waited a long time for these days,

and she thought of them as sacred. While she'd always celebrated Good Friday and Easter weekend with deep sorrow
and reverence and, finally, joy, she felt that somehow this
Easter was different. It would be the first of her new life. It
would be the first during which she'd truly understand what
it was like to be given a new life, to be risen.

Was that the gift of cancer? she asked silently. Was it so
that I could feel just a little, tiny bit of what You experienced?

She entered the cottage, smiling. She'd stopped expecting God's answers to smack her on the forehead. She had a
feeling that the freedom, the faith, to question might be the
only answer she would get. Or should need.

She dressed swiftly in a black jersey dress she'd purchased specially for today. Most people bought new clothes
for celebrations and parties. She bought a new outfit every
year for Good Friday, always something black. The admittedly
odd tradition had started over 40 years ago when, as a child,
she'd seen all the pictures of the people dressed in black for
President Kennedy's funeral. A few months later, when her
mother took her shopping for an Easter dress, she'd refused
to even try on any of the lace-trimmed pastel frocks until her
incredulous mother agreed to first buy her a simple black
dress. She told her mother she wanted to wear it "on the day
of Jesus's funeral."

It was not easy finding black for such a small child, particularly because Margaret had promptly rejected any dress
with a white lace collar or cuffs and stubbornly insisted on
unrelieved black. Her poor mother, probably wondering what
had happened to her usually compliant daughter, had finally
agreed. Only after Margaret had tried on a severe dress they
managed to find and carefully watched her mother pay for it,
would she agree to model any prospective Easter dresses.

Her mother had bought her two dresses each year
thereafter, never again questioning her wish to wear black

on Good Friday. Eventually she'd bought them for herself. But the memory of that first Good Friday, and her mother's wordless acquiescence every year from then on, now made her shake her head in wonder at such generous patience. How many times had she, as an adult, dismissed her mother as whimsical or even irrelevant? She was startled by a swift stab of sorrow. Would she and her mother ever share the kind of closeness she'd just felt with Christine? She'd never expected to, automatically assuming her mother could not possess the depth and sensibility for such a bond. But now she wondered which of them was truly lacking.

The procession was to start at noon at St. Peter's, where Father Dominick would bless the participants in the presence of parishioners from every denomination and those who belonged to none at all. Arthur would then take up the cross and proceed on an established route through Key West, enacting the various stations of the cross on the way. They would, for the larger part of the remembrance, walk north on Simonton Street until they reached Caroline Street. There, the mayor and city officials had given them leave, after vigorous petitioning and even protesting by LEAST members, to turn left onto Caroline and then cover the block on Duval Street between Caroline and Eaton Street where they would mount the steps on the very large, very visible Episcopal Church.

This one short block had been the toughest sell. The Season was still in full swing, and the politicians and Chamber of Commerce members weren't convinced that a somber Good Friday reenactment in the midst of one of the busiest, loudest, most tourism-oriented blocks of the city was a great idea. Duval between Caroline and Eaton would be mobbed with vacationers and locals shopping and meandering through the myriad street-level bars and cafes on any

Friday afternoon. This one, suggested some of the more commercial-minded business owners and city leaders, would be no exception. Wouldn't the reenactment, they asked rhetorically, have a rather chilling effect on the typical Friday afternoon festivities?

Who cares, Marie had responded unrelentingly, speaking for LEAST and adding for good measure that they certainly *hoped* the pageant would have an impact on the non-stop party that was north Duval Street. Key West, she'd persisted, was internationally known as the street performance capital of the world. What better performance to offer than this one on this day?

Those who were not cowed by her blunt assessment, and most were, soon came around when she mentioned that perhaps the subject deserved a thorough airing in the Key West Citizen, the island's high-circulation daily newspaper. Should she call that reporter who'd done such a good series on corruption in city government and contract awards? That, it seemed, would not be necessary; the vital permits had been immediately forthcoming. Good Friday patrons of Duval Street were about to get the surprise of their lives.

Maggie arrived at the outdoor blessing just as Father Dominick was beginning. He stood in the entrance of St. Peter's, towering over the pageant actors who knelt on the steps below him. A sizable crowd, gathered on the sidewalk in front of the church, had already spilled over onto the spacious grounds. The church could have never held so many people; Maggie estimated there was double the number of those at the Ash Wednesday service or of any weekend Lenten Mass since then.

She looked around as Father Dominick, clad completely in purple vestments, raised his hands in preparation for a blessing. There were many familiar faces, and a rush of belonging such as she'd never felt in any Connecticut parish, suddenly filled her. It was a wondrous, welcome feeling, and not one that would be easy to leave behind.

She saw Marie, whom she'd agreed to meet and walk with, standing in the sideyard, a little apart from the others during this beginning scene. Maggie imagined how she felt: Marie had made all this possible, dealt with every detail, disposed of every obstacle. This single moment must be immensely satisfying to her, and Maggie held back for a few minutes, leaving her alone to savor it.

She saw Glendalynn and Bill among those kneeling on the steps. They were to participate in the pageant, Bill as an onlooker and Glendalynn as one of the weeping women who would lament over Jesus. The huge woman who'd been her kind-hearted neighbor on Ash Wednesday and whom she'd greeted at Mass several times since, was also among the marchers. She'd introduced herself shortly after Ash Wednesday as Minerva, saying, "Anytime you need a hug, honey, you just call on Minerva!" Maggie uttered a short prayer that the heat would allow her to finish safely.

Lorene and Patrick stood among a group of restaurant staffers and chefs she'd met last week at Jake's funeral. They hadn't spotted her, and she watched as Lorene leaned toward Patrick to say something in his ear. He inclined his head toward her, placing his hand casually on her shoulder to listen better. Maggie felt an ache that was, at once, sweet and bruising. She was watching a tableau she'd never be part of, and that knowledge filled her with grief. And at the same time, she knew she was watching something that was absolutely right.

And then, unaccountably, she had a sudden memory of Harry, holding her, curling around her, on that night before she left in January. In the space of a breath, her grief became a yearning so vast it made her gasp. That was a tableau she could be part of. Again. She hoped.

As Father Dominick completed his somber prayer, it was Arthur who wholly captured Maggie's attention. She realized he'd been right in front of Father Dominick the whole time, but she hadn't noticed him; or rather, she hadn't recognized him. He was dressed in a simple white shirt and shorts. Old, scuffed leather sandals were on his feet. But it was his aspect, more than his uncharacteristically bland garb, that shocked Maggie. His eyes downcast and his posture already defeated, there was nothing of the mischief or joy or even the gentle sensitivity she'd come to rely on. His eyes turned to greet no one. He was like an empty husk, drained of all vitality, strength, hope.

He barely lifted his head when Father Dominick intoned the final blessing. All eyes then fixed on Arthur, who lumbered painfully to his feet and trudged slowly over to the large rough-hewn cross that lay in front of the church on the top step. There was no sound, not even from a passing car, as he looked at the cross for a long, agonized moment. And then, as if it took his last bit of energy, he bent at the waist, grasped it and hoisted it to his shoulder. For the first time, he turned to the crowd and gave them one haunted, hollow look before he half closed his eyes against them and started down the steps.

It was all Maggie could do to keep herself from fleeing home. Nothing, not even the promise she'd made to accompany Marie or how much she'd been anticipating this very scene, could have kept her there. Nothing except the irrevocable sensation that Arthur, in that moment, had looked right at her. And she could not leave him.

Marie joined her silently as the crowd thronged behind Arthur and the others who would join him on this journey. People lined Simonton Street, many gathering along the intersections at Olivia and Angela to watch in silent awe as the huge, muscular man was transformed into a weak, faltering shell. Different stations were reenacted along the way, but Arthur had so utterly become a study in suffering that Maggie couldn't tell the staged stops apart from the whole wrenching portrayal. Here he faltered, there he fell, at another place Glendalynn and a number of crying, wailing women threw themselves in his path. Maggie watched Glendalynn as she looked into the eyes of her friend, broken by the weight of the cross he bore; and the tears she cried were real.

The sight of Glendalynn's raw grief ultimately freed the tears that had frozen, cutting like shards of ice, behind Maggie's eyes, and she felt Marie's hand grasp hers. She looked at her friend for the first time, cherishing Marie's warm, clear gaze and the comfort of that grip. They continued hand-in-hand, as the procession turned right on Angela, doubling back slightly onto Windsor Lane where they stopped at the Key West Cemetery which Maggie had passed so often on her way to church.

Here, in the eerily still, green, moss-covered graveyard with its many raised graves, Arthur fell prostrate on the ground for the third time. He lay there for an interminable time, motionless under the cross as it crushed him to the damp ground. Despite the pressing crowd, many of whom now wept silently, there might have been no one else present; it was that quiet. Everyone, it appeared, had ceased to breathe; nor did the slightest ocean breeze rustle the leaves and vines forming a canopy over the graves. Gradually, painfully, he rose, pushing the cross up as he struggled to his feet. He stumbled slowly out of the cemetery, his white clothes stained with mud and moss.

They followed him along Williams Street, turning onto Southard. When they passed Mark and Lily's house, Maggie glanced over and saw Lily standing on the porch. Like many along the procession route, she'd come out to watch. Her eyes were wide, riveted on the bent, staggering figure under the cross. Her alabaster skin was drained of even its usual slight blush as she beheld the man who was no longer recognizable as the cheerful counselor and T-shirt salesman.

Without seeming to know what she was doing, Lily started moving in a trance toward the crowd, many of whom were now crying out and lamenting. Mesmerized, Lily did not see Maggie, who maneuvered swiftly in her direction. At the moment Lily's habitual fear reawakened and she realized she was in the midst of strangers, Maggie was near enough to reach out and pull her close. Her panic and confusion subsided slightly as she recognized Marie beside Maggie, and she allowed herself to be led, huddling into Maggie's side. After a few moments, she began again craning her neck to get a glimpse of their leader. Almost to herself, she whispered, "Is he all right?"

Marie answered kindly, "No, dear. But he will be."

From Southard they turned right onto Simonton again and resumed the main route, crossing Fleming and Eaton. At the corner of Simonton and Eaton, Minerva suddenly shrieked in agony and plunged forward to the man under the cross, wailing, "My son! My son!" He stopped and slowly, as if he couldn't bear to lift the weight of his own head, raised his face to her as she stood, wringing her hands and weeping. When their eyes locked, she went abruptly silent. For a long moment they stood thus, and then he averted his eyes and struggled on. Minerva stood still as if paralyzed, and then, with a cry of despair, collapsed backward into the supporting arms of the crowd.

When the procession turned left on Caroline, the air grew tense with expectation. They were now a mere block from Duval; those leading the pageant could see the crowds ahead of them where Caroline emptied onto Duval. Marie, about to realize the objective she'd fought so diligently for, tightened her hold on Maggie's hand. Lily, oblivious to everything but the intensity of the reenactment, clung to Maggie's other arm as they turned the corner onto Duval.

And met with utter silence.

Whatever reaction Maggie had expected from the throng of Key West revelers, it was not this. Likewise Marie, who stood motionless, her mouth slightly agape. If they didn't know what to make of the Duval Street reaction, the Duval mob certainly didn't know what to make of this astounding group, some wearing tattered robes and veils or headwraps as they cried out in grief, while others, the silent onlookers, were dressed somberly.

Maggie was fleetingly reminded of a silent movie where filming suddenly transfers to slow motion. People who'd been engaged in every kind of conversation—discussions about where to dine, predictions of which bar served the best margarita, quarrels about how much money to spend in the shops, wagers about what time sunset would be tonight—went silent. Food and drink that had been progressing swiftly toward open mouths was suspended in mid-air. Children who had been pulling on their parents' arms stopped to stare wide-eyed. Men who'd been gesticulating wildly in support of various specious arguments, froze and slowly lowered their arms. Even waitresses at the outdoor cafes, appreciating the abrupt break in the action, turned curiously to see the source of their respite.

Only one man continued on, doggedly hauling the cross that had all but bent him to the filthy sidewalk until he reached a spot just in front of the famed open-walled Sloppy Joe's Bar where Hemingway was said to have engaged in public displays of fisticuffs. As usual, the bar was packed with afternoon partiers, most of whom could have easily given Hemingway a run for his money. But even the rowdies in Sloppy Joe's were awed into silence as the man with the cross stopped and stood, waiting.

Suddenly, a slender young man darted from the crowd, and taking a knife concealed in his copious woven tunic, slashed at the white shirt that was already stained and filthy from the journey. When the soiled shirt had been slit open from end to end, the young man grabbed an end of it and yanked. The dirty, ruined shirt came off, and the young man fled down the other side of Caroline Street, waving the scrap of cloth like a flag.

No one had time to react. It was only after he'd disappeared that the now merged crowd, Duval tourists with processional onlookers, gasped and shouted as though with one voice. Maggie felt the horror surge through her, tingling along her skin and leaving her arms and legs weak. Lily was trembling violently, sobbing with fear and sorrow. A long terrifying moment passed before Maggie noticed that Marie, though visibly moved, was unperturbed. When Maggie then turned to see that the Key West police officers who'd accompanied the pageant from St. Peter's had made no move to stop or pursue the knife-wielding man, she understood. The attack had been a planned part of the reenactment.

Stripped of his garments.

As the mingled crowd, disturbed and restive, watched at first in fear and then in slowly dawning stages of comprehension, the man with the cross stood, bowed and unmoving. He was utterly vulnerable in his weakness and shame, his exposed torso streaked with filth and glistening with sweat. Slowly he raised his head and fixed his sorrowing stare on a point far beyond all around him, a stoic portrait of cruel and hopeless abuse.

Within moments, the people had calmed and all eyes followed him as he lifted his cross with a grueling effort and began to pace unsteadily along the street. It was a short block to his destination, the Episcopal Church, but each step seemed to require an act of will that had all but deserted him.

With his shirt stripped away, his chest heaved and struggled for every breath. When he reached the steps of the church, the crowd, growing with every step as revelers joined mourners, heaved a collective sigh of relief.

But he was not done.

At a pace so slow as to be excruciating, he began dragging himself up the concrete steps. One at a time. After the first five, he fell, and after what seemed a long, long time, began to crawl on his knees and one hand as his other firmly gripped the cross. One of the young toughs from Sloppy Joe's, a Jimmy Dean look-alike with slicked back hair, impulsively moved forward to help him, but those surrounding him in the garb of soldiers, held him back. There was no Simon in this pageant.

When he reached the level space leading to the church, he lay down on the jagged ground and lowered the cross down upon himself.

It took a long while for the crowd, starting with the tourists, to dissipate. Many were still watching and whispering to one another when five of the men and two of the women in the pageant silently climbed the steps, and pulling the cross off, lifted him and bore him away. Two young men, no more than teenagers, went over to the cross and using all their strength, pulled it upward it until it was leaning half upright on the church landing. There it would stay for the rest of the weekend.

The remainder of those who'd stayed with the procession since St. Peter's gradually trailed after those bearing him as they walked east for a few blocks to the stark, unassuming Protestant Church. Maggie, who knew from the LEAST planning sessions that most participants would gather there, could not bring herself to go when Marie started in that direction. She knew that Arthur would not be there; Marie had already observed that he always went home, weakened and spent, to sleep for 15 hours after every pageant. The chance to see him, whole and alive, would be the only thing that could keep her from her own small haven now.

Marie understood, releasing her hand after a quick squeeze, and they parted. Lily, stunned and silent, now took Maggie's hand and did not let go until they'd reached home. Once there, Lily looked directly at her and said, "Thank you for taking me," before she disappeared into the house. Maggie, who'd begun to worry that she'd done Lily serious harm by bringing her along, rounded the corner to her own little cottage, marveling at the resiliency Lily managed to display at the most unlikely moments. She was still wondering about this changeability when she collapsed on her narrow little bed, her eyes heavy with sorrow. It was only late afternoon but she needed to sleep for an hour or two.

She woke only once after midnight, startled by some dream she couldn't remember. She was asleep again before she even stopped trying to recall it.

Her stomach woke her shortly after dawn on Saturday morning. Padding into the kitchen to fix the largest breakfast she could manage with whatever ingredients she found, she noticed the phone machine's blinking light. Pressing the play button, she heard Christine's familiar voice.

"Mom? You there? Guess not. Well, I got home OK. And Caro's fine. Still no signs of imminent popping. Looks like her doc was right, and she's not too happy about it. Dad's fine. He wants to know all about our time together. I'm not sure what to tell him, but I'll think of something. Love you, Mom. And thanks."

Chrissie. Could it be just 24 hours ago that she'd driven her daughter to the airport and said good-bye? It felt unbelievable. Maggie, relieved to hear that everyone was safe and Caro still in a holding pattern, turned back to her breakfast.

An hour later, she'd consumed a leftover pint of lemon chicken with peppers and brown rice, a cinnamon raisin bagel that required microwave-thawing from its frozen state, and a huge oatmeal chocolate chip cookie that she believed qualified as a breakfast food because of the oatmeal. If you do go home, she told herself, Harry will be shocked at what a hog you've become.

She knew she should check on Lily, but her good intentions were overruled by a driving need to simply be alone. To do normal, everyday things by herself. And besides, she had the growing sense that Lily would be just fine; indeed, that Lily was just fine. She passed the day cleaning the cottage, and by the time she was done vacuuming, sweeping, washing the slider windows, dusting, scouring the kitchen and scrubbing the bathroom, the little home was sparkling. Just like new, she thought, and suddenly wondered with a mixture of sadness and proprietary pleasure who would be the next occupant. Who would find it like this, a miracle, a shining new chance?

Because the clocks would not officially move ahead an hour until tomorrow, Easter Sunday, the Holy Saturday Vigil would take place earlier than usual. Most years it would start at 8 p.m. right after darkness fell, but tonight the sun would sink well before 6:30 p.m., and the total darkness traditionally required would reign by 7 p.m. At that appointed hour, the vigil processional would move from in front of St. Peter's to inside the church. Parishioners would light the way with hundreds of small candles.

Maggie intended to be among them, though Marie had bluntly refused an invitation to attend, noting, "After Good Friday's ordeal, there's just no way I'm up to a three-hour vigil. I'll take the Easter sunrise service anytime!"

Though Maggie had smiled at her friend's typical honesty, she felt a tug of sadness at this reminder that Marie's body was not as youthful as her spirit. Maggie did not like to consider how many more Easter weekends Marie would preside over. Many, she hoped fervently, many, many more.

She sat next to Minerva in the darkened church. The huge woman, apparently no worse for wear from yesterday's tragic performance, hugged her enthusiastically, forcing Maggie to smother a grin against the woman's ample neck. Maggie didn't see Arthur, but she wasn't alarmed. She knew tonight was his night to lead a rather large AA meeting. Holidays, he'd told her, were often the worst time for his flock.

As Marie had predicted, the service, though beautiful and moving, was a long one. St. Peter's was renowned for its extraordinary baptismal ceremonies, offering the full immersion often seen in certain Baptist and Southern Christian sects. A number of young families, and a few not-so-young, had chosen this holy night to celebrate this cleansing reception by water into the church, and the baptisms themselves took over an hour. It was well after ten before she'd gotten home and returned, gratefully, to her bed. She wondered hazily, as she closed her eyes, what it would have been like to be one of those who'd been baptized tonight. Did they feel cleansed and genuine, ready for a new life, a new spirit? A small ache of envy accompanied her as she slipped into sleep.

She'd meant to accompany Marie to the sunrise service, but had forgotten to reset her clock. She woke well after the sun was up and knew the early Mass was long over. Annoyed with herself, she couldn't help but acknowledge that she finally felt rested as she dressed for the 11 a.m. Easter Service. Her mind felt clear for the first time in days. She called Marie to apologize, but when there was no answer, remembered that LEAST was hosting an Easter picnic at Fort Zachary Taylor. It would begin after morning services at churches all over the island and run until, as Marie put it, "everyone goes home." Marie was probably already there, helping to set up.

Still dismayed at having missed the early service, Maggie hurried to St. Peter's and slipped into a back pew. The church overflowed with luminescent Easter lilies and sprays of tropical flowers as the sun spilled in, setting aglow everything it touched from the warm, dark skin of several little girls in pastel-colored dresses and patent leather shoes to the tabernacle which shone as if with sanctified fire. She thrilled to the sound of the sung Gloria, absent for over forty days and today vibrantly accompanied by Patrick on the organ. After reading the gospel description of Mary Magdelane encountering Jesus, Father Dominick rose. He gazed upon the crowded church for a long moment, and then began to speak.

"I am always struck by this particular, precious gospel. It tells us that against all odds, against all history, against all science, against all that had been known to man until that time, that Jesus rose from the dead. But it also tells us, against all odds, against all history, against all cultural mores, against all that had been known to man until that time, that the first person our risen Lord appeared to was Mary Magdelane. Not Peter, the future first pope. Not John, the beloved disciple. Not Thomas, the doubter. Not Annas or Caiphas or Pontius Pilate, the men who'd plotted His presumed death. Not even His grieving mother.

"But Mary. Mary, who—whether you believe she was a prostitute or a madwoman or simply a woman who'd been very, very ill—was, by all ancient and modern measures, a damaged woman. Not just any woman, and that He'd first appear to a woman at all was inconceivable, but this woman. This damaged woman. This broken woman. This sinful woman. This woman who had so publicly required healing and purging.

"This woman who was, in modern parlance, 'damaged goods.'

"Let us put aside our shock, our amazement, perhaps even our questions about why Jesus chose Mary. Let us simply know that He did and, instead, ask the only question that really matters: what does that choice mean for us? What does the fact that our Lord chose to first reveal himself to such an infamously damaged woman mean for us?

"IT MEANS THAT WE ALL HAVE A CHANCE!

"It means that we all have a second, a third, a fourth, an infinite number of chances, just as He gave chance after chance after chance to Mary, that ill and misguided and damaged woman. It means that we are *all* redeemable, all beloved, all worthy! It means that as He loved her, as He healed her, as He appeared to her; so does He love us, so does He heal us, so does He appear to us. And it means that we must not become so bogged down in our perceived unworthiness, in our perceived illness, in our perceived sin, that we miss the chance that Mary took.

"And that brings us to Easter's second question: are we ready to recognize Him and grasp that chance?"

An elderly woman next to Maggie pressed a tissue into her clenched hand. Her cheeks were soaked, her nose running, her shoulders shaking. She'd always been skeptical of people who claimed they wept with unspeakable joy. Now she understood.

Easter had not been in Arthur's anguish which she could only witness. It had not been in last night's baptisms which had excluded her in their innocence. It had not been in the sunrise service that she'd slept through and would have only experienced from the edges of a circle.

It was here! Easter was in this call to belonging. Easter was in this call to inclusion. Easter was in this call to *Rise!* and grasp that chance, regardless of how many had passed before it unnoticed.

Sorry I missed You so many times before, she said silently, and if I miss You again, help me to remember this.

Help me to recognize one of Your blessed, endless chances. And grab it!

She waited for Patrick after Mass. He made no comment about her ravaged face. He must have noticed though, because he took her arm as they walked, and as the familiar resentful sense of vulnerability tried to crawl into her heart, she swept it away with a flourish.

"I lost track of you in the crowd on Friday," he said.

"It became pretty overwhelming," she remarked, adding easily, "I saw you and Lorene."

"Mmmm. Yes. She's at the picnic now, helping Marie and the others."

A few moments passed silently before he added, "I'm going there now. Can I give you a ride?"

Maggie stopped abruptly and then laughed at herself. "I'd completely forgotten I've no way to get there! I'd planned to ride over with Marie, but missed her this morning. I could always go home and get Lily's bike ... but if you don't mind, I'd be grateful for a ride. I can always ride home with Marie later."

He drove a beautifully preserved, fire engine red Mustang that even Maggie, who knew virtually nothing about cars, recognized as valuable. Without thinking she said, "I'd not thought of you as, um, a car buff."

He laughed. "You mean you'd not thought of me as someone who would waste all that time or money on a mere car?"

She grinned sheepishly. "Well."

"It's my one vice. At least it's the one I admit to. Jane, my wife, loved old cars, and I caught the bug from her, I guess. We got this one together."

"Do you miss her?" Maggie asked as he opened the door for her.

"Every day. First thing in the morning is the worst. That split second between sleeping and waking before I remember she's gone? I always think she's right there with me, right next to me in bed. And then I'm awake. I start every day with a stone sinking in my stomach." Maggie touched his hand briefly; he took a breath and continued, "We never had a chance to have kids, so there's no one to remember her with. I guess that's why the car's so important. Stupid, huh?" His smile was lopsided, and for the first time since she'd met him, he looked away from her.

Maggie turned to him in her seat. "No," she said decisively, "I don't think it's stupid. I think memories are vital. I've learned that they can shape our present and influence our future, and that they should. I'd forgotten that, and my life went off track all too easily because I'd forgotten."

He smiled, sweetly this time, and started the sleek little car. Still without looking at her, he asked, "Do you think Lorene needs me too much to know whether she really cares about me?"

"Do you?"

"Maggie," he remonstrated, "don't start that again. Please."

"OK, fair enough," she said, "I think she needs you, but that doesn't mean she doesn't, or won't, love you. Now, really, what do you think?

"I worry sometimes that I'm attracted to women who've suffered and who need me. I worry that I'm trying to make up for losing Jane."

Maggie was silent, hesitating. But once this level of honesty had been reached there was no point in turning back. She asked, "Were you attracted to me because I'm so needy?"

They'd reached the parking lot at Fort Zachary Taylor, and he turned in astonishment to look directly at her. "What? You're kidding right? Maggie, you're one of the strongest women I've ever met. In fact, you were the exception to the rule when it comes to me being attracted. You were a real challenge."

She felt suffused with warm pleasure. He hadn't thought she was pathetic, needy or broken. She wasn't ready to agree with his assessment of strong, but it certainly sounded good. "So what made you give up on the challenge?" she teased, not wanting her delight to be too transparent.

"I didn't give up so much as come to the realization that you would go back. I guess I knew it before Christine came, but once I saw you together I knew it for certain."

"And there was Lorene," she added for him.

"Yes, there was Lorene," he repeated and then added earnestly, "You know she's really extraordinary. I know it doesn't come across with all the Southern Belle stuff, but she's amazing. Before Jake needed her, she was extremely successful on Wall Street, and to stand out there, a woman has to be truly . . ."

"Strong." Maggie supplied for him, smiling widely. "So I guess you're not just attracted to weak, sick, needy women after all. Sounds to me like you picked the two strongest women on the island."

"Well," he laughed, "besides Marie. Neither of you stand a chance next to her."

They left the car and climbed over the knoll. In the distance they could see a large group already gathered, and as they strolled closer, Lorene gave them an uncertain look. Seeing it, Maggie nodded once and smiled gently at her; then she parted from Patrick and went to embrace Arthur.

It was close to midnight by the time Maggie and Marie left, though many others, including Patrick and Lorene were still going strong. Arthur, Glendalynn and Bill had left earlier to take the Meals on Wheels gang home. They'd all attended, but by dusk, Melanie and Maude looked about ready to keel over after all the food and excitement. Though they wouldn't admit weariness, Arthur had cajoled them into the van and they were soon off.

Maggie gave Marie a quick hug farewell and promised to meet her for lunch the next day. She entered the cottage, realizing with some surprise that she'd not been home in over 12 hours. The phone machine was blinking with what she knew would be an Easter message from Harry and the girls. They'd planned an Easter brunch together if Caro felt up to it. Smiling with anticipation, she pressed the Play button and heard Harry's voice.

"Margaret. It's about seven o'clock here. We've tried a few times to get you in person. Didn't want to leave this on the machine. Caroline went into labor around noon, but there's something wrong. I'm not sure what. They're getting her ready for an emergency Cesarean."

CHAPTER 10

A NEW SEASON

ON Maggie's second flight to Key West, the plane landed smoothly on the first pass. More important, this pilot was friendly and talkative. He'd been speaking to them all along, pointing out the Everglades and the dark mass of the Coral Reef under the glimmering seas. When he told them where to look to catch the first glimpse of Key West, Maggie felt a surge of excitement that easily surpassed her anxiety. Craning to see the island materialize in the distance, she tightened her grip on Harry's hand.

He gave her a small smile, taking pleasure in her excitement. It had been a long year, and this trip, a year to the day after her first, had been his Christmas present to her. Privately, he knew the gift was as much for him as for her; he was sharply curious about this place, and when he was being honest with himself, more than a little interested in the people she'd met here. An avid curiosity was as much as he would admit; the twinges of something else he'd felt while she was gone, certainly not jealousy, he would not acknowledge.

But there was one thing he knew for certain: were it not for her shocking decision to come here last January, they would have never made it through the past year. Nor would he be so confident in their future. Her time here had forced both of them to change in ways that made it possible to confront the extraordinary challenges that had come. Had she not developed a disconcerting and finally, comforting, independence, and had he not learned a brutal lesson about how deeply he needed her, their lumbering, stoic marriage would never have grown into the partnership it had become.

* * *

The memory most irrevocably burned into his mind was the vision of her walking into the intensive care waiting room at dawn on Easter Monday. He was the only one awake; Chrissie was dozing fitfully, curled in an uncomfortable chair, and Tom was stretched out over three chairs, mumbling anxiously even in his sleep.

But Harry hadn't been able to sleep at all, and so he was staring straight ahead into empty space when the movement of someone coming toward him caught his eye. He'd studied her carefully, not sure she was real, as she walked down the hall and into the stark reception room. He was still staring at her as she walked up to him and wordlessly put her arms around him, cradling his head to her body. And Harry, who'd not shed a tear or raised his voice once in the past 24 hours, turned his face into her and wept.

They remained so for some time until Christine stirred and, seeing her mother and father, gave one renting sob of relief and walked into their embrace. It was Christine who told her mother that Caroline and the baby had survived the ordeal, but that the doctors weren't sure if the baby had been deprived of oxygen for too long. They'd rushed her to intensive care, where she now slept fitfully. It would be a while before they would be able to determine whether there'd been any damage to the brain or nervous system. Caroline, exhausted and fearfully weak after the complicated birth, was disconsolate.

Tom, at first stunned and then unaccountably enraged, had only distressed her more with his ranting as he blamed everyone from the intake nurse to the obstetrician to the hospital itself. When he'd started raving that Caro should have never taken a job at the hospital because now it would be harder to sue, Harry had forcibly hauled him from the room. Listening to his daughter sobbing wretchedly as he pulled the door closed, it was all he could do to keep from slapping Tom in the face.

"Why didn't you?" Maggie asked him quietly, interrupting as she sat between him and Christine. Harry took some time to reply, and when he did, Maggie knew she'd come home.

"As mad as I was at him, I understood what he was doing," Harry answered slowly as if working it out for the first time himself. He glanced over at Tom, still tossing restlessly on his makeshift cot. "He had to blame someone. Or something. If not, he'd have to look at his own behavior. He was already feeling guilty for how he'd treated Caroline; always sniping at her and acting like he really didn't want them to have a baby now. So he had to be feeling terrible, like somehow maybe it was his fault because he hadn't been excited about the baby and hadn't cherished Caro enough. When I dragged him out of there and took a good look at him—he looked absolutely miserable—I guess I just understood. I wasn't angry anymore. Just sad. For both of them."

"For all of us."

Maggie, blinking, had reached over and taken his hand. The three of them then rose as one to go see Caroline. They left Tom to what rest he could get and whatever nightmares tortured him while he tried.

Caroline had been released by the end of Easter week, and the doctors saw no reason to keep the baby longer. She'd recovered physically as much as possible, and it would simply be a matter of time before they could judge whether she would develop normally. Caroline wanted her to be called Ruth, and Tom, whose anger had become an alarming listlessness, made no objection. Ruth was baptized at St. Patrick-St. Anthony on April 24, three weeks after her Easter birth. Christine and Harry had been godparents. Despite Caro's returning optimism and driven determination that Ruth would be fine, Tom had been morose throughout the ceremony and even at the buffet brunch afterwards. Caroline, with an almost desperate enthusiasm, had ignored him.

Harry and Maggie had become increasingly troubled about their son-in-law's capacity to be a good father, or for that matter, husband. They'd finally admitted their concern to each other that Sunday night as they drove back to Old Saybrook after Ruth's baptism. Tom's demeanor all day had been impossible to dismiss.

"I don't know what to do." Maggie acknowledged when Harry brought it up. Though quietly pleased at how Harry continued to demonstrate his newfound ability to broach troubling subjects, she was very concerned for Caroline. "In fact, I don't know what to do for either of them. Caroline's as bad as he is, the way she's ignoring the problem. Ignoring him. He's drifting further and further away, and it's as though she hasn't even noticed. I can't imagine what it must be like in their apartment when no one else is around."

"Apparently, it's pretty much the same—like Tom's not even there," Harry answered, surprising her with this knowledge. Noting her questioning gaze, he explained, "Chrissie's been staying with them—it's almost as close to the University as her apartment, so she moved in when Ruth came home. She promised me she's keeping up with her rehearsals for the recital, and she wants to help Caro however she can." Maggie tried to ignore a pang of jealousy at the thought of Harry knowing the important details of her daughters' lives, details that not so long ago would have been shared only with her. Unaware of her discomfiture, Harry continued, "Christine says the atmosphere at the apartment is constantly tense, not so much because Caro and Tom are fighting, but because each acts like the other doesn't exist.

"Caroline is wholly occupied with the baby; it's as if Tom isn't even there. Christine says Caro acts like she made a deal with God when the birth started to go wrong: if she was granted Ruth, she would give up Tom. Myself, I think she might have truly given up on him in those moments after the baby was born when he became infuriated, and all she needed or wanted was to be comforted. And Tom just didn't have it in him to give. I think it was at that moment that they were set adrift from each other.

"According to Christine, Tom's not helping matters any. He's working longer hours than ever, and when he is there, he evidently spends a great deal of time just staring at Ruth as though he's perplexed about how she got there or who she is." Maggie cut him off furiously, blurting, "I can't believe he's still spending all that time at that job. I know it's important work, but doesn't he get it? Doesn't he understand how much he almost lost?"

Harry, who'd spent their entire married life avoiding any type of confrontation, had countered readily, "I think Tom believes that work is the only thing he can do to show whatever love he feels. Caro and Chrissie may not see it that way, but I think that's exactly what he's trying to do: be useful in the only way he can. He has to know at some level that he's failed Caro, failed himself. Work is the only thing he's done well, and I imagine he thinks at least he can be a good provider, if not much else."

Nonplussed, Maggie made no reply and after a few minutes, Harry went on. "Whenever Chrissie suggests he pick the baby up or change her or just hold her, he backs away as though he's been asked to manhandle fragile porcelain. It's like he's afraid of the child. Chrissie's caught Caroline shooting him a look of utter disdain at such a moment, and that's about the extent of their communication. Christine says it's the saddest thing she's ever seen. 'Sad to the point of despair, Dad,' was how she put it."

Maggie, still unaccustomed to being the spouse who does all the listening, had nevertheless asked, "Do you think there's anything we can do? Or should do?"

"I think we have to," Harry answered gravely. "I'm just really not sure what."

The next day Maggie had discussed the situation with Christine who made an astounding suggestion. "How about if you and Dad, and Caro and Tom, did a Retrouvaille weekend together? They're holding one at St. Pat-St. Anthony at the end of May, so it would be just around the corner for all of you. I really don't think Tom has the gumption anymore to resist, and Caro would probably do it if you and Dad put on the pressure. I could work on her from this end."

Maggie had been unconvinced and frankly astonished that Chrissie would even consider such a prospect. But Christine had replied impishly, "Hey Mom, desperate times call for desperate measures."

Pointedly ignoring the teasing in her tone, Maggie all but dismissed the idea, "Christine, Caro would never leave Ruth right now. You yourself told Dad that she absolutely dotes on the baby, practically watching her every breath and move."

"I know, Mom, but I could offer to watch Ruth. I've been living here and know her whole routine. Caro trusts me completely with the baby, more than she does Tom, that's for sure. Besides, the recital and graduation will be over by then, and I'll have a few weeks to kick back."

Maggie, refraining from asking her daughter just how long she expected to "kick back," agreed to mention it to Harry despite her misgivings. There had been no more talk of Retrouvaille between them since Maggie had returned home, and she frankly believed that the crisis of Ruth's birth had brought her and Harry together in a way that no religious weekend or counseling ever could. She assumed Harry felt the same and expected him to reject Christine's "desperate measure" out of hand.

"Let's do it," he said when she mentioned it to him over supper.

She'd looked at him in amazement, barely managing to swallow a mouthful of meatloaf before she croaked, "What? You're joking, right?"

But he'd held her gaze, his face clear and his eyes dancing. "Listen, I learned a lot about Retrouvaille while you were gone," he began, and Maggie thought wryly, *yeah, don't I know*, remembering Chrissie's tale about Macy. But Harry was hurrying on as if hoping to convince her. "It's based on a really great premise; all about caring communication and honest listening."

Maggie interposed, her voice slightly hurt, "I guess I thought we were doing pretty good on our own with caring communication and honest listening."

Harry regarded her across the small kitchen table they'd shared, often silently, for over three decades. Putting down his fork, he pushed aside his plate and took both her hands in his. Looking directly into her eyes in a way that managed to thrill her despite those three decades and her lack of enthusiasm for Retrouvaille, he said, "We have been doing pretty good. But Caro's crisis didn't give us much of a choice. I think you came home before you were ready. I'm not saying we haven't done well and learned a lot. But we're pretty new at this, and it might do us a lot of good to learn more about what we seem to be doing naturally. It could be sort of a booster course for us, a way to be more confident about the future."

Maggie murmured, "I may have come home before I planned to, but I don't think I came home before I was ready."

Harry had smiled then, that rare, lovely, open grin that she'd seen so little of in the past few years. "Maybe not," he acknowledged happily, "but even if we don't do it for ourselves, I think Chrissie is right: we need to do it for Caro and Tom. You know as well as I do that it's the only way they would go. And while the weekend may only be a helping hand for us, it could be a lifesaver for them. Frankly, I'm not sure they'll make it even with Retrouvaille."

Despite her initial reluctance, Maggie had not been able to gainsay this compelling argument. It had taken nearly two weeks for Maggie, Harry and Christine to convince Caroline to join her parents on the weekend. At first she used Tom as an excuse, but when Christine had pointedly asked Tom when he returned home late from work one night, he'd merely shrugged and said it was up to Caro. Aggrieved at having been so easily bested by her sister and, though unwittingly, her husband, she continued to resist, now using Ruth as the source of her adamant denial. But when Christine offered to care for Ruth for the weekend, Caroline had no real out. Still she fought the idea, and it took a private talk with her father to convince her. Maggie had not asked Harry what was said, and he'd not broken whatever confidences he'd shared with his daughter. Maggie couldn't deny a niggling curiosity as to what had passed between father and daughter, and thought someday she might ask him. And maybe someday, he would tell her.

Christine's recital had been a resounding success, staged in the University of Hartford's newly minted Performing Arts

Center. The center had been designed, not only to showcase the university's theater, dance and performing arts programs, but to integrate the university with the people and neighborhoods of Hartford. It had succeeded in both objectives; even Harry had commented on the striking architecture and spacious design that merged rather well with its northend Hartford site.

Christine's performance was exquisite, and for just a few moments, both Maggie and Harry managed to lose themselves enough in their pride to forget the sullen young couple seated next to them. Caroline had come for her sister's sake, but her own resentment and discontent had begun to spill over. After fussing grouchily at leaving Ruth for just a few hours, even though the sitter was a neighbor and experienced mother herself, Caro proceeded to scowl throughout the entire afternoon, her face lighting briefly only while Christine danced. Tom might as well have been watching cars go by, for all the interest he showed. Abu, Chrissie's friend from last Christmas, helped lighten and liven the atmosphere, clapping loudly and cheering at the end of Chrissie's dance. Actually, he clapped and cheered loudly every time she paused in the dance, but Maggie and Harry easily forgave him his exuberance. Indeed, after a sidelong glance at her grim daughter and son-in-law, Maggie could have kissed Abu. And when the entire audience followed his lead and, defying convention, stood to applaud when Christine finished, Maggie *did* kiss him.

Christine had been breathless and flushed after the recital. She knew it had gone well, and for a dance student, even graduation paled next to a successful senior recital. In her excitement, she managed to overlook her sister's subdued demeanor. But when Caroline insisted on returning right home to the baby rather then joining them at Max's Downtown as planned, Maggie was out of patience.

Christine had been there to help Caro in every way since Ruth had come home, and Maggie felt this was poor thanks for Chrissie on her one special day. But her younger daughter's anxious glance kept Maggie from taking Caroline to task right in the parking lot outside the Performing Arts Center. Instead, she'd maintained a barely civil silence when Tom and Caroline bid a distracted goodbye and drove back to their apartment. Abu's irrepressible good cheer helped dissipate the tension, and they'd ended up having a lovely celebration anyway. "Look at it this way," Harry had said on the way home, "It wouldn't have been nearly as much fun if they'd come."

Maggie had been less forgiving. "I can't *wait* for the Retrouvaille weekend," she'd said sarcastically, "It's going to take a miracle for that to work out."

And it had, though the miracle was merely the beginning. The last weekend in May was gorgeous, the type of perfect spring weekend that allows New Englanders to tolerate, if not justify, the long, gray months of winter. On their way to St. Patrick-St. Anthony, Maggie managed not to recite how many other wonderful things they could be doing in the warm sunshine, but Harry read her mind and, grinning, patted her hand as he drove.

In a stern tone he seldom used with his daughters, Harry had called Caroline to say that he and Maggie would pick them up, not giving her a chance to object or cancel the weekend. Caroline had been ready to do just that, but at the sound of her father's voice, she ended up agreeing, albeit with ill-grace. Caro and Tom, each carrying their own bag, hurried out of the apartment as soon as Harry pulled into the drive. "Looks like we're being punished by not even getting a chance to see Ruth," Maggie had murmured to Harry as the two young people stormed toward the car. They got in, one on each side, but when Caro took a deep, aggravated breath to launch into some complaint, her father turned and quelled her with one long look.

At that moment even Harry, who'd determinedly made this happen against the will of all involved, had had his doubts. Forty-eight hours later, his faith had been justified. At some point during the weekend, he and Maggie had stopped keeping track of what—if any—progress the children were making, and had given their full attention to each other. They'd discovered that each had been correct in their presumptions about Retrouvaille: Harry realized that Maggie had been right in claiming that they'd already started communicating in a more honest and caring way, and Maggie learned that Harry had accurately gauged their growth as new and uninformed. What cancer, Key West and Ruth's birth had started between them needed to be nurtured and continued.

Within the structure and spirit of Retrouvaille, the issues that they still hadn't frankly confronted in the two months since Maggie's abrupt return came flooding through the walls they'd carefully built. Maggie was able to pour out the fear she'd lived through after the diagnosis and during the treatment. When she told Harry how abandoned she'd felt, he wept openly with dawning comprehension. When she described the emptiness and disconnectedness that had sent her to Key West, he listened silently. When she told him how the terror of a recurrence sometimes still woke her in the night or forced her to pull the car over to the side of the road until it passed, he held her until her heart slowed.

And when Harry, more tentatively at first, began to describe the helplessness and confusion he'd felt for the whole of the previous year, Maggie made no attempt to hide her relief that he'd felt something beyond burdened. When he spoke of his fear to distress her by expressing desire during that time, she heard her faith in his kindness and courtesy affirmed. When he told her of the bottomless chasm he'd faced after she left, it was her turn to cry. By the end of the weekend, Maggie understood that the kind of loving, forgiving communication and attention she expected from God was what He expected them to give each other.

She didn't know whether Caroline and Tom, silent and drained on the drive home Sunday, had had the same revelation. But when the younger couple climbed out of the car at the apartment, Tom holding the door for his wife, Maggie knew they'd experienced their own miracle.

It was one they needed. By mid-June, Ruth was showing the first signs of problems. Both Caroline and Maggie, who spent two days a week caring for Ruth in Hartford while Caro worked half days at St. Francis, noticed that the baby was frequently ill. She seemed to catch every virus that entered her atmosphere and took a long time recovering from each. One of the benefits of Retrouvaille turned out to be a mixed blessing: Tom was now working shorter hours and constantly interacting with his daughter at home, holding, feeding and changing her whenever he could. Unfortunately, every invisible germ he picked up during his people-intensive work day easily passed to Ruth. Their doctor, during a scheduled follow up appointment, confirmed this, explaining that Ruth's immune system had been compromised during the birth and was underdeveloped. Whether or when she would grow out of the problem could not be predicted.

Meanwhile, Ruth was weak and ill too often for anyone to tell whether she was lagging in other areas of development. Maggie, just a little more objective than Caroline or Tom, felt that Ruth, during her all-too-brief healthy periods, was as alert and bright as any infant her age, but this was more hopeful opinion than informed judgment. And though Harry and Maggie feared that the baby's problems would again drive Caroline and Tom apart, the opposite appeared true. They drew closer together, sometimes even seeming to cling to one another for comfort and hope. Maggie and Harry had happily cared for Ruth three times as the year passed so that her parents could attend as Tom put it, "A Retrouvaille Refresher" weekend.

As the summer waned, Harry and Maggie kept their questions to themselves about exactly what Chrissie intended to do next. After Tom and Caroline had returned from Retrouvaille, Christine had moved out, renting an apartment near the University with another recent graduate whom Harry and Maggie had not yet met. She seemed to have no real plans. Harry grumbled that a beautiful dance recital was one thing, but a job was quite another. Chrissie had been volunteering at the University's Performing Arts Center, teaching dance to mostly Black and Hispanic children from Hartford. And while Harry was pleased with her generosity and commitment, he waited in vain for some sign that she might actually try to earn a living. Though still impressed with the depth she'd seen in Chrissie during their time together in Key West and unwilling to underestimate her, Maggie nevertheless understood Harry's dismay. But by the end of summer, both were wishing Christine had been as truly directionless as they'd so easily assumed.

She announced at a Labor Day picnic that she had joined the Peace Corps and had received permission to return to Nigeria with Abu in late October. Everyone's attention, which had been focused on the antics of little Ruth, suddenly turned to Christine. This time Abu, by now a fixture at most family gatherings, did not applaud. However, his eyes danced with intelligent merriment as he met Maggie's gaze. *Not quite the silly charity case you'd all thought, am I?* his eyes seemed to say, and Maggie, despite herself, smiled back at him.

Apparently Abu was, indeed, not anyone's silly charity case. He did not utter a word as Christine calmly explained that he was a doctor in Nigeria who'd come to the U.S. to study business and administration as well as solicit equipment and financial donations for the clinics he hoped to establish at home. The University of Hartford, well-known for aggressively recruiting international students, had given him a partial scholarship to their respected business administration school, not to mention introductions to key administrators at St. Francis Hospital and Hartford Hospital. For the year in which Abu had been in and out of their lives as an unwavering source of light and good humor, he'd also carried a full course load and managed to cajole Hartford medical administrators into shipping over $50,000 worth of funds and used equipment back to Nigeria. Now he himself was ready to return to the distressed and sometimes volatile country to continue his work.

And Christine would be going with him.

She looked sedately around the circle of shocked faces. All faces she loved dearly, and all faces she was willing to leave for this extraordinary and increasingly mysterious man and his work. Even Ruth, having a particularly robust day, stopped her gurgling and arm waving to stare solemnly at her aunt as if she understood that her family of adults had just reached a particularly sober pass. Harry, uncharacteristically, was the first to react.

Turning to Abu, he asked bluntly, "How old are you?"

"Thirty-one, sir." Abu answered in his deep lilting voice, apparently untroubled by the shock Christine's pronouncement had caused.

"And you're a doctor." Harry made it a statement, as if by repeating the facts he could more fully comprehend what was happening. Maggie meanwhile stole a glance at Caroline and realized in one flashing moment that her eldest had known precisely what Christine's plans were, and probably had for some time. It had always been this way between the two girls: silent allies in anything they knew might be opposed by their parents. And despite her very real dismay, Maggie felt a shiver of pride. In both of them.

"And you're taking my 21-year old daughter, who's never left Connecticut except to see her mother this past spring, to a potentially dangerous country with you to work at a barely established, underfunded clinic." Continuing his dogged analysis of the facts he'd been given, Harry might have gone on for sometime, but Christine decided it was time to intervene.

"He's not taking me, Dad. I'm going with him," she said firmly without raising her voice in the least. In this even temperment, she was much like her father, but Maggie wondered if in this case Harry would hold his temper. He did, but just barely, saying, "Christine, did it occur to you that we might have wanted to discuss this as a family, privately?"

Again, there was no rancor in her voice. "If by privately, you mean without Abu, this is as much about him as about me. We're going together, and he's part of the reason I'm choosing to do this. Besides," she added with just a touch of ironic humor, "No one here seemed to mind having him around when his sole purpose was to cheer and entertain."

Touché! thought Maggie as Christine gave everyone a chance to think about that before adding more gently, "And Dad, I'm not raising this as an issue for discussion. I'm telling you my plans, and I hope you'll all be happy for me."

And that had been the end of it. After the kids all left, Harry and Maggie had argued for much of that evening about how to react to the stunning news, but in the end, Maggie's perspective had won by default. "Harry," she finally said in exasperation, "Even if you think we should express our disapproval—and I don't think we should—there's nothing we can do to stop her. She's an adult, and she certainly seems to know what she wants. In a way, we should be proud of her.

How many 21-year olds would be willing to take on such a commitment? And you have to admit, we all underestimated Abu. If we'd been paying attention at all, we would have seen this coming."

Harry had given her a sidelong glance and mumbled softly, "He's the 'recent graduate' she's been living with all these months, isn't he?"

"I would imagine so," Maggie answered neutrally.

"Do you think she loves him?" was the next barely audible question.

"I think she loves him, and yes, I think he loves her."

"It's going to be awfully hard on them, whether they live here or there," Harry worried.

Maggie had wisely kept her response to herself: she suspected Christine and Abu had a lot more going for them at the outset then she and Harry or Tom and Caroline had.

Two weeks before Christine was to leave, Tom had an overnight conference to attend, and Caroline invited her mother and sister to a farewell slumber party. "Just us four girls," she'd told her mother, jiggling Ruth on her lap one afternoon when she'd returned home from work. Maggie and Chrissie had thought it a great idea, though Harry seemed a little forlorn when Maggie left for Hartford on the appointed afternoon. At the sight of her husband waving good-bye in the same picture window she and the girls used to watch for him from, Maggie did a U-turn in the middle of their quiet street and pulled back into the driveway. He was at the door before she'd even made it up the steps.

"Did you forget something?" he asked with a boyish eagerness that erased 30 years.

"I forgot to tell you that this time I'm coming home. Tomorrow."

He was smiling widely when she pulled out the next time.

The 'four girls' spent the afternoon drinking tea, eating popcorn and watching *Oprah*. Ruth, who was limited to mashed peas and applesauce, seemed to at least enjoy the company. She crowed every time Oprah's audience erupted into cheers as the mother-daughter makeover candidates emerged with their brand new looks. "I can't believe this is the theme of today's show!" Caro exclaimed. "What a perfect coincidence."

Christine had glared at her somberly and intoned, "There are no coincidences," and they'd all burst into laughter. Ruth, though still small and uncoordinated for her age, giggled and waved her arms in excitement. For dinner they decided on takeout, finally settling on barbecue from Black Eyed Sally's in downtown Hartford. Chrissie offered to go pick up their order, but Caroline, taking a slightly nervous breath, suggested they all go together. Knowing Caroline seldom brought the baby into any crowded public place, Maggie asked quietly, "Are you sure, Caro? We can stay here, and Chrissie will be back in a few minutes."

"No." Caroline replied, a hint of the old stubborness in her voice. "I want us all to go. I want her to go. We can't live our whole lives in fear. Can we, Ruthie?" she lifted the baby into the air, eliciting a grinning gasp of delight. Maggie heaved an inward sigh of relief: this was the beginning of healing.

They made the short trip without incident, returning home with enough barbecued chicken, pork and beef, accompanied by massive servings of the sloppy, sumptuous side dishes that had made Black-Eyed Sally's famous. Caroline opened a bottle of wine, and they dug greedily into the feast, Ruth looking on with a scowl that might well have been aggrieved envy. Caro, watching her mother polish off a substantial rib, said, "Mom, are you making up for lost time or what?"

Before Maggie could form an adequate retort, Chrissie supplied helpfully, "She turned into a real pig in Key West." And as Maggie cried out, "Hey!' the two girls erupted into a bout of giggles.

It was much later, after Ruth had been put to bed and they'd demolished a quart and a half of Starbucks Mudslide ice cream while watching an hysterical video Caroline had rented called *My Big Fat Greek Wedding,* that they got ready for bed. They'd decided to all sleep in the small living room, Maggie on the pull-out couch and the girls in sleeping bags. "Like a real slumber party," Caroline had enthused, but the real reason went unsaid: none of them knew when they would next be together this way. If ever.

They talked well into the night. About Christine's plans. About Key West. About Nigeria. About cancer and, blessedly, Maggie's most recent good and hopeful exams. About Ruth, and Caroline's hopes and fears. About Harry. And as they finally dropped off, the girls first, Maggie thought how strange it was that the things we most love are the things most likely to provoke our deepest terrors. It must be that way for everyone, she told herself, and then whispered, smiling slightly, "Except for You."

The real irony, she thought as she too slipped into sleep, is that the state of true and final faith leaves no room for fear. But who, really, ever reaches that hallowed place?

Harry and Maggie drove Christine and Abu to JFK Airport at the end of October. The young couple seemed to have reversed roles. Abu was unusually quiet, while Christine chattered nervously for most of the trip. Maggie, frequently glancing out of the corner of her eye at her husband as he drove grimly down Interstate 95, had never seen Harry so tense. And Chrissie's apparent jitters were doing nothing to help reassure him. Maggie was much calmer; she understood that Christine was distressed about disappointing her parents, not about leaving them to pursue an unknown future in an unfamiliar place. About that, and about Abu, Chrissie had no doubts.

Still, everyone except Abu was sobbing by the time they parted at the airline check point. Harry, who'd been unable to see Abu in quite the same friendly light, nevertheless shook his hand firmly. But when he muttered in a choked voice, "Make sure you take care of her," neither Christine nor Maggie could hold back their tears. The three embraced, trying futilely to laugh at their tears, while poor Abu stood by helplessly. He kept lifting his arms and flapping them a little, as if that would somehow help. Finally, Christine broke away from her parents, took Abu's outstretched hand, and walked rapidly away with her head down. Maggie and Harry stood there hand-in-hand until they could no longer see her, but she did not once look back.

* * *

Their next trip to the airport had been today's. They'd boarded the plane to Miami early this morning and had easily made the connecting flight with the friendly pilot who'd just landed with hardly a bump in the small Key West airport. Harry had given Maggie the tickets just two short weeks ago on Christmas Day, as Caroline, Tom and Ruth watched with happy anticipation. They'd been in on the secret since November, and the gift had been the highlight of the day next to the long international call they'd placed to Christine in the afternoon. As with all such precious calls since October, Chrissie was bubbling with an energy and enthusiasm that even Harry knew could not have been fabricated. As usual, she did most of the talking, supplying the little details that Maggie cherished because they provided such a vivid description of her daughter's life and surroundings. After a while, they put Ruthie on the phone, and she made a series of delighted cries and gurgles that Caroline steadfastly maintained were early words. Tom watched her wistfully, his eyes brimming with love for them both, as she repeated the claim bouncing Ruth on her lap.

The days since Christmas had been filled with Key West. Maggie was so excited, Harry feared just a little that he could never love it as she did, and therefore, may disappoint her. But when he finally shared his concern, she dismissed it, saying, "You don't need to love it the way I do; just the fact that you're willing to go with me is enough." He relaxed after that, and simply enjoyed her anticipation as she packed and told him more about the island in two weeks than she had in the previous nine months. She called Marie to let her know when they'd be arriving, and ended up talking for over an hour. Her delight helped quell his private worries about leaving the store for two months in January, one of the busier seasons. Maggie, who knew just what it took for her work-a-holic husband to make these plans, keenly felt the value of this gift and told him so at every opportunity.

And now they'd arrived. Maggie finally released his hand when the plane came to a full stop. They stood together in the small jet, stretching as other travelers busily retrieved carry-on bags from the overhead compartments. Maggie knew a group—summoned and led by Marie, of course— would be waiting for them inside the airport. But this moment was hers and Harry's, and she lingered as others streamed by them.

Harry looked at her quizzically and said, "I thought you'd be the first off the plane."

Most of the other passengers had filed out, and the stewardess, smiling patiently, looked down the aisle at them. Maggie slipped her arms around Harry and moved into the comforting circle of his embrace. "Haven't you heard?" she murmured, "The last shall be first."

BOOK DISCUSSION GUIDE

INTERVIEW WITH MARCI ALBORGHETTI

Q What made you decide to write a novel about the impact of cancer on one woman's life?

A Several years ago, I was diagnosed with malignant melanoma. While God has blessed me with healing and a brilliant doctor, I needed to learn to live with the reality of cancer in my life. The brutal shock of hearing the word "malignant," absolutely shakes everything, right down to the foundation of one's life. I found myself looking for ways to cope, and eventually, looking for others who HAD found ways to cope. I've met some extraordinary people and heard some wrenching, wonderful stories. All together, we ARE Margaret/Maggie.

Q Margaret/Maggie has a unique relationship with God. What did you draw on to develop that bond?

A Maggie's communication with God mirrors my own. Even as a kid, I felt very close to God, not in a pious or traditionally religious sense, but more because He is a constant Friend, a Companion. The anecdote Margaret tells about how her mother used to marvel at how quiet and self-sufficient a child she was is really MY mother's story. So I wanted to write about prayer-as-conversation, and how devastating it would be to lose that. Margaret's prayer crisis is nothing less than a "dark night of the soul."

Q What made you set the book in Connecticut and Key West?

A I lived right across from St. Francis Hospital in Hartford, and I graduated from the University of Hartford, so I was very familiar with that landscape. I grew up in Old Saybrook, so that was a natural setting, too. I selected Key West for Maggie's flight/journey for two reasons: one, it is about as far—geographically and philosophically—from staid, stolid Connecticut as you can get; and two, I AM one of those people described in the book who absolutely and utterly fell in love with the island.

Q So are a lot of the Key West characters based on people you actually met there?

A Not really. I borrowed one or two traits of people I knew in Key West, and then created a new personality using that basic material. But many of the scenes were directly from my experience. For instance, I did see Leon Redbone perform on the beach, and it was incredible.

Q Who is your favorite character?

A It depends on what day you ask me. I guess if I had to choose one, it would be Marie, because she is most like a very dear friend and mentor I met in Key West. So "writing" Marie felt like I was actually visiting with her, and that made the whole story flow more easily. But I also loved Arthur.

DISCUSSION QUESTIONS

1. Would Margaret have ever confronted the emptiness in her life and marriage if she hadn't had cancer?

2. Which character changed, grew or developed the most during the course of the book?

3. Is Harry's reaction to Margaret's cancer selfish or merely inept?

4. Are Caroline and Christine responding to their parents' model of communication/marriage in their own lives and relationships?

5. Is Margaret's relationship with God typical of most people who have faith?

6. What would have happened if Margaret, in the midst of her physical, emotional and spiritual crises, had stayed in Connecticut?

7. Should she have?

8. Should she have stayed in Key West?

9. Both Harry and Maggie express concern that she might come home before she's ready. Did she?

10. In general, does it take a significant crisis for people to truly examine their lives? Can an illness or tragedy truly be a "gift" from God?

Additional Titles Published by Resurrection Press, a Catholic Book Publishing Imprint

A Rachel Rosary *Larry Kupferman*	$4.50
Blessings All Around *Dolores Leckey*	$8.95
Catholic Is Wonderful *Mitch Finley*	$4.95
Come, Celebrate Jesus! *Francis X. Gaeta*	$4.95
Days of Intense Emotion *Keeler/Moses*	$12.95
From Holy Hour to Happy Hour *Francis X. Gaeta*	$7.95
Grace Notes *Lorraine Murray*	$9.95
Healing through the Mass *Robert DeGrandis, SSJ*	$9.95
Our Grounds for Hope *Fulton J. Sheen*	$7.95
The Healing Rosary *Mike D.*	$5.95
Healing Your Grief *Ruthann Williams, OP*	$7.95
Heart Peace *Adolfo Quezada*	$9.95
Life, Love and Laughter *Jim Vlaun*	$7.95
Living Each Day by the Power of Faith *Barbara Ryan*	$8.95
The Joy of Being an Altar Server *Joseph Champlin*	$5.95
The Joy of Being a Catechist *Gloria Durka*	$4.95
The Joy of Being a Eucharistic Minister *Mitch Finley*	$5.95
The Joy of Being a Lector *Mitch Finley*	$5.95
The Joy of Marriage Preparation *McDonough/Marinelli*	$5.95
The Joy of Music Ministry *J.M. Talbot*	$6.95
The Joy of Preaching *Rod Damico*	$6.95
The Joy of Being an Usher *Gretchen Hailer, RSHM*	$5.95
The Joy of Worshiping Together *Rod Damico*	$5.95
Lights in the Darkness *Ave Clark, O.P.*	$8.95
Loving Yourself for God's Sake *Adolfo Quezada*	$5.95
Meditations for Survivors of Suicide *Joni Woelfel*	$8.95
Mother Teresa *Eugene Palumbo, S.D.B.*	$5.95
Personally Speaking *Jim Lisante*	$8.95
Practicing the Prayer of Presence *Muto/van Kaam*	$8.95
Prayers from a Seasoned Heart *Joanne Decker*	$8.95
Praying the Lord's Prayer with Mary *Muto/vanKaam*	$8.95
5-Minute Miracles *Linda Schubert*	$4.95
Sabbath Moments *Adolfo Quezada*	$6.95
Season of New Beginnings *Mitch Finley*	$4.95
Season of Promises *Mitch Finley*	$4.95
Soup Pot *Ethel Pochocki*	$8.95
St. Katharine Drexel *Daniel McSheffery*	$12.95
Stay with Us *John Mullin, SJ*	$3.95
Surprising Mary *Mitch Finley*	$7.95
Teaching as Eucharist *Joanmarie Smith*	$5.95
What He Did for Love *Francis X. Gaeta*	$5.95
Woman Soul *Pat Duffy, OP*	$7.95
You Are My Beloved *Mitch Finley*	$10.95
Your Sacred Story *Robert Lauder*	$6.95

For a free catalog call 1-800-892-6657